MURDER
in
PLAIN
SIGHT

**Center Point
Large Print**

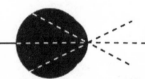

**This Large Print Book carries the
Seal of Approval of N.A.V.H.**

MURDER
in
PLAIN
SIGHT

MARTA PERRY

CENTER POINT PUBLISHING
THORNDIKE, MAINE

The text of this Large Print edition is unabridged.
In other aspects, this book may vary
from the original edition.
Printed in the United States of America
on permanent paper.
Set in 16-point Times New Roman type.

ISBN: 978-1-60285-969-2

Library of Congress Cataloging-in-Publication Data

Perry, Marta.
Murder in plain sight / Marta Perry.
p. cm.
ISBN 978-1-60285-969-2 (lib. bdg. : alk. paper)
1. Amish—Fiction. 2. Amish Country (Pa.)—Fiction. 3. Women lawyers—Fiction.
4. Trials (Murder)—Fiction. 5. Large type books. I. Title.
PS3616.E7933M87 2011
813'.6—dc22

2010046137

MURDER

in

PLAIN
SIGHT

This story is dedicated to
William and Carolyn Baillie,
with thanks for your support.
And, as always, to Brian, with much love.

ACKNOWLEDGMENTS

I'd like to express my gratitude to all of those whose expertise, patience and generosity helped me in the writing of this book: to Erik Wesner, whose Amish America blog is enormously helpful; to Donald Kraybill and John Hostetler, whose books are the definitive works on Amish life; to my daughter-in-law, Karen Johnson, for legal advice; and to my family, for giving me a rich heritage on which to draw.

Dear Reader,

Thank you for choosing to read the first book in my new Amish suspense series set in the Pennsylvania Dutch country, which I know and love. I enjoy writing about the unique traditions of my native Pennsylvania, especially since I'm able to draw on my own Pennsylvania Dutch background.

The difficulties the Plain People face in dealing with the outside world's legal institutions aren't readily understood by our litigious society. It would be hard to find more law-abiding people than the Amish, but they do not easily turn to the law when things go wrong, perhaps because of their history of persecution by the law in Europe. They fled to Pennsylvania to escape that, forming communities that rarely have anything to do with the legal system. They don't sue each other and are reluctant to seek legal help even when accused. It's something that I've seen close-up from time to time in my area, and that experience, when outsiders had to step in to form a defense, has inspired this story.

I hope you'll let me know how you feel about my book, and I'd love to send you a signed bookmark or my brochure of Pennsylvania Dutch recipes.

You can write to me at HQN Books, 233 Broadway, Suite 1001, New York, NY 10279, email me at marta@martaperry.com, or visit me on the web at www.martaperry.com.

Blessings,

Marta

The course of the righteous is like morning light,
growing brighter until it is broad day;
but the ways of the wicked are like
darkness at night, and they do not know
what has been their downfall.
—*Proverbs* 4:18–19

PROLOGUE

Amish Youth Arrested in Murder

SPRINGVILLE, PA—The body of a local woman was discovered early Sunday morning in a remote barn in rural Lancaster County. The woman, whom police say had apparently been beaten to death, has been identified as Cherry Wilson, 24, of Springville. Police have detained a young man who was found at the scene. Thomas Esch, 19, of Spring Township, son of a local Amish family, is being questioned in connection with the death. Police declined to say what the motive might have been in the grisly crime.

In what appears to be a related incident, an unidentified older woman was warned away from the suspect by police. She apparently attempted to interfere when the suspect was being taken into police headquarters. No further information about this incident was released by the police spokesperson.

CHAPTER ONE

A SUMMONS TO THE OFFICE of Dwight Henderson, senior partner in the Philadelphia law firm of Henderson, Dawes and Henderson, seldom resulted in good news for a junior associate, but Jessica Langdon didn't intend to let her apprehension show. Assuming her most professional expression, she straightened her suit jacket with icy fingers then tapped lightly and opened the door.

"You wanted to see me, Mr. Henderson?"

Henderson frowned across the expanse of a massive mahogany desk, balancing a gold fountain pen between his forefingers. He let the engraved pen drop to the desktop and nodded to the chair across from him.

The penalty box. That was how she'd thought of that seat recently. She sat, smoothing her skirt down over her knees.

Center City's skyline, seen through a wide window, made an impressive backdrop, not that Henderson needed any help to impress. Over sixty, he had a heavily lined face that no expensive facial treatments could make resemble anything but a bulldog's, a shining bald dome that reflected the light from the window, and a pair of remote, piercing dark eyes. Whatever his appearance said, he was a highly successful attorney whose clients could afford, and got, the best.

Jessica waited out the frowning silence that had such a demoralizing effect on reluctant witnesses on the few occasions when Henderson Senior deigned to appear in court himself. Henderson had summoned her. It was for him to speak first.

"Your time here has not been particularly successful, has it, Ms. Langdon?"

That didn't seem to require an answer. Her heart sank. This was it, then. Termination. She tried not to think of her father's reaction. A superior-court judge tended to expect better of his only child.

"After the business with the Clements boy . . ."

The Clements boy, as Henderson called him, was the sixteen-year-old scion of one of the firm's wealthiest clients, currently embarked on an escalating pattern of vandalism and violence. Her comment that perhaps he should for once have to face the consequences of his actions had not been well received.

". . . to say nothing of your failure in the Altmiller matter . . ."

She had to bite her tongue at that. Dwight Henderson Junior had dropped the ball in that situation, but it had been made abundantly clear that her duty was to accept the blame and say nothing. Dwight Henderson's son could not possibly have mishandled a case. Junior associates fell on their swords.

". . . only my respect for your father has allowed . . ."

Her father, Theodore Belmont Langdon, superior-court judge and law-school crony of Dwight Senior. His influence had secured this position for her, but it was apparently not enough to ensure that she stayed.

Henderson cleared his throat. "However, a case has come up which you've been requested to handle." He shoved a file folder across the desk.

She was so astonished that his words took a moment to sink in. She picked up the folder by its edges. Some response seemed called for. "Yes, sir?"

"You'll have to drive to Lancaster County immediately to deal with the matter. The Morgan family has decided to fund the defense for this unfortunate young man. Take your lead from them as to how to handle the case. It shouldn't involve anything more complicated than negotiating a plea bargain."

"May I ask—"

"That's all, Ms. Langdon. Satisfy the Morgan family, and perhaps . . ."

He let that trail off, but she got the message. *Perhaps we won't be letting you go.*

She'd like a little more information, but his peremptory gesture sent her to the door. She escaped, clutching the file to her chest. She'd have to trust that its contents could salvage the remnants of her career.

• • •

FACE IT—SHE WAS LOST. Jessica glared at the GPS system that was supposed to get her wherever she needed to go. It worked fine in Philadelphia, or out on the interstate. But once she'd gotten entangled in a network of narrow roads that wound past neat farms and through patches of woods, the system seemed to get as lost as she was. At the moment, it was blinking, its automated voice informing her that it was recalculating the route. Unfortunately, it had been doing so for the past ten minutes.

She slowed the car, pulling off onto the graveled verge, and reached for a map. Since she didn't know where she was, it seemed unlikely that the map would help her much. The last road sign she'd seen had marked an even narrower road than this one, called Creek Road. No Creek Road appeared on the map. It was undoubtedly one of the many thin, unnamed lines that wound through Lancaster County, presumably connecting the apparently endless patchwork of dairy farms.

Propping the map against the steering wheel, she tried to find the spot at which she'd gotten off the main road. Following her prospective employer's directions so far had resulted in nothing but trouble. She could only hope that wasn't a portent of things to come.

A noise behind her brought her head up. If she could flag down a car and ask for directions—

But it wasn't a car. A gray-and-black buggy came into view over the gentle rise of the road behind her, seeming to fit into the pastoral surroundings far better than her year-old hatchback. The horse's hooves clopped rhythmically on the blacktop, slowing as the animal approached.

The faintest apprehension brushed her nape, and she shook it away. She was surely far safer here than on some of the city's streets, strange though the equipage looked to her.

The buggy came to a halt next to her. She had to open her window and crane her neck to look up at the person who leaned down toward her.

The young woman's face was framed by a black bonnet, oddly anachronistic. Her long-sleeved, dark green dress had a matching apron. Jessica had to remind herself that she'd been driving through Center City Philadelphia only a couple of hours ago. Beyond the woman, the man who held the buggy lines had the sort of haircut achieved by cutting around a bowl on the head, topped by a straw hat. Well, maybe their dress wasn't that much stranger than that of the Goth couple she'd spotted yesterday, the woman wearing a studded leather dog collar around her neck.

"You are lost, ja?" The woman gave her a tentative smile. "Can we help?"

Her English was accented, almost singsong in quality, but understandable enough.

"Yes, thank you." Did she sound relieved or desperate? "I'm not sure where I am. I'm trying to find an address off Dale Road near Springville."

"Ach, you are not so very far wrong at all." Her face broke into a smile. "I am Anna Mast, and this is my brother, Aaron. We are chust coming home from delivering eggs in Springville."

"It's not far, then?" Surely it couldn't be, if these two had come from there in a buggy. "Can you give me directions?"

The brother leaned over, squishing his sister against the side of the seat. "Directions depend on how far along the road you are going already. Who are you going to see?"

Her ear must be adjusting to the dialect, because she could understand him even though his English was more heavily accented than his sister's. She hesitated. Normally she wouldn't give out information like that to a stranger, but these were not normal circumstances. If she didn't want to spend what was left of the afternoon wandering these lanes, she'd better not alienate the only help that was offered.

"I have an appointment with Mrs. Geneva Morgan. Her address—"

"Ach, everyone knows the Morgans." His face split in a grin, blue eyes crinkling. "Anyone would help a friend of Mrs. Morgan."

His sister was nodding agreement. Evidently Mrs. Morgan was well-known in the area.

"You chust go down the road past the Stoltzfus farm—"

"She won't know which is the Stoltzfus farm," his sister said, elbowing him. "Go about a mile and you'll see a big red barn on the left-hand side of the road. Turn right there—it's the first paved road you come to. Follow that for about five miles, and it will take you to Dale Road. Then go left, and you'll see the Morgans' mailbox only a little piece down the road."

"Right at the first paved road, go five miles, left on Dale Road," she repeated.

"Ja, that's it." Anna beamed down at her.

"Thank you so much. I really appreciate your help."

"It makes no trouble." Aaron gestured her to go ahead of them, sitting back on the seat again.

"Well . . . goodbye." It seemed an oddly abrupt way of ending a conversation, but what did she know about Amish ways?

She pulled back onto the road, lifting her hand in a wave, and watched the buggy recede in her rearview mirror. She'd just met her first Amish people. She could only hope that the boy she was supposed to defend was as cooperative as that pair.

LAST CHANCE. THE WORDS echoed in the back of Jessica's mind as she got out of the car, squared her shoulders and headed for the door of a

23

sprawling Pennsylvania farmhouse. The drive into the pastoral reaches of Lancaster County had taken longer than she'd expected even before she'd gotten lost, and she'd delayed leaving the city in an attempt to obtain a few more facts.

A futile attempt, as it turned out. The file had contained little to prepare her. It contained only the baldest listing of the defendant and the name and address of the woman who'd retained her. The Philadelphia paper hadn't had much more.

She raised her hand to knock, but the door jerked open before her fist reached it. The introductory speech she'd so carefully prepared during the long drive vanished from her mind. The person who stood there could not be the woman who'd sent for her.

Tall, male, glowering. Definitely not someone named Geneva. The khakis and open-necked shirt said casual, but the square jaw and the fierce glint in the man's golden-brown eyes said, "Keep out." As if to reinforce the message, he braced one hand against the door frame, effectively stopping her from entering.

She'd faced worse in the courtroom, she reminded herself. "Good afternoon. I'm Jessica Langdon. I have an appointment with Geneva Morgan."

He gave a short nod. "Blake Morgan. Geneva is my mother."

Still he didn't move, and his gaze was as frosty

24

as if she'd just crawled out from a crack in the stone wall that surrounded the nearby flower bed overflowing with tulips and roses.

"Is Mrs. Morgan in?" She kept her tone polite but put a sliver of ice in it.

"Not at the moment." Level brows drew together forbiddingly. "I'm sorry to tell you this after you've driven out from Philadelphia, but the family has decided we don't require your services."

The words hit her like a slap in the face. Was that a polite way of saying they didn't think her competent? Mrs. Morgan wouldn't have hired her in the first place if she thought that.

"There must be some misunderstanding. I spoke briefly to Mrs. Morgan just before I left the city, and I gave her my cell-phone number. Surely she would have called if she didn't want me to come."

He didn't move. Didn't speak.

"Do you mind if we discuss this someplace other than the porch?"

He took a step back, with an air of giving ground reluctantly. "I suppose you can come in."

But not for long, his body language said.

Jessica stepped into a center hallway, cool and shady after the June sunshine outside. Yellow roses spilled from a milk-glass pitcher on a marble-topped table, and a bentwood coatrack was topped with a wide-brimmed straw hat.

Morgan gestured toward an archway to the right, and she walked through it.

In the moment before she faced the man again she had a quick impression of Oriental carpets against wide-planked wooden floors and ivory curtains pulled back from many-paned windows. The furniture was a mix of periods, comfortable and well-used but holding its beauty.

She faced Morgan, tilting her chin. He must top six feet, and his height gave him an unfair advantage. That, and the fact that he was on his home turf. Still, she was the professional, called in when things went wrong.

"Mrs. Morgan retained me to defend a client named Thomas Esch on a charge of murder. She asked me to come immediately, which I did. If you have decided on another attorney—" She let the thought hang. He owed her an explanation, and he must know it.

"It's not a question of that," he said quickly. "Not at all. We've simply decided that it's wrong for us to be involved in the case. Naturally we expect to be billed for your time and trouble. Now if you'll excuse me . . ."

It was an invitation to go. She didn't take it. Blake Morgan had that air of command down to an art. He was the type you had to stand up to at the start or always be steamrolled, not that she expected to have enough of a relationship with him to care.

When she didn't move, a glint of anger showed in his face. "I'll have to ask you to leave now, Ms. Langdon."

Fight back? Or roll quietly away and say goodbye to what was left of her career? Not much of a choice.

"I was retained by Geneva Morgan. If she no longer requires my services, I'll have to hear it from her."

His jaw hardened until it resembled one of the rocks in the stone fireplace that dominated one wall of the living room. "Thomas Esch is accused of a brutal murder. I don't want my mother involved, even in the background, in such a thing."

"Are you saying you speak for her?"

"Yes." He bit off the word.

"Do you have a power of attorney to do so?"

His teeth seemed to grind together, and he leaned toward her. She'd scored, but she wasn't sure she wanted to hear what he'd say next.

Quick, light footsteps crossed the hall behind them. "Trey, my dear, there you are. You must have gotten the message wrong, dear, and that's so unlike you."

Jessica watched, fascinated, as the woman trotted across to Blake and patted his cheek. She had to reach up, very far up. If this was his mother, he clearly didn't take after her.

"You must write things down," the woman scolded gently, as if he were about six.

She spun, swooping toward Jessica and holding out both hands. Bright green eyes sparkled, and the full sleeves of the filmy tunic she wore fluttered. Silvery curls bouncing, she moved with the quick light step of a girl, although she had to be in her sixties.

"You're Jessica Langdon, of course." The woman caught Jessica's hands in a warm, surprisingly strong grasp. "My dear, I can't tell you how delighted I am to see you. You're the person I've been praying for." Tears glistened suddenly in the green eyes. "You are just the person to defend Thomas in this terrible matter."

That answered the question of whether Blake Morgan had really spoken for his mother. Jessica glanced at him over Mrs. Morgan's shoulder. He had made one effort to get rid of the attorney his mother had hired, and Jessica suspected it wouldn't be the last. At the moment, his glare seared.

She stared back, unmoved. She had more to lose in this situation than he did, and she was in this to stay.

CHAPTER TWO

TREY WAS FLOODED BY his usual mixture of frustration, affection and bemusement at his mother's return. He'd been confident he'd deflected her attention long enough so he could send this Philadelphia lawyer packing. If he'd been able to get the woman's name and cell number, he'd have headed her off before she'd ever reached here.

But Geneva Morgan, despite acting as if she had the attention span of a butterfly, inevitably disconcerted him by fixing on the one thing he wanted her to ignore. She'd been doing that since his first attempt to deceive her, having to do with a homemade slingshot and a broken window when he was six, and he shouldn't have been surprised that she'd done it again today.

But today's problem was considerably more serious than a broken window, and he didn't want his mother to get hurt trying to defend someone the whole county thought was guilty of an ugly crime.

The Langdon woman stared at him, suspicion darkening blue eyes that had so much green in them they were almost turquoise. "I thought your name was Blake."

His mother's irrepressible laugh gurgled. "Blake Winston Morgan the Third, to be exact. Isn't that

29

a pompous name to hang on a helpless little baby?"

"Mom . . ." Business, Mom. This is business, remember?

"So I took one look at the pink cheeks and that fuzz of blond hair, and I decided to call him Trey. For three, you know."

"I'm sure Ms. Langdon figured that out," he said drily.

"It's not my concern." To his surprise, Jessica Langdon looked faintly embarrassed. "I just . . ." She paused, evading his gaze. "Perhaps we could clarify whether Mrs. Morgan wants me to continue with the case or not."

"Of course I do." His mother shot him a reproachful look. "Trey, we've been through this already. That poor boy couldn't possibly have done what they say, and if no one else will stand up for him, I will. I spoke with his mother, and she agreed to let me handle getting a lawyer."

"If I'm going to represent the young man, it would be helpful to know a bit more about the circumstances." Ms. Langdon looked at his mother, probably figuring she wasn't going to get anything out of him.

"Yes, of course. Do come and sit down. I don't know why we're standing here." His mother led her to a seat on the Queen Anne chair and then perched on the arm of the sofa opposite, head tipped to one side, as if waiting for questions.

The Langdon woman opened her briefcase, took out a yellow legal pad and prepared to take notes. Trey couldn't help it—his lips twitched at the image of the two of them, despite the seriousness of the situation. Mom, still seemingly caught in the '60s of her youth, wore her usual filmy Indian-inspired tunic over a pair of jeans that were frayed at the knees. Her face was bare of makeup, and a favorite pair of turquoise-and-silver earrings dangled from her ears.

His gaze lingered on Jessica Langdon. The carefully tailored, lightweight gray suit, cream silk shirt and ridiculously high heels might be suitable for the woman's usual round of clients, but not for an excursion deep into the country, where a pair of khakis and a button-down shirt were practically considered formal wear. She had auburn hair, worn in a shining, chin-length style, a heart-shaped face, skin so fair she probably didn't dare go out in the sun and deep blue eyes. Not quite beautiful, but striking enough that any man would notice—any man who liked the cool, sophisticated type, anyway.

". . . so you see, he couldn't possibly do anything like that," Mom was saying, leaning toward Jessica with the look of an earnest child. "Why, Thomas helped me plant all those roses along the back fence, and he even brought a load of chicken manure to use on the rhubarb bed. Besides, he's Amish, and the Amish simply don't commit violent acts. A more law-abiding people you'd never want to meet, and—"

"But about the crime." The lawyer sounded a little desperate, and he noticed that she hadn't written anything on her yellow pad. "I need to know—"

"Thomas Esch is accused of the beating death of a young woman named Cherry Wilson," he said bluntly. He might consider that Thomas was guilty as sin, but the boy deserved a defense attorney whose mind wasn't muddled by roses and rhubarb. "Thomas was found near her body, unconscious, in a remote barn where they'd apparently been partying. The hammer that was used to kill her was in his hand."

"Trey, dear, you don't need to be so graphic." His mother's face crinkled in distress. "I'm sure Thomas didn't—"

Impelled by the probably futile need to protect her, he crossed the room, bending over to take his mother's hands. "I know you don't want to believe it, Mom. But you have to face the truth. He's guilty, and if you become involved in trying to get him off, your friends and neighbors won't thank you. Please, just drop this."

His fingers tightened on hers, and he felt the wedding ring she'd never removed since the day his father put it on her finger forty years ago. A spasm of pain shot through him. Dad ought to be here now. He'd always protected her.

It had been over a year, and Trey still hadn't stopped wanting to talk things over with his father. Maybe he never would.

"I can't forget about doing what's right just because the neighbors might disapprove," his mother said, with that odd little dignity that could crop up now and then when she felt strongly about something.

"This isn't a matter of belief," he said, sure it was useless and hating that they were having this conversation under Jessica Langdon's cool, critical eyes. "It's a matter of facts. Evidence."

Mom freed her hand so that she could pat his cheek. "Dear Trey. You're just like your father. Always acting on reason, never on instinct."

He stiffened. "Dad had very good judgment." And acting on reason wasn't a fault.

"I'm not criticizing him, Trey. I'm just saying that sometimes you have to listen to your heart, not your head."

He straightened, trying not to give an exasperated sigh. Arguing with his mother was like . . . like boxing with a bumblebee, and about as effective.

The Langdon woman slid the cap back on her pen, apparently giving up on getting any useful information out of them. Three small lines appeared between her eyebrows.

"I really need to talk to the client before I make any recommendations. But if the physical evidence is very strong, we may need to think about a plea bargain. Will the district attorney . . ."

"Oh, no," his mother said. "You mustn't do that. Why, that's what Bobby wanted to do right away when I talked to him, and I just won't hear of any such thing."

"Bobby?" Jessica's frown deepened.

"Robert Stephens. He's our financial manager," Trey explained, his gaze fixed on his mother. "Are you telling me you talked to Bobby about this and not to me?"

"Well, I knew you wouldn't approve." His mother looked as guileless as a kitten. "So I just thought I'd talk to Bobby first. He's always so accommodating, but this time I had to practically force him to do as I asked. I finally threatened to call Eva Henderson myself if he didn't take care of it, so he did."

Did that mean that she had gone to Bobby Stephens on other occasions, instead of turning to him? Trey's temples began to throb. His father had expected him to take care of his mother—that was a given. But maybe it would have been helpful if he'd left behind some written instructions.

"Anyway, Bobby finally did what I wanted and hired a topflight Philadelphia lawyer to look after poor Thomas," his mother said. She clasped Jessica's hand suddenly, looking at her with that melting, elusive charm which had all sorts of people lining up to do as Geneva wanted. "You will handle this for us, won't you, Jessica? I just know you'll be brilliant."

The woman was succumbing. He could see it in her face. Then she sat up a little straighter, clutching her legal pad as if it were a shield.

"I'd better speak to the young man before doing anything else." She rose. "If you'll just give me directions—"

"Of course, of course." His mother glanced at him. "But there's no need for directions. Trey will be delighted to take you."

JESSICA SUCKED IN a breath, trying to think of a polite way to say she'd rather walk. But she wouldn't need to say anything, surely. Trey Morgan had made his feelings only too clear. He wouldn't touch this situation with a ten-foot pole.

"Mom," he began, looking harassed.

Geneva swung on him. "Blake Winston Morgan, don't you dare argue."

He lifted both hands. "I'm not." He turned to her. "If you're ready now, we'd better get into Lancaster before the traffic gets bad."

She doubted Lancaster traffic would bother her. "There's no need for you to accompany me. I'm sure I can find the county jail without help."

He took her elbow and piloted her toward the door. "Trust me, if you want to see Thomas and get back to the city today, don't start an argument with my mother."

She waited until they were out on the porch and presumably out of earshot before she spoke. "I know you don't want to be involved in this—"

"If my mother's involved, I am." His tone was curt. He nodded toward a dark green pickup. "I'll drive you. It'll be easier than giving directions. You can pick up your car afterward and head back. It's not out of your way."

Obviously the sooner she left Lancaster County, the happier he was going to be. Still, what he said made a certain amount of sense, and maybe she could get some information about the case from him on the way. She hated going into a situation blind.

She climbed into the high seat, trying to pull her skirt down at the same time. This suit was definitely not made for riding in pickup trucks. Come to think of it, she'd never been in a pickup before in her life.

She eyed Blake as he swung easily into the seat and started the vehicle. "So, do you prefer that I call you Mr. Morgan, or Blake or Trey?"

His jaw tightened. "Trey." He bit off the word.

"I take it you don't agree with your mother that Thomas Esch is innocent." She knew the answer to that, but she wanted to hear him articulate his reasons.

"I think he's guilty as sin."

"Why?"

The tight jaw was very much in evidence. "Do you know anything about the Amish?"

She scoured her memory. "I think I saw that movie with Harrison Ford once."

"Great." It was almost a snarl. "Well, to condense a lot of culture into a brief summation, Counselor, the Amish believe in living apart from the world. That means no electricity, no television, no movies or video games or all the other things kids take for granted. They don't believe in going to the law. They settle problems with the help of the church, not the courts. They even have their own language, a Low German dialect, although the kids learn English in school."

She thought briefly of the accented English of the young couple in the buggy. "Fascinating, but what does it have to do with the case?"

"Everything. You can't possibly defend Thomas if you don't understand what he comes from. Amish kids live a sheltered life, but in their late teens, they're allowed more freedom. They're supposed to be socializing with each other with a view to finding a mate, but plenty of them want a taste of the outside world before making the decision to be baptized into the Amish church and give it up forever. That period of running around is called *rumspringa*. That's what Thomas was doing when he got involved with Cherry Wilson."

She pondered that explanation, trying to fit it into a possible defense. "How old is Thomas?"

"Nineteen. But a young nineteen in the ways of the world."

"And the woman—Cherry Wilson, you said?"

His lips moved in an expression of distaste. "Cherry was in her mid-twenties. Had a reputation of liking to party. She worked as a waitress at the inn in Springville. You probably passed it on your way to the house."

She hadn't, since she'd gotten lost instead. "What was she doing alone in a barn with a nineteen-year-old? She sounds a bit old for teen parties."

"Rumor has it she got a kick out of partying with younger kids. I don't know how she hooked up with Thomas." He frowned a little, as if getting past his initial distaste to actually think about the case. "That is odd. The Esch family has a farm not far from our place. A close family, I'd say. Thomas always seemed a bit shy, but maybe that made his reaction all the worse."

"What do you mean?" She didn't like the idea that he was taking it for granted that her client was guilty. He seemed a reasonably intelligent man, behind the slightly tyrannical attitude of his. If he thought the boy guilty . . .

Well, her job was to provide the best defense she could, regardless. Since she'd taken the position with Henderson, Dawes and Henderson, she'd certainly defended clients who'd have been the better for a guilty plea. Things had been a lot clearer, in a way, when she'd been a prosecutor.

Trey's forehead knotted, and his hands moved restlessly on the steering wheel. "Take a kid like that—inexperienced, shy—and put him in a situation where he'd been drinking with a woman who led him on. He might, I guess, get carried away, not knowing what he was doing."

"Carried away enough to batter her with a hammer? It still seems out of character for the person your mother described."

His frown lingered. "Maybe. It's hard to say what happened. All we have are the facts, and they don't look good for Thomas."

No, they didn't. If she ended up trying to plea-bargain the case, Geneva would be disappointed in her. She'd be disappointed in herself, for that matter, but she'd do what was best for the client.

"When did this happen?"

"They were found in the early hours of Sunday morning in a barn outside of town." Trey negotiated the narrow streets of Lancaster with ease. "Thomas was passed out, drunk. Cherry had apparently been dead for several hours, if the rumors are true, and they usually are."

"He's been in custody over twenty-four hours?" Her voice rose. "Without an attorney?"

"Relax, Counselor," he said. "A local attorney has been handling the situation, basically advising the boy to say nothing. The local man doesn't want to continue with the case, though."

Trey sounded as if he didn't blame the man.

In fact, if Trey was right, the entire community was convinced of the boy's guilt. Everyone, apparently, except Geneva Morgan.

A random thought popped into her mind. The newspaper piece she'd read—

"Your mother tried to speak with Thomas when he was being taken into the police station, didn't she?"

She could almost hear his teeth grinding.

"Yes. She did. Except that it was when he was being taken to the county jail. The newspaper got that wrong. Fortunately they didn't get her name, either." He clamped his lips shut on the words.

It didn't take a genius to figure out that Trey was worried about his mother. She'd give him credit for that, although she wasn't convinced Geneva needed all that protection.

Jessica subsided, staring out the window at the fields on both sides of the road, lush and green. White farmhouses sat well back from the road, as if to protect their privacy. Here and there she spotted people working in the fields, looking like figures in a landscape painting.

"Amish," Trey said, nodding at one farmhouse. "You can tell because no power lines go to the house."

"No electricity." She tried to imagine it. "What about phones?"

Trey's shoulders moved in a shrug. "Not in the house. Often there's a phone shanty at the edge of the field, so they can use a phone for business or in an emergency."

This was the life her client had led. She tried to reconcile it with drunken parties and found she couldn't.

Springville appeared—a collection of shops and a few restaurants facing the road, with residential areas spread out behind them. She took a second look at the Springville Inn, where the dead woman had worked. A visit to talk with her coworkers might be in order.

Then they were in the countryside again. Neat farms, neat houses, twin silos flanking barns, contented-looking cows grazing in fields . . . it was like something off a calendar.

The truck overtook a gray horse-drawn buggy. Trey passed with care, raising a hand to the driver. The bearded man nodded, face impassive, and the two towheaded children with him grinned and waved.

"They know you," she said. She thought again of the pair in the buggy she'd met earlier. They'd known the Morgan family, too.

"I know most people in the township. Morgans have been here for a long time."

She let that revolve in her mind. If he knew the place that well, she couldn't ignore his sense of what the community believed about this crime.

Farmland gave way abruptly to residential areas, a few strip malls, and then they were in Lancaster proper. Trey wove his way through a maze of narrow streets easily, still wearing a slight frown. No doubt he'd like to divorce himself from this proceeding entirely.

"The county jail is in the next block," he said at last. "Anything else you need to know before you see Thomas?"

"Just one question." She probably shouldn't ask this, but she was going to, because when you were swimming in a strange ocean, it helped to know who the sharks were. "Given how you feel about the case, why did you want to come with me?"

The stone jaw returned with a vengeance. "I don't want my mother involved in this at all. She's too trusting, and she doesn't have the slightest idea how serious it is. But if I can't stop her, I'm at least going to make sure it's handled appropriately." He pulled into a parking space and stopped, turning to face her, crowding her in the small space. "You do one thing to turn this situation into a media circus or to manipulate my mother, and I'll make you wish you'd never heard of the Morgan family."

Well, that was clear enough. She had a client who was probably guilty, an employer who was acting on instinct and a very formidable man who was determined to dog her every step. And she hadn't even met the client yet.

CHAPTER THREE

THE ROOM ALLOTTED TO lawyer/client meetings was typical of such places—cement-block walls, a high barred window and a bare wooden table bolted to the floor, flanked by two chairs. The wire-meshed window in the door allowed a police officer to peer in on the conference but hear nothing.

Trey Morgan had walked with her through the maze of corridors. He'd seemed to know, or at least been recognized by, most of the people they encountered, and he'd had an easy, laid-back manner for everyone but her. She'd half expected him to try to stay with her, not that she'd have allowed it, but he hadn't, merely saying he'd be outside in the truck when she finished with Thomas.

Jessica tried not to fidget as she waited for the client, but she couldn't forget that Thomas Esch had been accused of beating a woman to death. Any normal woman would feel a sliver of anxiety in this situation. The table was only about three feet wide. If he decided to come after her, how long would it take the guard to get to her?

Nonsense. She'd certainly confronted worse during the three years she'd spent as an assistant D.A., prosecuting domestic-abuse cases. She'd burned out on that, finally, unable to look at another battered woman, knowing chances were good that the woman would change her mind about prosecuting at the last minute and go right back to her abuser, maybe ending up dead.

There'd been value in the work, certainly, but nobody could do it forever. Her father had been relieved that she had come to her senses, as he put it. From the day she passed the bar, he'd been ready to set up a position for her with a good firm. There'd also been his unspoken opinion that she wasn't tough enough to deal with criminal cases. Unspoken, maybe, but it had come through. Too bad he hadn't had the son he'd always wanted to follow his footsteps.

The door creaked, startling Jessica into an involuntary flinch. It opened. Two burly guards dwarfed the boy they ushered into the room.

At her first glimpse of Thomas Esch, the apprehension slipped away. He was nothing more than a boy, with frightened blue eyes in a round face and blond hair that looked as if someone had put a bowl on his head and cut around it.

She stood, giving him what she hoped was a reassuring smile. "Hello, Thomas. I'm Jessica Langdon. I'm the lawyer Mrs. Morgan hired to defend you." She held out her hand.

Thomas looked at the outstretched hand as if it held a trap and then cautiously shook it. His palm was hard with calluses, and her opinion pivoted again. He might look like a boy, but he was strong as a man.

Strong enough to beat a woman to death? Thomas was innocent until proved guilty in the eyes of the law, if not the community. He deserved that same assumption from his attorney.

She sat again, nodding to the chair opposite her. Still looking uncertain, Thomas slid onto the seat, moving back as if to get as far away from her as possible.

She waited until the door closed behind the guards, its slam resonating through the bare chamber. She focused on the client, keeping her mind away from the locked door.

"Thomas, do you understand that Mrs. Morgan wants to help you?"

He nodded, eyes still very wide, not blinking.

"Good. She's helping you by retaining— hiring—me to represent you with the law."

He looked down at his hands. "Mrs. Morgan is very kind." He swallowed, Adam's apple moving.

At least he could talk. His speech was formal, like that of the young pair in the buggy, and she remembered Trey's doubts over her ability to represent the boy when she knew nothing of his culture.

That was ridiculous. The law was the law, no matter what the defendant's background.

"Thomas, I want you to understand that

anything you say to me is private. I can't tell anyone, and you can trust me."

His only answer was to stare at his hands—big hands, bony and strong. Strong enough to kill. Did he get any of this? She couldn't be sure, and her frustration rose.

"Mrs. Morgan wants me to help you," she tried again. "But I can only do that if you talk to me about what happened."

He looked at her face then away again. "My parents—they would not want me to be involved with the law."

Trey had said something like that, but she'd disregarded it. Apparently she should have paid more attention. "Mrs. Morgan spoke with them about hiring me, and they agreed. And I'm afraid it's too late, anyway. You are already involved. The police believe you killed Cherry."

There was no mistaking the emotion behind his expression now: fear. She expected a denial, but he was silent.

"Did you and Cherry see a lot of each other?"

He shrugged. "Sometimes at parties she would talk to me."

"Were you dating? Did you go out just with her?"

He shook his head, the muscles in his face working.

"You were found alone with her. Did you go out together that night? Saturday night?"

Again he shook his head.

"Thomas, you were found with her. You must have gone out together, or how did you get there?"

"The other lawyer. He said not to talk to anyone. Not to answer questions."

"He's not representing you now. I am."

His face took on a mulish expression. "Mr. Frost said not to talk to anyone. Not to answer questions. I know him."

The implication was clear. Thomas didn't know her. He didn't trust her. Would it do any good if she could arrange for Mrs. Morgan to talk with him? She could imagine Trey's reaction to that.

"Suppose I talk to Mr. Frost. If he tells you it's all right, will you answer my questions?"

The big hands tightened briefly, then relaxed. He nodded.

She blew out a breath. Patience. Obviously that was what was required just now. Plenty of patience.

"All right, then. That's what I'll do. I'll bring Mr. Frost to vouch for me." She stood, repressing the instinct that wanted to demand answers, to move, to get on with the case. She could do nothing without her client's trust.

He looked up at her, his eyes as wide and innocent as a child's. "They took away my clothes."

"I'm sorry. You will get them back, if . . . when you are released."

"It is not proper. For an Amish man to be dressed this way." He touched the front of the orange jumpsuit he wore. "Not proper," he repeated.

"People who are being detained by the police are required to dress that way. I'm afraid there's nothing I can do about it."

"If you told them I need my clothes . . ."

"It wouldn't do any good. They won't change their minds."

He just stared at her, eyes wide with expectation. She'd said he could trust her, but she couldn't do the first thing he asked of her. Clearly he didn't understand the situation he was in.

And just as clearly, she didn't understand him. Trey had been right about her. She didn't know enough to defend this boy.

TREY SAT IN THE TRUCK, waiting for the Langdon woman to come out of the red sandstone building that was the county jail. With those circular Norman towers, it looked more like a castle. Its builders had intended it to impress everyone who looked at it with the weight and majesty of the law. No doubt it intimidated a kid like Thomas.

With the radio on, he was treated to the views of the local station's public, conveyed through the station's call-in show. Opinion was running high—all of it against Thomas, it seemed. There were always those who harbored a prejudice against the Amish, just because they were different. Thomas's arrest was feeding that feeling.

He switched the radio off. Neither Jessica Langdon nor his mother had a good grasp of the situation.

Trying to explain to his mother was useless. She wasn't swayed by facts. She believed in Thomas, and she would do what she felt was right.

Jessica wasn't in this for idealistic reasons, however. Worry tied his stomach in a knot. If Jessica thought this the sort of sensational case that would make her reputation, who knew what tactics she might resort to?

Was she that kind of person? His immediate impression had been of someone pretty hard-boiled, with her elegant clothing and her cool manner. But there had been a brief glimpse or two of someone not so easily categorized.

He didn't think he liked that. He wanted to know where he was with people. And she'd challenged his opinion of what was best for his mother—he knew he didn't like that. His mother could be devastated by this case, no matter how it turned out. Would Jessica even care?

His hands tightened on the steering wheel, and he deliberately forced himself to relax. Since Dad's death, he'd been responsible—for his mother, for the family-owned businesses and rental properties, for all the people in the township who depended on the Morgan family. His thoughts flickered briefly to the office. He'd had to cancel a couple of appointments today, and no doubt there'd be more of that in coming days.

He couldn't go to the office, deal with the day-to-day running of the family properties, handle the investments his grandfather and father had entrusted to his care and still deal with the ramifications of his mother's interest in defending Thomas. So Morgan Enterprises would have to run along without him until this was settled.

In one way, he'd been preparing all his life for his role. It had governed his choice of summer jobs, his business major, even his Wharton MBA. He'd just never expected it to come so soon. He wasn't ready. Maybe he'd never have been ready to lose his father, but to lose him that way . . .

Why, Dad? Why did you do it? How could the father I thought I knew do something like that?

He'd asked that question a thousand times. He'd never gotten an answer.

His gaze, idly scanning the street in front of the jail, suddenly sharpened. That dark blue van bore the logo of the local television station. The building entrance was out of his view from here, but the chance that the news crew camped out at the jail for any reason other than to cover the murder was nil.

He shoved the door open and slid out, worry and

irritation edging his nerves. He reached the corner and stopped, stunned. Not only had the news crew clustered in front of the entrance, so had probably thirty or forty other people. A couple of them carried signs, leaving no doubt as to their opinion on Thomas's guilt.

As if that wasn't bad enough, the television news reporter was busy interviewing them. Anyone who hadn't already thought it a good idea to voice their uninformed opinion would probably be inspired by the sight on the five-o'clock news.

The crowd blocked the steps. Unless someone warned Jessica, she'd walk out right into the arms of the television news reporter. Was it coincidence the news people were waiting at this precise moment? He doubted it. He moved faster. If he could get into the building, find Jessica, take her out another exit—

Too late. The heavy door in the front of the building moved, and Jessica came out. In an instant the reporter pounced, calling Jessica's name.

Her name. He hadn't even known that until she'd arrived. They'd been tipped off, then. By Jessica? If she wanted attention, there was no better way to get it.

The crowd, alerted by the reporter's question, closed in, waving their signs. He had a glimpse of a startled face through the narrow glass slit in the door. It quickly vanished, to find help, he hoped.

Trey elbowed his way through the mass of bodies with murmured apologies. Ridiculous that at a moment like this his mother's training in proper manners held. Except that in Mom's universe, people didn't yell obscenities to express their opinions. If he could reach Jessica before she said anything that would focus attention on his mother . . .

Jessica seemed to be holding her own. He shoved his way between two burly bodies. She'd looked surprised when the reporter ambushed her, he had to say that, but she could have been faking it.

"Come on, Ms. Langdon. A Philadelphia lawyer doesn't just show up here. Who hired you?" The reporter had the looks of a movie starlet and the aggressive instincts of a puma. She thrust the microphone in Jessica's face.

"Every defendant is entitled to the best possible representation. I'm sure you'll agree." Jessica's professional manner seemed unruffled.

"You want us to believe that an Amish family knew enough to bring in a topflight Philadelphia firm?" The reporter's voice expressed disbelief. "The public has a right to know who brought you here."

Trey pushed his way closer. If she mentioned his mother—

"Right now I'm more concerned with the rights of my client." Jessica smiled at the camera as if she did this every day. "I don't think anything will be gained by my discussing the case when I've hardly begun to assess the facts."

"Everyone knows the facts. He's a filthy murderer, and you're trying to get him off." The yelled words came from the far side of the crowd, and the mass of people seemed to surge forward.

Trey shoved his way through and caught Jessica's arm. "Let's go."

"Mr. Morgan." The reporter sounded like a woman who'd just been given an unexpected gift. "What is your interest in this case?"

"None at all." Taking his lead from Jessica, he smiled blandly. "I'm just giving Ms. Langdon a ride, that's all."

He turned to go, clasping Jessica's arm firmly, but the mass of people had closed in behind them. Push through them? Retreat into the jail?

Even as he thought it, the heavy door opened. "What's going on out here?" The cop had a deep voice to match his authoritative manner. "You people can't block access to the jail."

Trey seized his opportunity, piloting Jessica through the crowd and toward the pickup. She hurried to keep up with his long strides. Finally she planted her feet, forcing him to come to a stop.

He glared at her. "You eager to do another round with the television reporter? Let's go."

"The police are keeping them busy. And it looks

53

as if someone is waiting for us." She nodded toward the truck.

A figure dressed in Amish black stood motionless. Ezra Burkhalter, one of the three ministers of the local congregation, apparently unnoticed as yet by the reporters. What was he doing here?

"Ezra." He nodded, hoping the reporter wouldn't look their way. "Something I can do for you?"

"I came to this place to see Thomas Esch, but the officers would not allow it." Ezra's narrow, bony face seemed to grow more rigid as he looked at Jessica. "This is the Englisch lawyer you have brought down on us."

It would be too much to hope that every Amish person in the county hadn't heard by now that his mother had hired a lawyer to defend Thomas. But the Amish weren't likely to be chattering about that to outsiders.

"This is Jessica Langdon. She'll be representing Thomas in the Englisch court. Ms. Langdon, this is Ezra Burkhalter. He is one of the ministers of Thomas's congregation."

"I'm glad to meet—"

"It is not fitting." Ezra didn't raise his voice, but it rasped like a saw blade, cutting through Jessica's words. "The boy has brought disgrace to his family, and now you would have this exposed in an English court for all to see."

Jessica stiffened. "Mr. Burkhalter, my only job is to give Thomas the legal defense to which he is entitled."

"You can do nothing for him. Nothing." The anger in Ezra's face was unmistakable. "Stay out of this, and leave us alone."

He turned and walked away. Jessica stared after him, looking stunned.

The television crew, freeing themselves from the crowd, hurried toward them. Trey hustled Jessica inside the truck. Climbing in himself, he slammed the door on a shouted question and pulled away from the curb, narrowly missing the cameraman who'd darted into the street. A glimpse in the rearview mirror showed him the television reporter trotting down the street after Ezra. Lots of luck. She wouldn't get anything out of him.

They rounded the corner and Jessica let out an audible breath. "Well. That was . . . odd. I didn't expect it."

She sounded genuine, but how could he be sure? "You mean the television people, the crowd or Ezra Burkhalter?"

"Any of them. All of them. I guess the Burkhalter man particularly. Why is he angry that I'm here? I'd think he'd be grateful that Thomas has someone to defend him."

Trey shrugged, trying to get rid of the tension in his shoulders. "The Amish don't want to find themselves in the news. There's prejudice enough against them without that. They believe in living separate, and they don't go to the law."

"Thomas said something like that, but in this case the law has come to them. I'll do the best I can for Thomas."

"I don't think Ezra Burkhalter will see it that way."

Her mouth set as she considered that. "If all the Amish react that way, it will make the situation more difficult."

Difficult enough to make her go away? He was tempted to paint a black picture, just to achieve that, but he couldn't.

"Not all. I'm sure there will be those who welcome your help. Thomas's family, certainly."

She nodded, brushing a wing of auburn hair back from her face. "I suppose. I certainly didn't expect the crowd at the jail. Is there really that much prejudice against the Amish?"

"Not so much out in the country, where people know them." He tried to answer fairly, but the Amish were such a constant part of his life that it was hard to see them as an outsider would. "They're different, and plenty of misconceptions float around among people who don't know them."

He'd known there would be strong feelings about the ugliness of the crime and the Amish connection, but he hadn't expected a mob at the jail, either. If people were this worked up now, what would it be like by the time the case came to trial?

He drove automatically, his mind turning the situation at the county jail over in his mind. It still rankled, having the television people there exactly when Jessica would be coming out. It was too pat.

"Were you really surprised by the news crew?" He put the question abruptly, not sure how much good it would do. If she'd tipped them off, she'd hardly admit it.

He felt her gaze on him and flicked a glance in her direction. The blue eyes had widened.

"What do you mean? Why wouldn't I be surprised?"

"You wouldn't be if you were the one who told them you'd be there."

"Told them—that's ridiculous!" Her voice rose. "I'm not in the habit of headline-hunting."

"The reporter knew your name. That means that someone told her you were going to represent Thomas."

"I wasn't that someone." Her voice grew icy. "I understand that you want to protect your mother from any unpleasantness, but I'm not your enemy. All I want is to do my job for my client."

He shot another look at her as he turned onto the road that would lead them out of town. "If you didn't tip off the news people, who did?"

"Ask yourself that question," Jessica said tartly.

"It seems to me the leak was far more likely to come from your end of things than mine. My office would have no interest in tipping off the press at this point. Does anyone else know your mother was hiring an attorney for Thomas?"

A good question, and one he didn't have an answer to. "Who knows? My mother is not exactly a model of discretion, as you may have noticed."

"I found your mother delightful." The frost was back in her voice.

"Try being responsible for her and see how delightful it is." He muttered the words and was instantly sorry. He didn't need to be confiding in this woman, of all people. "She may have told any number of people. And there are people in Bobby's office who might think it worth a tip to the paper." He lifted an eyebrow. "The same might be said of your office, I suppose."

"You suppose wrong. Any hint of indiscretion in an employee of the firm would lead to immediate dismissal."

There was a note in her tone that he couldn't quite read. "Sounds like your boss runs a tight ship."

Her hands clenched on her lap, then eased, as if she made a deliberate effort not to show a reaction. "He does," she said shortly. He felt her gaze on his face. "You'd better get used to the publicity. There may come a time when I'll have to talk to the press. Thomas is going to need all the goodwill he can get."

"If and when that happens, I'd advise you to keep my mother's name out of it."

"If you wanted to keep attention away from your family's role in the case, you shouldn't have interfered with my handling of that reporter. I was perfectly capable of dealing with her myself."

His mood wasn't improved by knowing that she was probably right. He'd acted on instinct, just as he so often accused his mother of doing.

Maybe it was time to change the subject. "How did you make out with Thomas?"

Her frown looked worried. "Not well. I'll have to talk with this Mr. Frost as soon as possible. Thomas trusts him, and he's not going to open up to me until Frost assures him it's all right."

"That's easily done."

He drew the car to the side of the road and stopped, then pulled out his cell phone and touched the number for Leo Frost's private line. In a moment's time he'd set up an appointment for Jessica for the next morning. When he ended the call, he realized that she was looking at him with more than a little annoyance in her face.

"What?" he said, answering the look. "You said you had to meet with him."

"I didn't say I wanted you to make an appointment for me. Or to interfere in my handling of the case."

"Interfering? I thought I was being helpful." He gave her the smile that women usually found disarming. It didn't seem to have that effect on Jessica.

"I don't need your help. I'd hoped I'd made that clear."

He found he was gritting his teeth. "You've made your position clear enough. Now you'd better understand mine. As long as my mother insists on being involved in this case, I am, too. So you'd better get used to it, Counselor. We're going to be seeing a lot of each other."

CHAPTER FOUR

BY THE TIME JESSICA pulled into the parking lot at her town-house complex in Philadelphia, her head was splitting. She'd hit the city just in time for rush-hour traffic. Nobody wanted to be caught on the Schuylkill Expressway, known as the Sure-kill by locals, at that time of day.

Her headache intensified when her cell phone rang just as she walked in the front door. She frowned at the number.

Her father. That was unusual enough to give her a jolt of apprehension as she answered.

"Dad. Is anything wrong?"

"Perhaps I should be asking you that question, Jessica." Her father's voice was as crisp as if he were talking to an erring subordinate. "I understand you're on shaky ground at work."

She was tempted to ask how he knew that, but that would be pointless. Her father moved in rarified judicial circles, where everyone seemed to know everyone else's business.

"It's nothing I can't handle," she said, hoping that was true as she closed the door behind her.

"I hope that's true." His voice echoed her thoughts. "I've invested my own political capital in obtaining that position for you. Don't disappoint me."

That was all. No question about whether she

was being judged unfairly, no expressions of concern. She and her father didn't have that sort of relationship. Still, he loved her in his own way, didn't he?

"I'll do my best."

"Naturally." Unspoken was his obvious suspicion that her best wouldn't be good enough. "I'll talk with you on the weekend."

She hung up and blew out a frustrated breath as she turned toward her roommate. Sara Davenport was collapsed in their one recliner with her computer on her lap. "My father," she said in explanation. "He's heard about the job situation."

"Don't let it get to you," Sara said, her voice warm with sympathy. She was one of the few people who knew how just how rocky Jessica's relationship with her father was.

"I try." She dropped onto the sofa, leaning her head back. "I'm going to have to get a motel room in Lancaster County, at least for the next week or so. Driving back and forth is a killer."

"Don't you have a date with Brett Dunleavy on Friday?"

She closed her eyes for a moment. "I'd forgotten. I'll have to cancel."

"You'd forgotten. Need I point out that that is a sad commentary on your relationship with young Dr. Brett?"

She'd have thrown a pillow at Sara if she weren't so tired. "Brett understands. Given how busy his residency keeps him, he's no more eager to get seriously involved at this point than I am." She'd tried serious. It hadn't worked.

"Couple of workaholics. Sounds like a match made in heaven." Sara grinned. "So you're forgetting your love life. This case must be a stinker."

"It is, but what makes you think so?"

"If the partners were that ready to pass it off to you, that means they didn't want to deal with it themselves." Sara set the computer on the coffee table and shoved her glasses up on her head, using them to hold back her unruly tangle of red hair.

Since Sara had spent two years in a topflight firm in the city before escaping to a legal-aid office where she said she could at least help people who needed it, her advice was usually on target.

"You're probably right." Jessica rubbed her aching temples. "Henderson implied that the woman who's paying for the defense asked for me, but I don't see how that can be."

"What's the case? I haven't had anything more interesting lately than the usual run of rotten absentee landlords. I spent the day arguing with a housing inspector, trying to convince him to do his job."

"This would be right up your alley," Jessica said. "You always like taking on the hopeless cases. I've got an Amish kid accused of the beating death of a woman who was apparently something of a party girl."

"Amish? That is unusual. I can't remember the last time I saw anything about an Amish person suspected in a crime."

She hadn't thought of Sara as a source of information. Maybe she should have. "I take it that means you've never represented one."

"The Amish don't spend much time in the city. I've been on the usual tour of Lancaster County, but that's about it. Tell me about the defendant."

"There's not much to tell at this point." Jessica rubbed the back of her neck, trying to get rid of the tension there. "He doesn't trust me enough to talk to me, and I don't know how to get through to him. His minister wants me off the case, and as far as I can tell, most of the community thinks he's guilty."

"What about the person who's paying you?"

Jessica thought about how to explain Geneva Morgan. She wasn't sure she could even explain to herself the effect the woman had on her.

"She's totally convinced that the boy—Thomas Esch—is innocent, but it's based on instinct, not on facts."

Sara's nose wrinkled. "I wouldn't discount instinct, at least not if you thought her opinion reliable."

"I'm not sure. Geneva—well, she seemed a bit quirky, I guess. Warmhearted. I can't say what kind of judge of character she is on one brief phone conversation and an acquaintance of fifteen minutes or so."

"But you liked her," Sara said.

"Yes, I did." There was no harm in admitting that. "She certainly has faith in the boy. And faith in my ability to prove him innocent. As for whether she's right—well, her son doesn't think so."

"Her son? What does he have to do with it?" Sara snuggled into the chair, grinning. "Come on, give."

"He tried to get rid of me, because he doesn't want his mother involved in something this nasty."

"Overprotective," Sara said.

"Overprotective, arrogant, used to being the boss, I'd guess. And he's determined to dog my footsteps to make sure I don't do anything that reflects badly on the family."

"Sounds like a pompous jerk." Sara dismissed Trey with a wave of her hand. "If his mother retained you and the client agrees, he has nothing to do with it."

"Easy for you to say. You don't have to deal with him." And besides, Sara had more assertiveness in her little finger than Jessica had in her whole body. "It's curious that Mr. Henderson is so keen on pleasing the Morgan family. I'd have said they were big fish in a small pond, frankly.

Important enough in their little world, but hardly the type to impress Henderson."

"Let's see who they are." Sara straightened, leaning toward the laptop. She looked at Jessica inquiringly. "Geneva Morgan, you said?"

"That's right. The son's name is Trey—well, actually Blake Winston Morgan the Third. But I'm not sure it's appropriate to be looking them up." It always made her feel like a stalker to do that, but Sara never hesitated to check Google even for casual acquaintances.

Sara's fingers moved rapidly on the keys. "Hmm."

"Hmm what?"

Her roommate grinned. "Aren't you afraid it's inappropriate?"

"Never mind that." She crossed the room to perch on the arm of Sara's chair. "What did you find?"

"Geneva is from a Main Line Philadelphia family—the kind of people who go to the right schools, marry the right people and only appear in the newspapers when they're born, when they marry and when they die. That's probably the answer. Maybe she went to the same exclusive girls' school as your Mr. Henderson's wife. Those people all know each other."

Jessica couldn't help but smile at the description, thinking of Geneva. "She must have been the outlaw, then. She dresses like a '60s hippie. How did you get all that so quickly?"

Sara shrugged, not bothering to point out that she was a pro when it came to finding information about people. "I went on the assumption that Winston was Geneva's maiden name. Easy enough to find her birth and marriage record. The rest of it is informed supposition, based on a lifetime of knowledge of Philadelphia society."

"Come to think of it, she did mention something about Eva Henderson. What about Trey's father?"

Sara's fingers clicked on the keys. "Old county family, going right back to the original land grant from William Penn, it looks like. Nobody rich or famous, but solid citizens, all of them. Except . . ." The sassy tone in which she'd been reciting her research died away.

"Except what?" Jessica leaned over, trying to read the screen.

"Blake Morgan the Second. Your Trey's father, I suppose. It seems he committed suicide about a year ago."

"Suicide." Jessica repeated the word, shocked and saddened. "I didn't think—well, how could I know?" That would explain why Trey was so protective of his mother.

"The obituary is carefully worded. A newspaper report won't be as tactful. If I can find anything else—" Keys clicked again, and Sara frowned at the screen.

It took only a few more minutes to find a

newspaper account of the tragedy. Sara turned the laptop so that Jessica could read it for herself.

Trey's father had shot himself in an isolated hunting cabin belonging to the family a few days after receiving a diagnosis of cancer. The photo showed a rustic cottage surrounded by dense woods. His son had been the one to find his body.

Jessica's stomach twisted. "Poor man," she murmured, not sure whether she was talking about Trey or his father. Maybe both.

"Yes," Sara said, her normal ebullience muted. "But you can't let it change how you deal with him. If he's interfering in your case, you still have the right to brush him off. Politely, of course."

She hadn't been able to brush him off even when she'd resorted to rudeness. This made it a hundred times harder. She would have been better off not knowing. And poor Geneva . . . how difficult that must have been for her.

"What did you say the client's name is?" Sara was clicking away again, undeterred.

"Thomas Esch. But you're not going to find anything about him. I told you—he's Amish. I don't know much about them, but I'm pretty sure they avoid publicity. The original account I read gave only his name and age."

Sara nodded, scanning quickly down through her search results. "You're right about that. There's nothing here except accounts of his arrest. He was taken into custody right after the body was discovered. He was still at the scene, either asleep or unconscious."

"Right." That was what Trey had said. "I'll read through the rest of the coverage later." If it came to asking for a change of venue, she'd need that ammunition. She rose, stretching. "Is there anything left of that chicken soup your mother sent over?"

Since Sara was a native Philadelphian, Jessica had benefited from her mother's apparent conviction that they both needed quantities of home-cooked food every week in order to survive.

"You can have the rest of it," Sara said absently, her gaze still intent on the computer screen. "Wait a minute. Here's something you didn't mention. Did you know that the barn where the body was found actually belongs to the Morgan family?"

Jessica stopped in the middle of a yawn. "Are you sure?"

"That's what the paper says. They didn't tell you?"

"No. Neither of them did." Her mind whirled for a moment then settled. Geneva, in all her protestations of how innocent Thomas was, in all her talk of the gardening he did for her—was that only meant to establish that Thomas had access to the barn they owned?

And Trey. How could Trey have talked about the case as much as he had without mentioning the fact that he owned the barn where the murder occurred? He'd glossed over the finding of the body without so much as a hint of it.

The sympathy she'd been feeling for Trey after learning of his father's suicide vanished. He'd lied to her. Well, maybe not lied, exactly, but he'd omitted an important piece of the truth. Which meant that she couldn't trust Trey Morgan any farther than she could throw him.

TREY'S STOMACH CHURNED mercilessly as he pulled into the rutted track. Not because of the road. Because it led to the cabin where his father died.

Jonas Miller waited, leaning against a tree as if he had all the time in the world to spare, although Trey knew perfectly well that any Amish farmer had a long list of chores. Still, Jonas took all his responsibilities seriously, including looking after the Morgan hunting cabin and the surrounding property. It was a message from Jonas that had brought Trey here so unwillingly this morning.

He stopped the truck and climbed out, trying not to look at the cabin. "Morning, Jonas. I got your message."

Jonas nodded gravely, his blue eyes serious in a weathered face above the beard that marked him as a married man. "Trey. I wish I had not had to bring you out here already."

Trey shrugged, trying to ease the tension out of his shoulders. "It's all right. I know you wouldn't have sent for me unless something was wrong."

The last thing that had been wrong at the cabin had been his father's lifeless body, slumped over the table, the gun fallen from his fingers.

Jonas was silent, as if he knew and respected what Trey was thinking.

Trey took a breath and blew it out. "So. You came over and found the door open."

"Chust cracked a bit, it was." Jonas sounded troubled. "The padlock was lying on the porch floor."

"Did you look inside?" The longer they stood and talked, the longer he could put off the moment at which he'd have to go in.

Jonas inclined his head. "I took a look, ja. Thinking it might have been teenagers, tearing places up. It did not seem anything was disturbed, so I thought it best to let it be until you could see."

He couldn't delay any longer. "Let's have a look, then."

He strode toward the cabin. The hunting cabin, they'd always called it, although Dad had never had much taste for hunting. Trey and his brother had gone through a phase of wanting to bag a buck when they were in their teens, and Dad had gone along with them, more to see them safe, he supposed, than because Dad wanted to shoot anything.

Still, they'd come out here often enough, whenever Dad wanted to get away from the telephone and have a bit of quiet. They'd fish the stream, cook out over an open fire and go to sleep watching the stars.

Good memories, plenty of them. Unfortunately they didn't seem to cancel out the one terrible one.

Jonas stood back to let him go up the steps first. Trey crossed to the door and bent to examine the padlock. It wasn't obviously damaged. He put his hand on the rough wood panel of the door, blanked out his thoughts as best he could and opened it.

At first glance, nothing seemed wrong. His gaze touched the kitchen table and skittered away. Nausea rose in his throat. He wanted to leave. The need pushed at him, pounded in his temples.

He couldn't. Jonas's sense of responsibility had brought him here. Trey's own sense of responsibility forced him to stay, even though he ought to be back at Leo Frost's office right now, keeping tabs on Jessica's activities.

The cabin wasn't large—a big room downstairs, divided into kitchen and living area, three tiny bedrooms upstairs, the smallest not much bigger than a closet.

He moved cautiously around the living room area, feeling as if any sudden gesture would set loose the pain that clawed at him.

Jonas made his own circuit. He stopped at the massive fieldstone fireplace that took up much of the outside wall. He squatted. "Someone has had a fire here. The hearth was clean and empty the last time I looked."

Trey looked for himself. Jonas was right. "So someone's been here, but not the usual teenage party crowd. They'd make more of a mess than this."

"Ja, they would. A tramp, you think? Chust looking for shelter?"

"Could be." Trey frowned. That didn't feel right. They didn't have tramps any longer, and Lancaster's homeless wouldn't be likely to come clear out here to find a roof.

Jonas had moved on to the kitchen, and Trey forced himself to follow. The memories were out in the open now. His mother's worries when Dad didn't come home that night. His own conviction that Dad needed a little time alone to deal with the bad news the doctor had delivered. Cancer. Serious, but something that could be fought.

But Dad hadn't chosen to fight. The man Trey had always thought the bravest person he knew had put a gun to his head instead of battling the cancer. It didn't make sense to him. It never had. He'd spent months trying to find a way to make that fact fit, but he couldn't. If there had been something else troubling his father—

Trey looked at the table. He'd come in the door cautiously that morning, calling his father's name, embarrassed at intruding on what he'd thought was a spiritual retreat on his father's part. And found him dead.

The table and floor had been scrubbed clean since then, the table moved to a slightly different position. Jonas must have done that—Trey had certainly been in no shape to think of having it done.

He cleared his throat. "You cleaned up in here, after. Thank you."

Jonas looked embarrassed at being thanked. "Ach, it was little enough to do for him. Your father was a fine man. Everyone knows that."

Trey could only nod. Yes, everyone had known that.

"Trey—" Jonas hesitated for a moment. "It seems to me that only God can know what was in your father's mind and heart in the last moments of his life. Only God can judge."

Endless comforting platitudes had been aimed at Trey when he'd been in no shape to listen to them. Now, oddly enough, he found comfort in Jonas's simple words.

"Thank you."

Jonas was already turning away, with the typical Amish reluctance to accept thanks or compliments. He moved to the sink and stopped. "Look at this."

Trey looked. An empty wine bottle lay in the sink. A moderately expensive bottle, not the sort of thing he'd expect the local teenagers to favor.

"Someone has been here," Jonas said again.

"Yes. But I doubt we're going to know who. Or

why." Some married man, meeting with a girlfriend on the sly? The thought sickened him—that someone would use the place his father died for such a purpose.

He straightened abruptly, leaving the bottle untouched. "I'll get a new padlock and drop it off at your place, if you don't mind putting it on. That's all we can do."

Jonas nodded. "It makes no trouble. I will take care of the lock."

Turning his back on the table, Trey headed for the door. Maybe the best thing would be to put the place on the market. He didn't see the family wanting to spend time here ever again. Let someone else worry about break-ins.

He was nearly at the door when a shaft of sunlight from the side window picked up a pinpoint of light reflecting from the leg of a wooden straight chair. He bent, running his hand down the leg.

His fingers touched a rough spot, jagged enough to snag a piece of fabric. He pulled the fabric free and looked at it.

A tiny red scrap, maybe an inch long and not more than an eighth of an inch wide. Tiny red sequins glittered when he moved it in his fingers.

Nothing. It meant nothing. It was the sort of thing someone who liked cheap finery would have worn. An image of Cherry Wilson popped into his mind, and he pushed it away. This had nothing to do with her.

CHAPTER FIVE

"THANK YOU, MR. FROST." Jessica held out her hand to the elderly attorney. "I really appreciate your sharing your expertise with me." Her interview with Frost had been helpful, and he'd been cooperative. Because of the Morgan connection with the case? Maybe, but she still appreciated it.

Gray eyes twinkled behind wire-rimmed glasses. "For a small-town fuddy-duddy, you mean."

Was her embarrassment showing? That had been exactly the impression she'd had when she'd entered an office that looked as if it hadn't changed since the 1930s and met the white-haired, stooped gentleman who'd risen from his rolltop desk at her approach. It had only taken a few minutes of conversation to realize how wrong she was.

"You're as up-to-date as I am, and you have years more experience, as well. I'm surprised you're not defending Thomas yourself." An unpleasant thought occurred to her. "Is it because you're convinced he's guilty?"

Frost shook his head. "Even if I did, I'd still think he deserved a fair trial, unlike some people I could name, such as our esteemed district attorney."

He sent an annoyed glance toward the

newspaper lying on the corner of his desk. She'd already seen it. It contained a front-page interview with the district attorney, who seemed, by the way he spoke, to have Thomas already convicted and on his way to the state penitentiary.

"Is he usually that—" she considered several words and eliminated them "—outspoken?"

"Preston Connelly is ambitious. A case like this has already drawn regional attention. He'll make the most of it, I'm sure."

"Does that mean it would hurt your practice if you took on the case?" That would be a very good reason for bringing in an outsider.

"No, I'm stepping aside on doctor's orders." Frost patted his chest. "The old ticker's been acting up a bit. Oh, I'm fine for routine jobs, but I'm afraid a high-profile murder case is too much."

"I'm sorry." She wasn't sure what else to say.

"Don't look so mournful." He chuckled. "I'm not going to drop dead yet, but I am in the midst of retiring. Still, if you need any help, you can come to me. Strictly in confidence. Henderson, Dawes and Henderson don't have to know a thing about it."

"Thanks. I just might take you up on that." Somewhat to her surprise, she realized she meant it. It wasn't in her nature to trust easily, but Leo Frost's integrity seemed to shine through everything he said.

She walked out of his office smiling, and there was Trey, waiting for her. Her smile faded, and she went toward him with a sense of inevitability. Of course he would show up. Just as well. Before much more time passed, she was going to confront him about what he'd been holding back.

He stood, laying aside the well-thumbed magazine he'd been looking at.

She lifted her eyebrows. "A little late, aren't you? I expected you to be lying in wait the minute I arrived in town."

"I had . . . something else to do this morning." His normally pleasant expression went somber, and she thought she saw pain in his eyes. Before she could react, the impression was gone. "How did your meeting with Leo go?" he asked.

"Fine." She wanted to confront him, but she could hardly do that here, with Frost's elderly secretary pretending to look through a file while she listened to every word. "He's meeting me at the jail at one o'clock to talk with Thomas."

"Good." His tone was brisk, as if whatever bothered him had been swept away. "What are you going to do until then?"

"I have a reservation at Willow Brook Motel in Springville, since I'll be staying until after the arraignment, probably longer. I may as well go check in."

She caught an expression of distaste on his face.

Was he really that bothered by her presence? "Something wrong?"

He shrugged. "Not if you like faux Pennsylvania Dutch tourist traps. You might be more comfortable at one of the local bed-and-breakfasts, or at the Springville Inn."

Was that really all that was behind his reaction? She couldn't trust anything he said, knowing he'd already lied to her once.

"I'll be fine. After all, I'm here on business, not a vacation."

They had reached the ground floor of the building, and Trey continued walking with her down the hall toward the parking lot in the rear where she'd left her car. They were alone, doors closed on both sides of them. This might be the best chance she'd have to confront him.

"Tell me something," she said abruptly.

He halted, looking down at her with a quizzical expression. "What?"

"Why didn't you tell me you own the barn where Cherry Wilson was found dead?"

If she expected an explosion in return, she didn't get it. Trey simply looked blank for a moment.

"Didn't I?" He frowned. "Maybe I didn't. I suppose I didn't think it that important."

"Not important that the murder happened in your barn? Do you really expect me to buy that?"

His face hardened at her tone. "I'm not sure what to expect from you, Counselor. But that happens to be the truth. And it's not exactly 'our' barn. Our barn is the one behind our house."

"But you own it. The police had to have questioned you about that."

"They did." He bit off the words. "I didn't even realize the crime happened on a piece of land our corporation owns until they brought it up. I told them just what I'm telling you. The barn where Cherry was found is on an abandoned farm my father bought years ago, miles from our place. Anyone could have had access to it."

"That person would have to know it was there, and that he could get in."

A muscle twitched in his jaw. "Meaning Thomas? That's what the police think, I suppose. But almost anyone in the township might know as much. Country people are aware of things like that."

"You said it was abandoned. Doesn't anyone use it?" Her suspicions couldn't be allayed that easily.

"No one, much of the time. A neighboring farmer sometimes uses it for storage, but I don't think he has anything in it right now."

"So you just let it sit there."

"Believe it or not, we do. The land is too cut up to be good farmland, but eventually it may be ripe for development. Look, this is not really that unusual, no matter how it might seem to you. That land is one small parcel out of hundreds of acres Morgan Enterprises owns in the county. A large part of our business is involved in real estate. I don't necessarily know the details of every parcel. Naturally I looked it up, once the police told me."

"I see." Did that make sense? She supposed so. It would be like expecting her father to know instantly the status of every investment in his portfolio, she'd guess. "Does your mother know?"

"I didn't tell her. It would just make her feel more responsible."

"She might easily find it out. It's been in at least one of the newspaper reports."

"If and when she does, I'll deal with it." He started walking. "Look, I'm not going to keep trying to convince you. Either you accept my word or not."

She trailed after him to the door, fighting with herself. She wanted to believe him, and the strength of that feeling dismayed her. Trey hadn't given her much of a reason to trust him.

He held the door for her, and she went through it without speaking. She took a few steps and stopped dead.

"My car . . ." It sank to the pavement, both tires flat on the side facing her. Anger flickered through her. She hurried to the car, circling it. Not just two. All four tires were flat.

Her breath caught. A knife stuck out of the front tire on the driver's side, piercing a piece of paper.

Trey grasped her arm, the warmth and strength

of his hand penetrating the sleeve of her jacket. "Wait. Let me take a look."

She shook herself free, bending to read what was scrawled on the paper. *Go back where you belong.* The words were followed by an ugly obscenity.

She started to reach for it, but Trey caught her hand, holding it as firmly as he'd gripped her arm. A wave of warmth went through her. She wanted to lean on him, to rely on him. But she couldn't, because he might be the very person responsible for this.

THE POLICE HAD COME, had taken statements and photographs, and gone again. Trey leaned against his truck, watching Jessica, who in turn watched the garage mechanic now circling her car, shaking his head and clucking softly.

Jessica had surprised him a little by her seeming reluctance to call the police at their discovery. He'd done it for her, and she hadn't liked that, either. Face it, she wasn't going to like anything he did.

He pushed himself away from the truck, feeling a little reluctance of his own. This situation was spinning rapidly out of control. Despite the ugly crowd at the jail, he hadn't expected outright vandalism, and the sight of that knife sticking out of the tire had twisted his stomach.

Jessica had turned to him in her shock and

distress—for about half a second. Then she'd pulled away, determined to stand on her own. An admirable quality, he supposed, but in this case . . . well, he wasn't sure what he thought.

The destructive act had sickened him, but looking at it in a hardheaded way, it could get him what he wanted. It could make Jessica think twice about this case.

He approached, noticing the way her shoulders stiffened as he neared. "I'll drive you to the jail. You'll be late if you wait until they get the tires on."

She gave him a wary look that seemed to put him at a distance. "It might be better if I stayed with my car. Apparently it's not safe in your municipal lot."

"Not 'my' lot," he said mildly. "Hey, Tom." He raised his voice. "How long is this going to take?"

Tom, owner of Tom's Garage, shoved his ball cap back and scratched his head. "I got Tom Junior bringing the tires over now. Shouldn't be more'n an hour, I'd say." His round, mild face puckered into a frown. "Nasty business. Gives the town a bad name, somethin' like that."

"It does," he agreed. That was the attitude he hoped for from folks around here. "I need to take Ms. Langdon over to the jail on King Street for a meeting. You mind dropping the car over there when you're done?"

"Sure thing, Trey. No problem at all." He settled

his cap firmly on his head and nodded toward Jessica. "I'll take care of it. Don't you worry. I'll bring the keys in and leave 'em at the desk, okay?"

"Good." He clapped Tom's shoulder. "Thanks, Tom. You tell Tommy I said hi, too."

"Will do."

Trey raised an eyebrow at Jessica. "That all right with you?"

"I suppose so." The words came out grudgingly. "I can get a cab . . ."

"My truck's right here." He took her arm. "By the time you wait for a cab, you'll be even later."

She pushed back her sleeve to glance at the gold bracelet watch that circled her wrist. Nice. And expensive. A gift, maybe, from a boyfriend or fiancé? She didn't wear a ring, but that didn't mean she wasn't involved with someone.

"All right. Thanks."

He opened the door for her. She climbed in, smoothing her skirt down over her knees. The skirt didn't quite make it.

Removing his gaze with an effort, he rounded the truck, got in and started the engine. He shouldn't be looking at her legs, much as they were worth a second glance. And he shouldn't be wondering whether she had a man in her life. The only thing that should interest him at the moment was whether this unpleasantness might make her back off from the case.

They drove for a block in silence. "I'm sorry that happened," he said finally. "I knew feelings were running high, but I never expected open vandalism. I hope it didn't upset you too much."

"Is that really what you feel? Or were you thinking that this might be what it took to drive me off?" Her tone was sharp, and he could hardly blame her. Jessica seemed to have an uncanny ability to read his mind.

He took a deep breath and sought for a rational answer. It wouldn't come.

"I suppose you're thinking that I might have done it myself to get rid of you," he said.

A glance at her face told him she'd been thinking exactly that. He clamped his lips shut on the angry words that wanted to pour out. He wasn't sure whether he was angrier at her for thinking that of him or at himself for caring.

He took a deep breath and held it for a count of five. Ten would probably have been better.

"I'm not going to keep protesting my innocence to you. But you ought to see that this is the very thing I'm trying to protect my mother against. I'm not pleased it happened to you, but—" He stopped. That sentence wasn't going anywhere good.

"But you'd rather it was me than your mother," she finished for him. "All right, I get that." She slanted a sideways glance at him. "And I'm willing to concede that you don't seem the sort of person to stick knives into people's tires."

"Thank you," he said stiffly.

She shook her head. "I just don't understand why anyone wants to take their anger at the crime out on me. Surely they realize that Thomas has to have a defense attorney. If not me, it will be someone else."

"I'm not sure the person who slashed your tires is capable of logical thought. Besides, you're a Philadelphia lawyer."

She looked at him blankly. "So?"

"You don't know the expression?" He couldn't help smiling. "I hate to be the one to break it to you, Counselor, but out in country places, the term is used as a not-very-complimentary comparison. As in, 'He's as slick as a Philadelphia lawyer.'"

"Charming," she said. "No, I didn't know that. But our vandal might as well get one thing clear." She turned toward him as he pulled up in front of the jail. "I'm not quitting this case. Not if I have to put new tires on my car every day of the week."

"That could get expensive," he said mildly, but he wasn't deceived. Jessica didn't just mean that for the vandal, whoever he might be. She meant it for him, as well.

He should be annoyed. He was. But he was also experiencing a certain sneaking admiration for Jessica Langdon. She might be a thorn in his side at the moment, but he had to admit that she had guts.

• • •

TRUE TO HIS WORD, Leo Frost was waiting for Jessica at the jail. She walked toward the spare, slightly stooping figure, forcing herself to focus on the task at hand. Thomas must be persuaded to talk to her. To give her something upon which she could build a case.

That was the important thing, not the vandalism to her car. And certainly not whatever random feelings and questioning doubts Trey had managed to raise.

"Mr. Frost." She gripped his hand briefly. "Thanks again for coming."

"No problem at all." He nodded toward the desk. "I asked the officer to have Thomas brought down. We may as well go on into the interview room."

Maybe he needed to sit down. Compunction hit her as she fell into step with him. "Have you been waiting long? I'm sorry I'm late."

"Not at all." He held the door for her and then sank into one of the straight chairs with a sigh. Someone had brought an extra chair in, she noted, showing more consideration for Frost's health than she had, it seemed.

"Mr. Frost, I do apologize . . ."

"It doesn't matter in the least. And call me Leo, please. I can hang on to an illusion of youth as long as a pretty woman calls me by my first name."

She smiled, making an effort to throw off the negative effects of the past hour. "Leo, then."

Sharp eyes zeroed in on her face. "Something's wrong. What is it? Something to do with the case?"

The concern in his voice cut through her reserve. She hadn't intended to tell him, but the urge to accept that concern was too strong.

"While I was in your office, someone let the air out of my tires." That wasn't correct. "Actually, whoever it was slashed my tires. And left me a nasty little note."

"That can't be." Leo's voice was sharp with disbelief.

She stiffened. "I assure you, that's what happened."

"I'm so sorry. Jessica, I didn't mean I thought you were lying. I'm just . . ." He shook his head, and she realized his face had lost whatever color it had. "I'm stunned. That's so out of character for people around here. Or at least it used to be."

His obvious distress touched her. She wanted to say something to ease the situation, but the door rattled. She turned toward it to see Thomas brought in . . . and to see the relief that flooded his face at the sight of Leo Frost.

The boy didn't speak until the door closed behind the guards. Then he leaned across the table. "You came. Denke."

"You're welcome." Leo gave him a reassuring

smile. "I told you I'd come back. Are they treating you all right?"

A trace of anxiety touched the older man's voice. Jessica understood. Thomas seemed ill-prepared to mix in with the general population of the jail.

"Ja." He plucked at the front of the jumpsuit. "I would like to have my own clothes, but the other lawyer said that I could not."

"Ms. Langdon is right about that." Leo leaned toward the boy. "Thomas, I explained that you would have another lawyer to take care of you. You can trust Ms. Langdon. You have to tell her everything."

Thomas's glance touched her face and then slid away. "Ja. I understand."

Jessica understood, too. Thomas would take Leo's word for it, because he had faith in Leo.

"Good." Leo started to rise. "I'll leave you two together then."

"Don't go." It was an anguished cry, and Thomas grasped the older man's hand, earning a sharp rap on the glass from the guard outside.

"Thomas, Ms. Langdon is your attorney now. You need to talk to her." Leo's voice was deep with sympathy.

Thomas nodded, but he looked miserable. Not exactly a ringing endorsement of her, was it?

She managed a smile. "Leo, if you don't mind staying . . ." She left it open, with a faint, apologetic thought for Henderson, Dawes and Henderson. Mr. Henderson would not approve.

Leo hesitated for a moment. Then he nodded and sat down, and the tension in the small room eased.

Jessica took a deep breath, feeling as if some barrier had been surmounted. Now, maybe, she could get to work on the case. She took a pad from her briefcase.

"Thomas, I . . . we . . . have to ask you some questions about what happened the night Cherry died. Just try to answer as fully as you can. Okay?"

He nodded, blue eyes filled with apprehension.

"All right, then." She started with some easy questions—who had planned the party where he'd met Cherry that night, where was it, how had he learned about it.

Thomas answered readily enough, sometimes groping for a word. She reminded herself again that English, according to Trey, wasn't his first language.

She made notes, sure that all this ground would have been gone over by the police. Still, they could have missed something, convinced as they were that their murderer had been lying there at the crime scene, waiting for them.

"You're doing fine, Thomas. Now, I want you to write down the names of the people who were at that party." She pushed the pad and pen over to him.

"They were mostly Englisch," Thomas said, taking the pen. "I don't know all the names."

"Non-Amish, he means," Leo said. "Just put down the names you remember."

Thomas nodded, beginning to print on the yellow pad. Mostly first names, she realized. It would take some work to track down everyone who'd been at that party, and even when she did, what would they have to contribute? The crime hadn't occurred there.

Leo was watching the movement of Thomas's hand on the paper. When it stopped, he spoke. "Now the names of all the Amish at the party."

Something that might have been rebellion tightened Thomas's face. "I don't—"

"We know you weren't the only Amish there." Leo's voice had a note of command. "Names. Ms. Langdon won't tell on them to their parents if she can help it."

She opened her mouth to say that she probably would have to talk to parents, especially if any of the party crowd was underage. Then she shut it again. Thomas was writing down the names. Leo had the knack of dealing with the boy.

When Thomas finally pushed the pad back across to her, she felt a sense of satisfaction. At least it was a place to start. But now she had to ask the tough questions.

"When did you and Cherry leave that party?" she asked.

The whites of Thomas's eyes showed. "I don't know."

"How did you get to the barn?"

"I don't know." His big hands clasped together.

"How can you not know?" Her voice sharpened. "Thomas, you have to be open with me if I'm going to help you."

"I don't know," he said again, desperation in his voice. "I don't remember." He looked at Leo, unleashing a torrent of words in a language she didn't understand.

Leo listened, then waved him to silence and turned to Jessica. "He says the last thing he remembers is being at the party, having a beer and talking to some English kids. Then it's a blank until the police woke him up."

Her heart sank. *I don't remember* wasn't a particularly good defense.

She wanted to ask if Leo believed him, but that was a question best left until they were alone. She put a few more questions to Thomas, not expecting much and not getting it. Ja, of course he knew the barn that the Morgan family owned. He hadn't been there in a long time.

When the guards had taken Thomas back to his cell, she stared at the single sheet of yellow paper. Not much to show for the interview with her client.

She glanced at Leo. He looked a little better than he had earlier, as if getting his teeth into the case had been good for him.

"You understood the language . . . Amish, is it?"

"Pennsylvania Dutch. Or Pennsylvania German, if you wanted to be more accurate, which most people don't." He shrugged. "Plenty of old-timers like me understand. My parents spoke it when I was a child."

"Your family was Amish?" She tried to get a grip on a situation that seemed to be slipping out of her hands.

"Not Amish, no. Of German-Swiss descent, like them. It's not that unusual in this area. Even some of the younger folks understand. Trey, for instance. He's quite fluent."

Trey, again. She could do without having Trey Morgan shoved in her face every other minute.

"About the other kids who were at the party," Leo said. "I don't want to interfere—"

"If you know anything that will help, just tell me," she said quickly. "I'm beginning to understand just how much a fish out of water I am in this case."

"The English kids will probably be easy. Some of them may have already talked to the police. But the Amish are another story."

"They won't willingly get involved with the law." Trey had said something like that, and Thomas had confirmed it.

"That's right." Leo looked relieved that she understood. "You'll need an entrée—someone

93

who knows them, if you're going to get anything out of them."

It went against the grain, but surely she was smart enough to know when she needed a hand. "If you're willing to help, I'd be grateful."

He nodded, smiling a little. "One last challenge before I retire. I'd like that."

She smiled back. Maybe she hadn't gotten what she'd hoped for from her client, but she began to feel she'd gained a friend. "Thanks, Leo."

"I'll do what I can. But you know who the kids might open up to more easily? Trey Morgan. You need to get him involved."

Involved? She nodded, but her heart sank. It seemed to her that Trey Morgan was already involved far too much for her peace of mind.

CHAPTER SIX

SOMEHOW JESSICA WASN'T really surprised when she went out to the street to find that Trey was leaning against her car. She stopped, frowning at him as he held out her keys.

"I thought your buddy Tom was going to bring the car over."

He shrugged. "I had time. You don't mind driving me back to pick up my truck, do you?"

She could hardly say no. She gave him a brisk nod and went around to the driver's side. Trey slid into the passenger's seat and adjusted the sun visor.

"So, how did it go with Thomas?"

"I can't discuss the case with you. Not unless my client wishes it." And her client was never going to be presented with that option, if she had anything to say about it. Leo's recommendation that she involve Trey in the case flitted through her mind, but she ignored it.

"Okay. I guess it's going to be a quiet ride, then. How do you like Lancaster County?"

"Considering that I haven't seen much yet except the jail, I think it's very . . . rural. You'd never guess it was so close to the city."

"That's what most people like about it." Trey attempted to stretch his long legs out and discovered he couldn't. He slid the seat back, making himself more comfortable.

"I appreciate your getting the mechanic moving so quickly on my car." If Trey hadn't done the calling, she might still be waiting, she suspected. "Did he leave the bill in the car?"

"We'll take care of it."

She frowned. "It's my car and my new tires."

"New tires you need because of your involvement in the case. We'll take care of them."

"That's very generous." She clipped off the words. Generous, yes, but she had a feeling he hadn't done it for that reason. He so clearly wanted to be in control of everything. "However, that's why I have insurance." She held out her hand, not looking at him.

Silence for a moment, and then she felt the flimsy paper being put into her hand.

"Are you this stubborn about everything?" Trey asked.

She shot him a glance. "Somehow I don't think I'm the only one."

For once, he didn't seem to have an answer. She pulled into the parking lot next to his truck just as her cell phone rang.

She flipped it open. Listened. And felt annoyance surge through her. She cut the connection. Glared at Trey.

"That was the district attorney's office. Thomas's arraignment is in—" she consulted her watch "—less than an hour."

Trey frowned. "Awfully short notice, isn't it?"

"Yes. It is." Her mind spun with possibilities. "I need to let Leo know. And Thomas's family should be told. He ought to have appropriate clothes, and I have to get to the courthouse in time to brief him."

Trey swung his door open. "I'll take care of getting Thomas's family and his clothes. You call Leo and head for the courthouse."

She was about to ask him why he thought he should take charge, but he was already striding toward his truck. Besides, it would do no good to ask—he probably hadn't figured that one out himself.

She and Leo made it to the courthouse with barely fifteen minutes to spare, and she was fuming. "What does the D.A. think he's doing, giving us so little notice?"

"Taking advantage of the publicity, I expect." Leo sounded a bit breathless, and she slowed her pace. "He's up for reelection, you know."

No, she hadn't known, and it didn't do a thing for her mood. "This should be fairly straightforward, in any event. I don't suppose there's much chance the judge will grant bail."

Leo shook his head. "Not sure it's a good idea anyway, as upset as people seem to be. Thomas might be safer in jail."

They entered the courtroom just as Thomas was led in. Jessica hurried down the aisle and slipped into a seat next to him, Leo right behind her.

Thomas wore a black jacket and pants with a pale blue shirt, so apparently Trey's mission had been successful.

Thomas's eyes were wide and frightened. No doubt he'd never been in a courtroom before, and he hadn't grown up watching reruns of *Law & Order* on television, either.

"Was ist letz?" he murmured. "What is wrong? Why have they brought me here?"

"Don't be alarmed." She patted the black sleeve. "It's just part of the legal formalities. The judge is going to ask how you plead to the charges."

He gave her a blank look.

Patience, she reminded herself. "He'll want to know whether you say you are guilty or not guilty, that's all. When that happens, you're going to say 'Not guilty.' Understand?"

A murmur of excitement behind her made her look around. Trey and Geneva walked down the side aisle, accompanying a man and woman dressed in sober black. Thomas's parents, to judge by the sob the boy choked on. Trey looked as if he'd rather be hanging over a seething volcano than walking into the courtroom.

They filed into the first row of seats, and Thomas reached out to clasp his parents' hands. Tears trickled down his mother's face as she murmured something softly to him.

Jessica hated to interrupt, but the judge could

enter at any moment. "You understand, Thomas? You say not guilty."

He blinked, fixing those wide blue eyes on her face. "But if I tell them I'm guilty, will they let me go home then?"

She managed to resist putting her hand over his mouth. He'd said it softly—no one but Leo was close enough to hear.

Leo leaned across her, compelling Thomas to look at him. "Absolutely not," he said firmly. "It doesn't work that way here. Understand? Just do exactly as Ms. Langdon tells you. Okay?"

Thomas nodded, reluctantly it seemed.

She looked at Leo, who shrugged. "That's how it's done in the Amish community. You kneel before the congregation and confess, and everything is forgiven. I've known people to confess to something even when they hadn't done it, just because the community means so much to them."

Appalled wasn't a strong enough word. "He can't do that here."

"No." Leo fixed Thomas with a firm gaze. "You say exactly as Ms. Langdon told you."

Thomas nodded.

The judge entered then, and they rose. The discomfort that had been weighing on Jessica slipped away.

Maybe, as Trey so obviously believed, she didn't belong, couldn't understand the culture, was an outsider. But in a courtroom, she was at home. This was her natural arena.

The gavel rapped. Jessica studied the judge, trying to get an idea of the woman's temperament. She was probably in her fifties. Judge Judith Waller's round face didn't give much away but the pink cheeks, the graying hair pulled back into an untidy knot and the gold-rimmed glasses through which she peered at the papers in front of her made her look like someone's grandmother, peering at a recipe instead of at the charges that could send Thomas to prison for life.

The judge looked up, her shrewd gaze moving from Jessica's face to Thomas's and then to the district attorney.

"Mr. Connelly, it's a bit unusual to see you for an arraignment."

"In view of the serious nature of the charges, Your Honor, I felt it advisable to handle it myself." Preston Connelly's voice was as smooth and assured as his appearance. He leaned forward, confidence in every line of his body. "The commonwealth—"

The judge held up her hand, palm out. "Save it for the appropriate time, Mr. Connelly. We have a counsel of record for the defendant?"

Jessica rose. "Jessica Langdon for the defense, Your Honor." Again she felt the impact of that shrewd gaze.

"Ms. Langdon. I don't think we've had the

pleasure of seeing you in our court before, have we?"

"No, Your Honor."

Judge Waller frowned down at the papers in front of her. "Ms. Langdon, has your client been given a copy of the charges against him?"

"Yes, Your Honor." She pressed her fingers against the sheet listing the charges.

The judge shifted her gaze to Thomas. "Thomas Esch, you have been charged with second-degree murder in the death of one Cherry Wilson. How do you plead?"

Jessica held her breath.

"Not guilty," he whispered.

From the corner of her eye, Jessica could see that Leo had his hand on the boy's black sleeve.

"Very well." The judge peered over the top of her glasses at the district attorney. "Let's set the dates for discovery and pretrial." She consulted her calendar and named the dates.

Jessica nodded.

"Mr. Connelly?"

"The sooner the better, Your Honor," Connelly said. "The heinous nature of the crime dictates—"

"I dictate procedure in my court." Judge Waller was crisp. "Anything else you wish to say, Mr. Connelly, may be said at the pretrial conference."

Jessica let out a breath she hadn't realized she'd been holding. The judge seemed determined to keep things under control in the courtroom, at any event. That was probably the best they could hope for at the moment.

A few more technical details settled, and the judge departed, her face grave, her black robe fluttering behind her.

Jessica exchanged relieved glances with Leo and turned to Thomas. The guards were closing in. "I'm afraid you must return to your cell now, Thomas. Say goodbye to your parents," Jessica said.

Tears filled the boy's eyes as his mother embraced him. He murmured something in Pennsylvania Dutch, his voice breaking. Then the guard's hand closed on his arm, and he was led away, looking over his shoulder at his parents until the closing door cut them from his sight.

"Mrs. Esch, Mr. Esch." She wasn't sure whether to shake hands with them, so contented herself with a nod. "I'm sorry to meet you under such circumstances. Did you understand what happened here?"

Thomas's mother looked at her husband. "Not all," he said. "The words, ja. Not the meaning."

"I'll be glad to explain it to you, if you want."

"Not now, I think," Trey interrupted. "The press is waiting outside, ready to pounce. I want to get them out the side door before it occurs to the television crew to cover that, too."

She had to agree, although she couldn't help wondering whether he was more concerned about

Thomas's parents appearing on television or his mother. "I'll come to see you soon," she said. "Please try not to worry." That was useless, of course, but she had to say it.

"It will be all right." Geneva slipped her arm around the woman's waist. "Come along, now. Jessica will take care of everything."

Jessica watched the four of them go out the side door and then glanced around the courtroom, emptying now. This was her place, and the law was the one thing she could count on. Thomas deserved the best defense possible, and she intended to give it to him.

JESSICA WASN'T QUITE SURE how she'd ended up at Geneva's house for supper the following evening. She'd put in a long day, nagging the D.A.'s office for discovery, trying to organize her materials for efficient work in her inconvenient room at the motel and finally driving back into the city to report at the office and pick up a few things. When she'd returned to Springville, all she intended was to pick up a sandwich, call Sara, whom she'd missed when she went to the apartment, and go to bed early.

But Geneva had been waiting for her. She'd insisted that what Jessica needed was a good dinner and a relaxing evening. She'd tried to make an excuse, but it was remarkably difficult to say no to Geneva.

So in the end she'd come, although how relaxing it was going to be with Trey sitting across from her at the long oval table, she didn't know.

"Won't you have some more noodles, Jessica?" Geneva passed a heavy earthenware bowl to her. "Or some more mashed potatoes?"

"Thank you, but I really can't eat another bite. Everything was delicious." The meal had tasted wonderful—crisp browned chicken, homemade egg noodles in chicken broth, mashed potatoes and asparagus fresh from the garden. Just . . . filling, to say the least.

"Jessica isn't carbo-packing, Mom," Trey said. "She's not used to the way we eat around here."

She shot him an annoyed glance. She didn't need him to speak for her. "As I said, it's delicious. Is this traditional Pennsylvania Dutch cooking?"

"Yep. The more starch, the better." Leo put another spoonful of noodles on top of his mashed potatoes. "Nobody makes noodles quite as well as Geneva."

Geneva beamed at the compliment. "My mother-in-law's recipe," she said. "Would you believe she waited until Trey's father and I had been married nearly ten years before she gave it to me? I think she wanted to be sure the marriage was going to last."

"Never any doubt about that, my dear." Leo spoke with the fondness of long friendship.

Geneva smiled, a shadow of sorrow in her eyes. Jessica's heart contracted. How terrible it must have been for her to accept that the husband she loved had taken his own life.

Jessica's gaze collided with Trey's from across the table. He looked . . . almost angry, she thought. As if he wasn't ready to have his father the subject of casual dinner-table conversation.

"She probably wanted to be sure her recipe didn't die with her." The fifth person at the table spoke and then looked up from his refilled plate at a stifled chuckle from his hostess. "Don't you think?" he added, flushing a little.

"I wouldn't be surprised, Bobby," Geneva said. "A few more potatoes?"

While Bobby—Robert Stephens—was accepting another spoonful, Jessica studied him. He was the one who'd contacted Henderson, Dawes and Henderson for Geneva. He'd been introduced as a business associate and old school friend of Trey's, and she couldn't help wondering at the relationship.

Bobby was slight, fair and diffident, with pale blue eyes partially hidden by glasses. He'd have been, she thought, the classic nerd in high school and an unlikely friend for Trey, who'd undoubtedly been the Big Man on Campus.

Trey's gaze caught hers again, and her speculation about Bobby drifted away. She hadn't thanked Trey for his assistance with the arraignment the previous day. He had been helpful, unexpectedly so. She appreciated it. She just couldn't help but wonder why.

Geneva's voice cut across her thoughts. "Why don't you all visit a bit while we clear? We'll have our dessert and coffee in the living room."

It was obviously meant to get people away from the table, and Jessica obediently rose. "Please let me help."

Geneva took the plate from her hands. "Not at all. Becky and I have it under control." She nodded toward the young girl in Amish dress who'd been helping her in the kitchen. "Go on, now." She made shooing motions. "I'm sure you want to chat with the others."

Chat? Well, she could talk to Trey, she supposed, but there was no guarantee that wouldn't end in an argument. The men had already gone into the living room, so she followed them.

Trey and Leo were deep in conversation in one corner of the room, while Bobby Stephens stared absently out the French doors. Geneva had said that Bobby "found" her for the case. Maybe this was her opportunity to find out exactly how they'd hit upon using her.

At her approach, he gave her a tentative smile. "Just admiring Geneva's garden." He nodded at the flower beds beyond the French doors.

"Lovely," she agreed. "I gather you're good friends with the Morgan family."

He gave an odd shrug that seemed to move only one shoulder. "You could say that. I work for them, of course, but I like to think our relationship goes deeper than that. If it hadn't been for Trey, I doubt I'd have survived high school."

"Really?" She suspected he wanted to tell her that story, or he wouldn't have brought it up.

He nodded. "Back then I was small for my age and too smart for my own good. Born to be picked on, I guess."

"Not by Trey?"

He looked shocked. "Of course not. He's not that kind of person. He noticed, you see. No one else did, but Trey noticed. He put a stop to it. And we've been friends ever since."

It was the sort of thing Trey would do, she supposed. His urge to take care of people extended beyond his mother. Jessica might find it annoying, but Bobby obviously hadn't.

"You work for Morgan Enterprises, I understand?" She made it a question. She'd intended to find out a little more about the Morgan businesses but hadn't been able to fit that into her day.

"Financial vice president," he said, a trace of pride in his voice. "Trey is CEO, of course. It's a private corporation, solely owned by the family."

"Trey mentioned that you do a good bit of business in real estate." Here was a chance to check up on that aspect of Trey's story about the barn, at least.

Bobby nodded. "That was a big interest of Trey's father. He was concerned that farmland would be gobbled up by careless developers, so he started buying up tracts years ago as they came on the market. Some have been sold to farmers, others held for future development. He wasn't opposed to development, you see." Bobby sounded very earnest. "He just wanted to be sure it was done in the right way."

"Now it's all up to Trey, I suppose."

"Well, that's what he intended to do all his life. He probably didn't really need an MBA from Wharton to handle the company, but it was what he wanted. And what his father wanted for him, too."

Bobby's words gave her a few more pieces to the puzzle of who Trey Morgan was. But she didn't want to give the impression she was pumping him about Trey. "I understand I have you to thank for hiring me for this case."

He didn't respond for a moment, and then he shook his head. "Not exactly. I mean, Geneva was insistent that I hire a Philadelphia firm. I was familiar with Henderson, Dawes and Henderson from some estate work they'd handled, so I called. I suppose they felt you were the best person for the job."

"I see." Everyone seemed to have a different

version of this story. Still, Bobby was the one who'd made the call, so he should know. "Well, thank you anyway. I guess you're still indirectly responsible."

His smile was deprecating, as if to say he had done nothing. "How is the case shaping up, or shouldn't I ask? I can't help but be interested."

He wasn't shouting angrily at her, but his avid expression when he asked about the case repelled her as much as those people at the county jail. "I'm afraid I really can't talk about it."

"Well, no. I suppose not. I guess you'll be looking for a plea bargain, under the circumstances."

She pasted a smile on her face. "As I said, I can't discuss it. Now, if you'll excuse me . . ."

She took a step back, turned and nearly walked into Trey.

JESSICA LOOKED, Trey decided, as if she needed to be rescued from Bobby, who tended to go on and on about the business until people's eyes glazed over. He put out a hand to steady her when she wobbled a bit on those high heels she insisted on wearing. She didn't need it, probably, but . . .

But what was he thinking? The last thing he should do was admit attraction to this woman.

He managed a noncommittal smile. "I hate to steal you away from Bobby, but I'd like a private word."

"Sure, sure." Bobby ran a hand over his hair, as if it needed taming. It didn't. "I'll just . . ." He let the sentence die out and backed away.

Jessica treated him to a frowning look. "That wasn't very polite."

"Bobby doesn't mind." He opened the French door that led out onto the patio. "Let's take a closer look at the garden."

She stared at him for a moment, and he thought she'd argue. Then, with a short nod, she stepped out onto the flagstones. He closed the door, and the cool evening enveloped them.

"My mother's roses are at their best right now." He ushered her a few more steps away from the door, intent on not being overheard.

"Beautiful." She cupped a yellow bloom in her hand, bending to smell it. "What's this one called?"

"I haven't the faintest idea."

"Well, then, suppose we stop pretending you brought me out here to admire the rose garden." She straightened, her eyes challenging him. "What do you want?"

All right, no small talk. "Did you see the local newspaper today?"

"Not today." She looked slightly confused, as if that wasn't what she'd expected.

He handed her the paper he had clutched in one fist, shaking it out. "Take a look." He didn't want to see it again himself. He'd rather forget it, but he couldn't.

Jessica held the paper up to catch the light that filtered out from the living room. "You and your mother with Thomas's parents, arriving at the courthouse. I'd have expected them to use one of Thomas."

Irritation filled him at Jessica's cool reaction. "This is exactly what I was afraid of—something that ties my mother publicly to this business."

Jessica tossed the paper onto the garden bench. "How, exactly, am I supposed to control what the newspaper prints?"

Common sense said she was right. It didn't help his disposition. "You can't. I just—"

"You just wanted to blame somebody, and I was handy."

He gritted his teeth. "If you hadn't taken the case, my mother wouldn't be involved."

"Do you really think that? Judging by the persistence I've seen in her, I doubt she'd let something like that stop her." Her lips curved. "I couldn't even turn her down for supper tonight."

"Did you want to?" His annoyance was slipping away. Stupid to hang on to it, when he knew it made no rational sense.

"I was beat, to tell the truth." She sat down on the bench, as if to illustrate the point. "But tonight's dinner was far better than anything I'd have gotten in the coffee shop at the Willow Brook Motel."

"I told you so." He sat down next to her. "But I know what you mean about my mother. When she's set her heart on something, she's relentless. Like water on stone."

"That's not a bad quality." She gestured toward the newspaper. "I don't know much about small country places, but I can't imagine anyone being angry with your mother for supporting those poor parents."

"I couldn't imagine anyone slashing your tires, either, but it happened."

"Yes." She glanced over her shoulder at the lengthening shadows on the lawn and shivered a little. "It seems out of place here, but I guess that kind of irrational violence can happen anywhere."

"A couple of years ago, I'd have said this place was a last refuge of peace." He stopped, wishing he hadn't said it. Jessica didn't need to see that far into him—into the terrible riddle of his father's suicide. She just needed to finish her work as quietly as possible and get out of here.

"If you're that upset at the photo in the paper, why did you take Thomas's parents to the courthouse? For that matter, why did you jump into helping when you heard about the arraignment? You didn't have to."

"Yes, I did." He said the words first and then thought about them, but they were true. He'd had to. Everything about his upbringing had prepared him for that. "I mean, I knew my mother would want to take Thomas's parents, and I certainly wasn't going to let her go alone."

"Is that all there was to it?" She linked her hands around her knee, seeming ready to stay there indefinitely.

"I suppose not," he admitted. "Do your friends enjoy being cross-examined about their motives?"

"My friends . . ." She stopped. "My private life has nothing to do with this."

"Sorry," he said. "My mother did teach me not to ask personal questions. I just forgot for a moment."

She shrugged, glancing over her shoulder again. "Forget it. If that's all . . ."

"Not quite." He said the words reluctantly. He didn't want to say them at all, but he'd promised. "Aaron and Molly Esch sent over a message that they're ready to talk with you anytime. I said I'd take you over there tomorrow." She'd think he was arranging things without asking again. "Is that okay with you?" he added, hoping to avert an explosion.

"I suppose so," she said slowly. For once, she didn't seem to take offense. "I probably should have gone to see them today. They must have been confused about the arraignment."

"Yes. I tried to reassure them, but it'll come better from you."

"At the risk of saying something personal, you seem to be involving yourself even more. For my client's sake, I appreciate it, but if you're hoping to influence Thomas's parents in some way affecting the case—"

"Of course not." He snapped the answer, but in his heart he knew he wasn't really annoyed with her but with the situation. "Look, I don't expect you to understand this, but the Morgan family has always looked out for people around here."

Her eyebrows lifted again, making him aware of just how laserlike those blue eyes could be, even in the dusk. "Like a feudal lord?"

His jaw tightened. "Like a friend. To the Amish especially. My father used to say that the Amish may not always realize it, but they need English friends. Thomas's family is totally unprepared to cope with his trial, so it's my responsibility to help them."

He waited. If she had a smart remark for that . . .

She didn't say anything for a long moment. Then she put her hand on his arm. He seemed to feel that touch running along his skin, carrying warmth, setting his mind spinning. Her eyes widened. Darkened. For an instant she leaned toward him, and the air sizzled.

She snatched her hand away as if she'd touched a hot stove. "I . . . I'm glad. I mean, that you'll go with me to see Thomas's parents. That will be very helpful." She rose, as if she couldn't wait to put some space between them. "Maybe we should go inside."

Maybe they should. And maybe he should stop putting himself in situations where he was alone with her.

CHAPTER SEVEN

WHAT WAS WRONG WITH HER? Jessica kept a smile on her face as she said goodbye to everyone, but once she got into her car and started back toward the lane, the expression slid away.

How could she have let that happen? She took a deep breath and focused on the turn to the two-lane blacktop road. The Morgan place was several miles from the village of Springville, and the road wasn't much traveled, it seemed. No other cars came along to distract her with their lights. She was alone, and at the moment that gave her too much time to think.

She tried telling herself that nothing had happened. Or that, if there had been some spark when she touched Trey, it had been entirely on her side, and he hadn't noticed a thing.

Wrong, said the judicial little voice at the back of her mind. Wrong on all counts.

It had happened, and it hadn't been just her. Trey had most definitely noticed it, too. When she'd scrambled to her feet and headed into the house, she'd seen the same stunned expression on his face that must have been on hers.

She took another breath, blew it out on a long exhale and tried to relax tense muscles. All right, face it. There had been a spark of attraction between them. A very strong spark. More like a flare gun.

For the most part, she kept her relationships on the light side, going out casually with people who were as wedded to their jobs as she was. People who would understand.

Not that she had any intention of letting something develop with Trey. Trey was still just as annoying, just as bossy, just as sure he was right as he'd been before.

She couldn't be attracted to him, for more reasons that she could enumerate. For one thing—

A deer bounded across the road in front of her, and she slammed on the brakes, catching a glimpse of the white tail as it vanished into the cornfield on the opposite side of the road. Her heart pounded with the suddenness of the animal's appearance, coming out of the dark and vanishing just as quickly.

She gripped the steering wheel and drove more slowly, eyes alert for movement on the berm of the road. As for Trey . . . she learned when she was just a kid that trusting someone with her heart wasn't wise or safe. She'd figured that out the day her father shipped her off to boarding school as if she were an inconvenient package, separating her from the woman who'd been the only mother figure she'd ever know. She'd learned to control her emotions, not let her emotions control her.

Sure, she thought about marrying someday.

Having a family. But she wouldn't approach that on the basis most people did. She'd use her mind, not just her heart.

She'd file that bit of attraction to Trey under the category of "Foolish Mistakes" and concentrate on the case.

She fished her cell phone out of her bag and checked for messages. None, but she'd promised to give Sara a call tonight. She almost pushed the button but dropped the cell phone on the seat instead. All she'd need was to have her attention distracted when another deer decided to wander onto the road. Or a skunk. Or a rhinoceros. Who knew what kind of wildlife they had around here?

The blackness all around her was beginning to make her nervous. She hadn't seen another light in miles, only the narrow ribbon of blacktop, shining as far as her headlights reached.

She switched on the radio, found nothing but hard rock and country, and switched it back off again. She must be almost to Springville. She just couldn't see the lights of the small town for the black bulk of the hillside.

Even as she thought that, a pair of headlights appeared in her rearview mirror. The car accelerated, gaining on her quickly. Her fingers tightened on the steering wheel. Was that idiot going to pass on this winding road? To be fair, it might be perfectly familiar to him. He could be fuming at the sedate thirty-five she was going.

She steered closer to the edge of the road, giving him more passing room, but apparently that wasn't his intention. He slowed about two car lengths behind her, keeping pace with her.

That was normal. That was what any safe driver would do. But for some reason the pair of lights, glaring at her from her mirror in the midst of all that darkness, began to get on her nerves.

Stupid, she scolded herself. *You're just not used to the country, that's all. Get you away from streetlights and traffic signals, and you panic.*

The stern lecture settled her nerves, but she was still glad when she rounded the flank of the hillside and the lights of Springville came into view. Once she got a bit closer, there'd be enough light to see the car behind her.

But that wasn't to be. The car turned off at the next intersection. All she could say for sure was that it was a car, not a truck, and it was dark in color.

The car didn't mean anything, any more than that ridiculous attraction she'd felt for Trey meant anything.

She drove down Springville's main street, turned in at the sign for the Willow Brook Motel and drove around to the back toward her unit. The motel must be full tonight. Most of the spaces were taken, and a laundry truck took up the one in front of her unit.

Annoyed, she went around the first rank of cars

in the lot, finally finding a space two rows back. She slid out, locked the car and headed for the motel.

Her briefcase—she'd left it in the trunk. Annoyed with herself, she stopped—and heard an echo of her step, as if someone else were in the lot, someone who stopped when she did.

Nonsense, she told herself briskly. An image of the knife stuck in her tire slid unpleasantly into her mind, like a snake slithering out from beneath a rock.

She would not let that vandalism turn her into a basket case. She walked quickly back to the car, took the briefcase from the trunk and slammed the lid defiantly.

Several large motor homes were parked in the middle row of the lot. Why would someone want to stay at the Willow Brook Motel when his or her home on wheels had all the modern conveniences? Maybe RV drivers got the urge to spread out once in a while. She walked between two of them, their high sides forming a tunnel, and heard it again.

It wasn't an echo. Footsteps. Distinct footsteps, keeping level with her on the far side of the motor home. A chill slithered down her back. Maybe it was nothing, but it paid to take precautions, especially after the incident with her tires. If someone would slash her tires, what might he do to her?

She reached into the pocket of her bag where her cell phone lived. Her fingers groped fruitlessly, and her stomach cramped. The phone wasn't there. It was on the seat in the car, where she'd dropped it.

Going back for it wasn't an option, not when she was aware of the person on the far side of the motor home. His footsteps had stopped when hers did, and she could almost imagine that she heard him breathing.

She pulled the key card from her bag, making sure she had it turned in the right direction. Then, before she could scare herself into immobility, she started walking again. When she stepped into the open, the other person would, too. She'd see that it was someone perfectly innocent, some late traveler headed for his or her room.

But when she stepped into the lane, the other person didn't. He stayed where he was, invisible in the shadow of the vehicle.

Then the shadow moved, and panic swept over her. She spun and ran for her room, unable to hear anyone for the sound of her own heart pounding in her ears, too breathless to cry out. She reached the door, shoved the key card in and stumbled inside.

She slammed the door and shoved the bolt home. She could breathe. Had she just made a complete idiot of herself? Probably.

Not turning the lights on, she sidled to the

window and moved the drape just enough to peer out. If she'd imagined this . . . but she hadn't. Beside the motor home she saw a shadow shift, detach itself and then move backward, disappearing into the darker shadows beyond.

SHE HADN'T CALLED the police, and Jessica was still wondering whether that decision had been the right one the next morning. They'd have come, but even after the incident with her tires, how seriously would they have taken her account?

Someone followed you in the parking lot, Ms. Langdon? Can you describe that person? Oh, all you saw was a shadow.

She could imagine the looks they'd exchange over that. No, she'd done the right thing. Maybe it had been nothing more than someone else going to his or her room.

She'd called Sara instead, and Sara's common sense had reassured her. Jessica frowned. She'd intended to ask Sara to do a little research for her on past cases involving the Amish, but she'd forgotten after that episode in the parking lot. She'd have to try to catch up with her later.

Trey's truck pulled up, and she hurried out to meet him, double-checking to be sure the door locked behind her. She'd said she could drive herself to this meeting with Thomas's parents, but Trey and his mother between them had battered down all her arguments. Besides, she didn't doubt

121

that the Esch family would talk more freely with him there.

"Good morning." She slid in quickly, circumventing his move to get out and open the door for her. "You're right on time."

"My father taught me to be punctual." He raised an eyebrow at her. "And my mother taught me to open a door for a lady."

"I'm perfectly capable of opening a truck door," she said.

She couldn't keep from glancing toward the spot where she'd realized someone was there, keeping step with her in the darkness. But it wasn't dark now, and the motor homes had vanished, their drivers off on their travels, presumably.

She turned back around in her seat, feeling Trey's gaze on her. She didn't intend to tell him, any more than she'd told the police, but for a completely different set of reasons.

Trey might believe her. And if he did . . . well, he'd jump in and try to take control, of course. She'd learned that much about him already. After that treacherous moment of weakness she'd felt with him last night, she had to keep her guard up.

"Is something wrong?" Trey frowned as he pulled out onto the street from the parking lot. "You look as if you didn't get much sleep last night."

She hadn't. "I'm fine."

She would not appear weak in front of him.

She'd started learning self-reliance the day she'd gone, a weeping eight-year-old, to boarding school. She wasn't going to regress now.

"You sure?" She could almost feel his gaze probing.

"Positive." She managed a smile. "Is it far to the Esch place?"

"Just a couple of miles down the road from our house." He didn't sound convinced, but at least he'd accepted her answer.

"Any words of wisdom about dealing with these people?"

He shot her a cold look. "First off, don't say 'these people' in that condescending way."

"I didn't mean—I don't look down on them. I just don't understand them."

"Amish aren't all the same." He sounded exasperated with her. Or annoyed. "They may dress alike and look alike, but they're individuals. Aaron, Thomas's father, has always been pretty strict with him, maybe because Thomas is the oldest child. Molly, his mother, well, I'd say she dotes on him a bit, maybe for the same reason."

She was tempted to ask if the same was true between him and his parents, but she didn't quite dare.

"There are seven younger children."

"Seven?" she murmured.

He grinned. "The Amish tend to have big families. I'm not sure how many of them you'll meet today. Aaron and Molly are trying to protect the younger ones from this. Oh, and Amos Long will be there. He's the bishop of the local congregation."

That news landed on her with a thud. "After our experience with the minister, I don't think I want a bishop mixed up in this case. It's complicated enough as it is."

"Trust me, you do want Bishop Amos involved. Without his urging, I doubt Aaron would even have agreed to talk with you. Aaron's pretty hidebound, and the Amish don't get involved with the law."

She kept hearing that, and it was starting to exasperate her. "I appreciate the bishop's influence, but in my experience, religion and the courtroom don't mix well."

"You can't separate the Amish from their religion." Trey's expression was that of someone pushing a rock up a steep hill—the rock in this case being her ignorance of Amish culture, she supposed. "They are Amish because of what they believe."

"Even so—"

"Look, I'm not saying this will come into the case." His tone said exactly the opposite. "But you'd do well to accept any help the bishop offers." He made the turn onto Dale Road. "Not far now."

He'd be relieved to be out of her company—that

much was clear from his voice. She was tempted to feel the same, except for one thing. Right at the moment she needed Trey.

He turned into a rough gravel lane leading between two fields. Brown-and-white cows looked up curiously as the vehicle passed then lowered their heads to continue munching.

Trey stopped the truck behind a gray Amish buggy. Maybe alerted by the dust they'd raised coming down the lane, a small group stood on the front porch. Motionless, their faces impassive, they waited.

Swallowing the qualms she felt, Jessica slid from the car. She hesitated at the edge of the grass until Trey took her arm and propelled her forward.

"Jessica, you remember Aaron Esch, Thomas's father, and Molly, his mother. This is Bishop Amos Long. That's Elizabeth, Thomas's sister. Everyone, this is Jessica Langdon."

Thomas's mother nodded, her face as pale and strained as it had been in the courtroom. His father stood as if carved out of stone. The sister, who must have been about fifteen or so, gave her a tentative smile.

Only the bishop, his face widening into a smile, came forward, extending his hand.

Jessica shook hands, surprised by the strength of his grip. The bishop had to be well up in years, with a weathered, lined face and an impressively long white beard, but the lively curiosity in his eyes belied his age.

"Wilcom, Jessica. Wilcom. You are the lawyer who is going to help our Thomas."

"I'm trying my best, sir." She wasn't sure how one addressed an Amish bishop, but that seemed a safe choice. Obviously, he didn't share the minister's opinion of her involvement.

"Bishop Amos," Trey murmured in her ear.

"Komm, komm." The bishop waved them into the house as if he were the host. "We must talk. Molly has the rest of the young ones busy so they will not hear."

Jessica had already glimpsed a small face peering at them from the barn behind the farmhouse, and another popped up from the vegetable garden momentarily and disappeared again. She had a feeling if she looked hard enough, she'd spot a few more, but already she and Trey were being ushered into the living room.

She took a quick glance around, hoping she didn't appear too curious. It looked like any farmhouse living room, she supposed, with bright braided rugs on polished wood floors and a tall bookcase next to a couch. No television, though, and the only ornament on the walls was a large, framed family tree.

She took the chair Bishop Amos pulled out for her, and Trey sat down next to her. Trey looked solemn, which befitted the occasion, but relaxed and at ease.

No butterflies danced in his stomach, obviously. Now that she was here, how was she going to communicate with the family? The father sat like a statue, and both the females stared down at their hands, folded in their laps, their prayer caps like white birds on their heads.

"Now." Bishop Amos settled himself in a high-backed rocking chair. "You must tell us how we can help you with Thomas's defense."

The father stirred slightly at that. "It is not fitting. Amish do not hire lawyers."

She opened her mouth to answer, but Bishop Amos beat her to it. "You did not hire the lawyer. The Morgan family did, and we should be thankful."

"The Ordnung says . . ."

Bishop Amos leaned forward, elbows on his knees. "The Ordnung is meant to show us how to live separate from the world. It is not meant to allow one of our young ones to go to jail for a wrong he didn't do. When we are forced into the Englisch courts, we must accept the help of those who understand."

The weight and pace of the words, combined with the bishop's grave stare, would have convinced her, had she been the target. Aaron stared back for a moment. Then he bowed his head in apparent agreement.

Her tension eased, but . . . "I appreciate your cooperation. When I met Ezra Burkhalter at the county jail, he led me to believe that my help wasn't welcome."

The lines in Bishop Amos's face seemed to deepen. "Amish are not all alike," he said, in an echo of Trey's words. "Brother Ezra and I do not agree on this matter."

"And the rest of your congregation?"

"Each has his own opinion," he said. "That is only right. I trust that Aaron and Molly will be guided by me in this trouble."

She hoped so, but she didn't miss the tightening of Aaron's lips at the words.

The bishop looked at her as if to say that they were ready for her questions. She took a small notebook from her bag.

"Why don't you start by telling me a little about Thomas? I've only seen him in the jail setting, and it would help to know how he is in his ordinary life."

"He is a gut boy." Aaron took control. "He works the farm with me. He is a gut worker." He looked at Trey, as if for confirmation.

Trey nodded. "Yes, he's certainly a hard worker. My mother thinks a lot of him."

The mother glanced up, as if she wanted to speak but wasn't sure she should. Jessica nodded at her encouragingly.

"Thomas likes to work for Geneva," she said

softly. "She was always kind to him. Talked to him while they worked."

He was a good boy. Everyone loved him. Except that the community, to say nothing of the D.A., was sure he'd committed an ugly crime.

"What about this . . . running around time that Trey told me about? Did Thomas give you any reason to worry about what he was doing?"

"No." Aaron snapped off the word. "He did what young people always do, but soon he would settle down. He wouldn't be gettin' involved with an Englisch girl. He knew better."

The mother nodded. But the sister—there was a quick, unguarded flash in Elizabeth's blue eyes. Then she lowered her face again, studying her hands, clasped on her apron.

"Elizabeth, do you know anything about who Thomas ran around with?"

Before the girl could answer, Aaron answered for her. "Elizabeth knows nothing."

"I know which Amish young people Thomas ran around with. I have made a list for you." The bishop took a piece of yellow lined paper from his pocket and passed it to Trey. "Trey can take you to see them. I will tell them to talk with you."

Trey nodded, scanning the list. "Do you know where they're likely to be getting together? They might speak more freely if their parents aren't around." He pocketed the list instead of handing it to her.

She suppressed a flare of irritation. "That's probably true."

"Ja, I suppose it is." Bishop Amos's voice was heavy with regret for that fact. "They will be at Miller's barn on Friday night."

"Fine. We'll be there," Trey said, not bothering to consult her.

He was right. That just annoyed her even more. "Do any of you know what time Thomas left here on Saturday night? Or where he intended to go?"

"He went after the milking and the evening chores were done." Aaron looked surprised that she needed to ask such a thing. "He said he was meeting Jacob Stoltzfus and some other boys."

"What time would it be when the evening chores were finished?" she asked, trying for patience.

"I did not pay heed to the clock," Aaron said.

"About eight, it was." Elizabeth murmured the words and then lapsed into silence again.

Elizabeth, Jessica thought, might know more than she was saying about her brother's activities. The problem would be getting her away from her parents in order to hear it.

"And you don't know anything else about where he went?"

Aaron's face tightened still more, if that were possible. "In the morning, we saw that he had not come home. It was not a church Sunday, so we thought he stayed over at a friend's house."

He couldn't have called, of course.

"We knew nothing until the police came." Thomas's mother finally spoke, and when she raised her face, Jessica saw the anguish hidden behind the stoic facade. "When will my boy come home? Can't you tell them that they are wrong about him?"

She'd thought she was hardened to the inevitable conviction of families that their child could not be guilty, but Molly's pain sliced into her.

"I'm afraid it's not that simple," she said gently. She leaned forward to touch the woman's hand. "I will do the best I can for him." For a moment they were eye-to-eye, hands clasped, differences in age and culture and education falling away to leave only the caring of two women.

Realizing the others were watching, Jessica straightened. "Is there anything that you'd like to ask me?"

The Esch family didn't speak, but the bishop nodded. Jessica turned her attention to him.

"I have heard talk of a plea bargain," he said.

"What is that?" Aaron asked, his tone sharp.

"A plea bargain is an offer from the district attorney to settle the case without a jury trial." Jessica couldn't help noticing that Trey had tensed. He'd be in favor of that, of course. Anything that would get the case, and his mother's involvement in it, out of the public eye. "The D.A. could offer a deal to Thomas, saying he'd reduce the charge if Thomas pled guilty."

"Thomas should do that," Aaron said immediately.

She studied his face, wishing she could read behind the stoic expression to the person. "Do you believe he killed Cherry Wilson?"

"No." The single negative was oddly convincing.

"Then why would you want him to confess?" She tried to keep the frustration out of her voice. She didn't understand these people, and they didn't understand the law. That didn't make for a good mix.

"He has brought shame to the community. If he went with that woman . . ." Aaron stopped. "He must confess that."

"To the church, ja," the bishop said. "That is not what concerns the law."

Aaron looked unconvinced.

"First off, the D.A. hasn't offered a deal, and I don't think he's going to." Why should he? He had a great case and an election coming up. "And even if he did make an offer, Thomas would have to say he killed Cherry Wilson. The best Thomas could hope for would probably be eight to twelve years in a state prison."

Molly seemed to choke on a sob, and Elizabeth's face was as white as the cap that covered her hair.

"I'm sorry to be so blunt," Jessica softened her tone. "But you have to understand how serious this is."

Bishop Amos nodded gravely. "Denke. It is best to understand." He touched Aaron's shoulder lightly. "We must deal with the law first, with God's help and Jessica's. Once Thomas has been cleared of his terrible charge, he will make things right with the church, ain't so?"

Aaron nodded.

Jessica felt herself relax, just a little. At least they seemed ready to go along with her recommendations. Or, more likely, their bishop's.

"You'll want to know what happens next," she said. "There will be at least one pretrial conference, at which the judge will meet with me and the district attorney. That's to decide some legal questions of procedure, and Thomas doesn't have to be there. I'll be working on building a case for Thomas, so I'll see him often. And you can go to the jail to see him, if you want, during visitor's hours. Or if there's anything you want me to take him, I'll be glad to do that."

"Would you? I could make some snickerdoodles. They are his favorite cookies." The mother looked relieved at having something concrete to do.

"I'm sure he'll like that. You can let me know . . ." She stopped, remembering they didn't have a telephone.

"I'll come by tomorrow and pick them up," Trey said quickly.

She'd have to be satisfied for the moment, but

Jessica couldn't dismiss the feeling that Elizabeth, at least, knew more than she'd said. She glanced at the girl, who had her arm around her mother's waist and was talking to her softly.

Not now. But at some point, she'd have to find out what Elizabeth knew. She suspected it couldn't be anything good.

CHAPTER EIGHT

THE URGE TO LEAVE WAS so strong that it nearly overcame Trey. Unfortunately, he knew exactly what caused the feeling.

Their grief. Their gratitude to him for what they imagined was his help. All it did was make him feel guilty, because he'd been thinking of nothing but protecting his mother.

What about the other people who needed protection? People like the Esch family?

He followed Jessica to the door. He'd like to blame her for getting him into this situation, but it wasn't her fault. He couldn't—

He stepped onto the porch and stopped dead. The lane behind his car was blocked by a television van and a couple of other cars. Two of the Esch children were surrounded by people, and the woman who was rapidly becoming his least favorite television reporter had stuck a microphone in their faces. He didn't stop to think—he just bolted off the porch and raced toward them.

Shoving his way into the knot of bodies, he grabbed the kids. Their two small faces flooded with relief at the sight of him.

"Come on." He turned to find that Jessica was right behind him. "Take them inside," he muttered. Aaron and Molly were coming toward them, holding up their hands to shield their faces from the cameras that were swung their way. "And tell Aaron and Molly to stay in, too."

Not waiting to see if she did what he said, he swung back to the reporters, glaring at a photographer who looked as if he might take a step toward the house. The man stopped in his tracks.

"Mrs. Esch, is your son guilty?" The television reporter shouted the question, and it seemed to ring in his ears.

"Mrs. Esch doesn't have anything to say to you," he said firmly, glaring at the woman.

Unconcerned, she shoved the microphone in his face. "This is the second time we've run into you while covering this case, Mr. Morgan. Care to tell us what your interest is?"

He'd asked for it, jumping to the rescue that way, but he couldn't possibly have done anything else.

"The Esch family are neighbors of ours. Naturally I want to help out in a time of trouble."

"So you're trying to get Thomas Esch off?"

"I'm trying to be a good neighbor."

"Does your mother agree—"

"All of you are trespassing." Jessica's voice sliced through the woman's question. He turned to see that she had a cell phone in her hand. "Trey, I'm not sure of jurisdiction here. Should I call the state police or the township police?"

"I'll do it," he said, giving her a grateful smile as he reached for the phone. "I'm sure the township police chief would be happy to cite a few people for trespass."

Several of the reporters started to back away, but the television reporter was made of sterner stuff. "You can't do that. The public has a right to know."

"Not when you're on private property," Jessica said. "Let me give you a little free legal advice. Leave now, or face misdemeanor trespass charges."

"Trust me, you're not getting near the house," Trey added. "I doubt your producer really wants the bad publicity involved in bailing you out of jail."

It hung in the balance for a moment. Then, muttering and discontented, the reporters straggled toward the road. He kept his eyes on them until the last vehicle disappeared.

Then he let out a breath of relief and grinned at Jessica. "Not bad, Counselor. You vanquished them."

She grinned back, eyes sparkling. "Not bad, yourself. You did as much as I did."

He held her gaze a moment longer, sensing the awareness that tingled between them. They'd no doubt be arguing again soon, but at the moment they were a team.

JESSICA SLID OFF the motel room bed, stretching her back, which had acquired a few more aches in the past hour. Working at a laptop while reclining on that bed was an exercise in torture. Leo Frost had been kind enough to offer her a desk in his office for the duration of her stay. Tomorrow she'd take him up on that. As he'd said, her superiors didn't need to know a thing about it.

The day had gone downhill after the triumph of routing the reporters at the Esch farm. The D.A.'s office had stonewalled her on the subject of discovery, saying the documents weren't ready yet. If that happened again in the morning, she'd have to go to the judge. Thomas's defense was entitled to see every piece of evidence the prosecution had.

And then there had been a call from the senior partner's assistant, wanting to know why she hadn't wrapped up a plea bargain yet. She'd danced around that, not wanting to get into a long-distance argument.

Frowning, she rubbed the back of her neck. Given the delicate situation she was in with the office, it seemed unlikely she'd get much help there. Sara had been interested in this case—she'd probably be willing to put in a few unofficial hours of research time to help her roommate.

She glanced at her watch. Sara ought to be back at the apartment by now. She picked up her cell phone.

"Hi, Jess." Sara was the only person in her life who called her that, ignoring Jessica's protests or saying that it was better than calling her Jessie. "How are things in the wilds of the country?"

"Moving slowly. I might almost think the D.A.'s office was being deliberately obstructionist."

"Wouldn't be the first time." Amusement filled Sara's voice. "You should know. You used to be one."

"Only a lowly A.D.A.," Jessica reminded her. "We were too unimportant to worry about politics. It seems the D.A. is running for reelection in the fall."

"And he wants to make some political hay on this case." Sara completed the thought for her. "Sounds as if you could use a little clout of your own. Maybe a call from the head honcho at Henderson, Dawes and Henderson would shake up the D.A."

"I don't think Dwight Henderson would extend himself for me right now. He just expects a quick plea bargain and an expression of gratitude from the Morgan family, but those two things aren't going to go together anytime soon."

"So the Morgans still think the boy is innocent?"

"Geneva does." She found she was thinking about Trey's face when he'd confronted the reporters. "It's possible that Trey—Blake Morgan—is coming around, too."

"Trey, hmm." Sara's grin seemed to come through the telephone. "So tell me, this Trey. Is he married? Engaged? Otherwise involved?"

"I don't . . . how would I know that?"

"Girlfriend, you can't fool me. You're interested, aren't you?"

"No. Well, maybe, but I'm certainly not going to pursue the man. Way too complicated. Besides, I get the feeling he's the kind to get serious over a relationship."

"Jess, there's nothing wrong with getting serious when it comes to the right guy." Sara's tone softened. "You ought to relax a little. If something's going to develop, let it."

"I can't." For a very long list of reasons. "Listen, let's forget about my love life, or lack of one, for the moment. I called to ask a favor."

"Sure thing. What?"

"I need someone to do a little research for me. Given the situation in the office, I don't think I can count on them."

She heard the sound of papers shuffling and pictured Sara searching for her pen, which was probably behind her ear. "Okay, shoot."

"I need any information you can find about previous cases involving the prosecution of an Amish person for a crime. Also anything else relating to a case like this one, where someone who lives in a sheltered religious community has been tried."

"You've got it. Anything else?"

"That's all I can think of at the moment. Listen, thanks so much. I know you're busy—"

"This is ten times more interesting than anything I'm working on now," Sara said. "You're trying a murder case involving an Amishman, while I'm still pursuing absentee landlords. I'm living vicariously through you."

That made Jessica laugh, which was as good a reason as any to call Sara. She said good-night, still smiling.

The motel room was too quiet once she'd hung up. It was too late to do anything else, and too early to go to bed. She stood, stretched and bent over to get the kinks out. If she didn't get some exercise soon, she'd stagnate. Maybe she could fit in a run tomorrow.

She started toward the television remote then stopped, listening. Footsteps, pacing quietly along the walk in front of the motel units. She took a quick look to be sure there weren't any gaps in the drapes. She'd never have taken a first-floor room if there'd been any option.

No gaps. No one could possibly see in, and she'd double-bolted the door when she'd come back after supper. She was perfectly safe. It was just another guest, heading for his or her room.

The footsteps stopped. On the other side of the window. It could be perfectly innocent. Someone looking for a room number, or stopping to admire the sky, or looking at his watch, or lighting a cigarette. All perfectly innocent reasons for someone to be standing on the other side of that window, inches away from her.

She could pull back the drape. Her hand reached for it and stopped before she touched the fabric. She couldn't. And anyway, she shouldn't. Common sense dictated that she do nothing to stir up unwanted attention.

She realized she was holding her breath. Waiting. Was he holding his breath, too? Looking at the window? Anyone could have found out where she was staying, and the thought of that knife in her tires sent a chill down her spine.

Call the desk clerk. That was the sensible thing to do, regardless of whether he thought she sounded like an idiot. She took a step toward the phone. The person outside moved, too, walking quickly away.

Receiver in her hand, she moved back toward the window. If she parted the drapes just an inch, she might be able to see whoever it was. Her fingers closed on the fabric, and she leaned close.

The fixture was on outside her door, casting a semicircle of sickly light on the walk. Her eyes, accustomed to the lamps she'd turned on inside, couldn't make out much in the parking lot.

She leaned closer, forehead touching the cool glass, and tried to look down the row of units. Nothing.

A movement from the parking lot caught her eye, but it was nothing more than a flicker of shadow against shadow. Suddenly something black hurtled toward her. She stumbled back, heart racing, as it thudded against the glass.

Silence. Nothing moved out there. Fingers shaking, she punched the button for the front desk.

"This is Ms. Langdon in Room 112." Amazing that her voice sounded so calm when she was trembling inside. "Someone just threw something against my window."

"Threw something?" He sounded about sixteen and unprepared to deal with anything other than a request for ice. "What . . . what do you want me to do, ma'am?"

"I want you to come over here and see what's going on." Call the police? She hesitated.

"Yes, ma'am. I'll . . . I'll be right there." He didn't sound particularly willing.

She waited, cell phone in hand, ready to dial 911 if anything else happened. But nothing did, except a tentative knock on the door.

"Ma'am? It's Benny, the night manager. The thing that hit your window . . . it's okay. Just a bird flying into it, that's all."

She opened the door cautiously. The kid looked sixteen, too. He held a flashlight, which he shone down on the object on the ground in front of the window.

A bird . . . black, large. It lay spread out on the sidewalk, wings limp, head twisted.

"A raven, I think it is." He knelt, poking at it.

"Dead. Must have broken its neck when it hit the window. Birds do that, sometimes, y'know."

"Yes, I know." She probably looked ridiculous to him. Still, after hearing someone standing out here, seeing movement in the parking lot, no one could blame her for overreacting, could they?

"I'll get something to clean it up." He went quickly back toward the office.

She stood for a moment, looking down at the bird. Then, unwillingly, she bent, touching it. The raven, if that's what it was, was dead. It was also cold and stiff.

She took a quick step away from it, grabbing the door. That bird hadn't flown into her window. Not unless it could fly when it was already dead.

JESSICA PUSHED OPEN THE door to Leo's office with the cardboard box she was carrying. At his questioning look, she put it down on the desk he'd insisted she use while she was in town.

"The box of discovery from the D.A.'s office. They finally came through with it, but there's not much, in comparison to some cases I've worked."

That was unfortunate. While it could be difficult to sort through tons of material, at least that gave the opportunity to pick holes in the prosecution's case. Clearly the D.A. thought he had a slam dunk in this one with the evidence he had.

Leo came to peer curiously into the box. Then he took a step back, as if recalling that it was

Jessica's case, not his. "Sorry. I just can't help being interested."

"Please, go ahead and look. You're assisting with the case, even if you don't want to formalize the arrangement." Jessica slipped off her suit jacket. She'd begun to feel that her clothes were a bit too formal for this setting, but she was stuck with what Henderson, Dawes and Henderson thought appropriate for an associate. "Given all the local antagonism, I can understand why you feel that way."

"If that bothered me, I wouldn't be insisting that you work here." He lifted the lid on the box while she hung her jacket from the old-fashioned coat tree in the corner.

"Well, no, I don't see you being worried about a little bad press," she said. Leo, like Geneva, would do what he thought was right, no matter what the cost. It was a refreshing attitude. Sara would like these people.

Thinking of Sara reminded her of what had happened after their conversation the night before. Once again, after a little consideration, she hadn't called the police, for two very good reasons. One, they wouldn't have been able to do anything with the only evidence, a dead bird. And two, if the press got hold of it, she'd undoubtedly be letting herself in for worse, as more people got the great idea of driving Thomas's defender away.

"I've lived long enough to know that even the

worst things fade eventually," Leo was saying. "And since I'm retiring, no one can hurt my business."

She opened her laptop and switched it on, sinking into the padded desk chair. "I can't tell you what it means to me to have the use of your office."

"Motel room getting you down?" he asked.

She nodded, opening her e-mail. "Too small, terrible lighting and a desk that wobbles hopelessly." To say nothing of too many uncomfortable . . . well, scary . . . moments that reminded her of how alone she was.

The truth was, quite aside from the convenience of the office, she enjoyed Leo's company. Unlike the premises of Henderson, Dawes and Henderson, this office wasn't permeated with the aroma of ambition.

"I enjoy having you here," Leo said. "Brings a little life into the old place." He glanced around the comfortably old-fashioned office, giving a sigh that he might not have been aware of. "I have to confess, I'll miss it."

"People will miss you, I'm sure." She'd already seen the parade of people with problems who came through Leo's office and left convinced their affairs were in good hands. Maybe they weren't the kind of cases Henderson, Dawes and Henderson dealt with, but they were important to the people involved.

"Ah, well, no use looking back. I've made my decision. It's time to retire." As if to belie his words, Leo sat down with a sheaf of papers from the discovery box and began going through them. "How did you make out with Thomas's parents yesterday?"

Now it was her turn to sigh. "Not bad, although I'm not sure I'd have gotten anything out of them if not for the combined efforts of Trey and Bishop Amos. And even at that, the family didn't have anything really helpful to say. I think the father would have jumped at a plea bargain, not that one will be offered, just to have it over with."

"I suspect his feelings are more complicated than that. Being separate from the world, living humbly—those things are the essence of the Amish. To be caught up in the English legal system and find themselves on the front page of the paper . . ."

Leo shoved his glasses up on his white hair and nodded toward the morning paper on the edge of his desk. The front page bore a photo of Trey pulling the Esch children away from the press. "Trey has a certain amount in common with the Amish in that respect. I don't suppose he's any too happy this morning to see that picture."

She couldn't help but smile. "Trey insists he doesn't want to be involved. Declares he's only in it to protect Geneva. But the instant he saw those children surrounded by reporters, he charged in like Sir Galahad."

Leo chuckled. "That's Trey all right. He inherited his mother's caring combined with his father's sense of duty. That can put a heavy load on a person, trying to take responsibility for everyone else all the time."

"Not everyone wants to be taken care of." The words came out sharply enough that she was afraid she'd given herself away.

Leo slid his glasses into place and gave her a speculative glance. "I suppose that's true, but you'd have a hard time convincing Trey of that."

She didn't intend to try, but maybe it was time to change the subject. This one was getting into uncomfortable territory. Her feelings on that subject went too deep—back to her mother's death, back to her sense of abandonment when her father sent her away. She'd survived by learning to stand on her own. Independence was a good thing. She didn't want, or need, to lean on anyone.

"Trey is going to exercise his need to take care of people by helping me interview the Amish kids that Thomas runs around with, especially those who were at that party. And I have to talk to the English kids, as well." *English*—she was starting to talk like these people. "I notice the police interviewed a man named Charles Fulton. Apparently he was an on-again/off-again boyfriend of Cherry's. Do you know anything about him?"

"Chip Fulton? I know who he is. Trey might be able to tell you more, since he's closer in age."

Naturally. Everything she needed, someone expected her to turn to Trey.

"He works at Walbeck's Garage and lives outside of Springville," Leo continued. "He's been in trouble with the law once or twice, as I recall, although nothing very serious. DUI, maybe assault."

Her eyebrows lifted. "He might be a more likely candidate for murderer than Thomas, but you can't get away from the physical evidence. You know as well as I do that 'I don't remember' isn't going to be an adequate defense. I have to provide the jury with a version of the crime they can buy into."

"Juries can be unexpected." Leo rubbed the back of his neck. "Unfortunately, every potential juror in the county is being affected right now by the press coverage."

"I've thought about filing a change-of-venue motion, but there are as many things against that as for it. At least here the potential jurors probably understand the Amish culture. I'm barely beginning to understand it myself, and trying to explain to a jury . . ." She let that trail off, sure that Leo understood.

Frustrated, she turned to the box. She had to go

through it carefully, searching for the bit of wheat among all the chaff it undoubtedly contained.

A few minutes later she sank back in her chair, looking in disbelief at a sheet of paper from the evidence box. She glanced over at Leo, to find him watching her, obviously noting the change in her expression.

"Something interesting?" he asked.

"Something that explains why the D.A. was so slow in releasing the evidence, I'll bet. This was buried at the bottom of the box. The results of the blood tests on Thomas and Cherry."

She handed it to him then went and stood behind him, reading it again as he scanned quickly down through the results.

"I don't understand," he said. "According to this, there was a whopping amount of Rohypnol in Thomas's system. Thomas's. And none in Cherry's."

"Date-rape drug," she said slowly. "That explains why Thomas doesn't remember anything. I've done some research on it in relation to a case." One of Henderson's wealthy clients, in fact. She'd been expected to make the case go away. "Victims experience amnesia in regard to anything that happened while under the influence."

He nodded. "Like Thomas. It wasn't the drinking. It was the drug. But it's all the wrong way around. Why would Thomas be drugged?"

"I don't know. But I'm not sure it would be possible for Thomas to have performed a violent act while under the influence, although I suppose the D.A. could argue that the murder happened before the drug had taken effect."

Leo reached for his address book. "We need an expert opinion. I know someone in Harrisburg, unless you have a person the firm uses."

"No, go ahead and call your guy." She wasn't sure how Henderson would respond to that request. He'd obviously thought this case would end in a simple plea bargain. If he'd imagined it could have turned into much of a case, he wouldn't have sent her. "In the meantime, I'm going to call the D.A. He can't be as sure of his case now as he was."

A spurt of enthusiasm flowed through Jessica, and her mind began ticking over possibilities. The D.A. might come forth with a more reasonable plea-bargain offer, although she doubted that Geneva would want to accept any deal. And maybe Geneva had been right all along. Thomas just might be innocent.

CHAPTER NINE

TREY WAS BACK BEHIND the wheel of the truck again, ferrying Jessica in search of kids who'd been at the party. Working together like this had begun to feel familiar—maybe too easy and familiar.

"Thanks again for helping out with this." Jessica sounded cool, as if she were as intent as he was on setting boundaries. "I'm sure I'm taking you away from work."

He shrugged. "I went into the office early to go through some papers that needed my attention. I'll catch up, eventually. And you'll get through this faster with someone who knows his way around. Besides, I know a few of these families, so it might help to have me along."

The truth was that he'd been ignoring a lot that should be done at the office because of this situation. But if he didn't help Jessica, he had a feeling his mother would, and he shuddered at the thought of Mom playing Nancy Drew.

"Your office is in Springville?" She glanced at him. "I confess, I hadn't pictured you in an office setting."

"Because of the khakis and sport shirt? This is considered dressy around here. Anyway, I'm the boss. I can wear what I want. You should see casual Friday."

That got a faint smile from her. "I'd intended to talk to Cherry Wilson's employer and coworkers today, but this drug-test report makes it more crucial to talk with people who were at the party."

"You figure that's where Thomas was given the drug?"

"I think so." Her forehead wrinkled. "According to the research I've done, Rohypnol causes a sleepy, relaxed, drunk feeling, and the victim may forget everything that happened. The last thing Thomas remembers about that night was being at the party."

"Makes sense." His fingers tightened on the wheel at the thought of someone doing that to any kid, let alone one as inexperienced and trusting as Thomas. "If that's the case, you might argue that he couldn't have become violent."

"We talked about that, but we need more than supposition. Leo is contacting an expert to go over the findings for us. The problem with experts is that juries tend to distrust them. The prosecution brings on theirs, we bring on ours . . . it can just be a wash. We need to find someone who saw Thomas either being drugged or under the influence. Unfortunately, teenagers tend to clam up in the face of authority."

He shot another glance at Jessica, reading the determination in the set of her jaw. "That sounds like the voice of experience speaking."

"Me?" She looked startled. "I had the most

boring adolescence of all time. We lived in Boston, but I didn't go to public schools. My father sent me to a strict girls' boarding school. Most of us were too scared of the administration to party, even if we could have gotten off-campus."

"That sounds a little . . . lonely." In comparison with his childhood, certainly. His younger brother and sister had kept things lively. And even though Mom and Dad could have sent them to private school, as far as he could tell they'd never even considered it.

Jessica shrugged. "It wasn't so bad. My mother died when I was young, and with my father's career . . . well, he didn't have much time."

He'd looked up Jessica's illustrious father when he was trying to find out more about her. It sounded as if his only child had been sacrificed to his judicial advancement.

"No other relatives?"

"No one we were close to." She seemed to shake off childhood memories. "Anyway, I'm sure you know more about the party scene around here than I ever could."

He had to respect her changing the subject. "I went to a few in my time," he admitted. "But I think those were pretty tame in comparison to what kids get up to now."

"That may make it even harder to get any of them to open up," she said.

"All we can do is try. I didn't realize defense attorneys had to be detectives, too."

Her lips curved. "I admit, it's not in the job description. But this isn't an ordinary situation. Right now . . ." She lifted her hands, palms up. "Right now I don't have much to take to trial." Her eyes darkened, and he could feel the tension building in her. "Maybe I ought to be trying harder for a plea-bargain offer."

"You said the only reason the D.A. would come up with an offer was because he didn't want to have to explain how the drug report fits into his version of the crime."

He'd been surprised that Jessica had confided that much information in him. Maybe she'd felt that he had to know that much in order to help with the teens. Or maybe she was beginning to trust him.

"True, but I still have to come up with an alternate version of the story. If not—"

"We'll find something," he said. They had to.

"We?" Her gaze seemed to sizzle on his face. "You're suddenly sounding like this is about more than keeping your mother out of trouble. I should think you'd be jumping at the chance to take a plea and get the case off the front pages as quickly as possible."

"You must not think much of me if you assume I want to see that kid go to prison." His fingers tightened on the wheel.

"If you still think he's guilty—"

"I don't." He might as well get this said. "Or at least, I'm not sure. That drug report—maybe my mother had it right all along. If there's a chance Thomas is innocent, I have to help."

"A lot of people wouldn't see it that way. A lot of people would say it wasn't any of their business."

"Those people weren't raised by my parents. They lived their beliefs every day of their lives."

"You were lucky, having parents like that."

Something in her voice made him look at her. She'd turned her face away, but the curve of her neck looked . . . vulnerable.

"Your family—" he began.

"There's the street." She cut him off. Clearly the topic of her family was off-limits.

He made the turn, letting the subject drop. But not forgetting it. He was fortunate in his family. Maybe Jessica wasn't so lucky.

Pulling to the curb, he took a moment to survey the house, a fairly new, upper-middle-class mini-mansion in one of the developments that had sprouted up recently on the outskirts of Lancaster. What was a girl from a house like this doing partying with an Amish kid?

Jessica was already getting out, and he followed her up the walk. The girl must have been watching for them, because she opened the door before they had a chance to knock.

"Hi. Are you Dani Cresswood?" Jessica struck a nice balance between formal and friendly.

The girl, in jeans and a T-shirt, hair pulled back in a ponytail, clutched the door. "I really can't tell you anything more than what I told the police. I don't remember anything else."

She meant she wouldn't admit to knowing, he suspected.

"Let's just go over it together," Jessica said. "Something may pop into your mind that you didn't think of before this. May we come in?"

Dani stepped back, still holding the door. She gestured them into the formal living room to the right of the center hallway. Probably the better to get them back out the door, he'd think.

"My mom will be back in half an hour. We'd better get this over before then. She doesn't want me talking about it." She rolled her eyes. "Like it will disappear if I don't talk about it."

"Let's get on with it, then." Sitting down, Jessica pulled a typewritten sheet from her leather briefcase. "I have here a copy of the statement you gave to the police."

Dani's eyes widened. "How did you get that?"

"The district attorney is required to turn over all evidence to the defendant's lawyer," Jessica said. "That's only fair. You want to be fair to Thomas, don't you?"

"If he killed Cherry . . ." She let that die out.

"If," Jessica said. "That hasn't been proved yet.

157

Everyone is entitled to a fair trial, don't you think?"

"You have an obligation to cooperate." Trey suspected Jessica wouldn't appreciate his interceding, but that's why he was here, wasn't it? He wasn't just a chauffeur.

That earned him a pout and a sideways glance from the girl. "It's none of my business."

"It's everybody's business to help when they can." What he'd said to Jessica about the Morgans wasn't just a family custom. It was the belief he lived by, even when his worries about his mother got the better of him.

The pout deepened, and Dani shrugged. "Well, I'd help if I could, but I don't know anything."

"Did you see Thomas at the party that night?" Jessica had her pen poised over the police report, probably ready to spring on any inconsistencies.

"Well, yeah, I guess. But I didn't talk to him." She sounded as if she thought she should get points for that.

"Had you seen him at other parties?"

She considered. "I guess, maybe. There were a few Amish kids who came around."

"And Cherry? Did you see her?"

Jessica sounded patient, even though it seemed like slow going to him. He'd plunge right into the pertinent question. Did you see anyone slip something into Thomas's drink? That was what they needed to know.

Dani nodded. "I didn't know who she was at first, but somebody told me she liked to come to parties. I don't know why." Her nose wrinkled. "She was old."

Twenty-four. Well, to this kid that probably seemed ancient.

"Was Thomas drinking?"

"Yeah. Well, he must have been. Everybody was."

"Think about it," Jessica urged. "Try to picture him in your mind the way you saw him that night."

Dani obediently closed her eyes. "Okay, yeah," she said finally. "He had a beer can in one hand. He'd put it down when he was dancing, but I'm sure I saw him with one."

And if he put it down to dance, anyone could have tampered with it.

"It looks as if someone put something in Thomas's drink at the party," Jessica said. "Did you see—"

"No!" Dani shied away from that. Apparently beer was one thing, even though she was obviously underage, but drugs were another. "I don't know anything about any drugs. Nobody was doing drugs at that party. They wouldn't, and if they had been, I'd have left." She rose. "I think I shouldn't talk to you anymore without my folks being here."

"Dani, I'm just trying to get at the truth about

what happened. I'm not accusing you. If you saw anything to indicate that Thomas was under the influence—"

"I didn't, okay? It's not like I was watching him, but when I saw him, he looked fine." She clamped her mouth shut. Then she marched to the door and opened it.

They followed her. Jessica paused on the doorstep to press a card into the girl's hand. "If you think of anything, call me."

No response. This kid was so intent on protecting herself, and probably her friends, that she wouldn't do a thing to help.

And that was exactly what he'd been doing . . . so eager to protect his mother that he'd forgotten that there were other people who needed help. He glanced at Jessica as they walked toward the car. She needed his help, although she didn't want to admit it. Thomas did, too.

What he'd said to Jessica was the simple truth. He'd been brought up to take responsibility. And from this point on, he was in this to stay.

JESSICA SHOULD HAVE SAID no to the invitation to dinner at Geneva's that night. Just as she should have done something to stop the growing attraction she felt for Trey. She missed on both counts.

She set the plate that had contained a slice of rhubarb pie on the end table next to her. The living room glowed with a mellow light from a pair of brass table lamps. The other three probably felt as sated as she did after the meal Geneva had served.

Trey sat in a worn leather armchair that must have been his father's, although *sat* wasn't exactly the right word. He'd slid down to the base of his spine, his long legs stretched out on the leather ottoman. He looked practically boneless in that position.

Geneva and Leo, on opposite ends of the sofa, were scanning the newspaper spread out between them. A golden retriever lay on the floor, his heavy head resting on Geneva's foot, his graying muzzle a testament to his age.

If she didn't say something, she'd fall asleep. "I didn't see Sam the last time I was here." She nodded at the dog, and his plumy tail waved a bit at the sound of his name.

"He can get stressed if there's company," Trey said, not moving.

The likeness between dog and man, both stretched out in almost-comatose relaxation, made her smile. "He doesn't look particularly stressed at the moment," she observed.

"Like me, you mean." Trey hadn't moved, but he seemed to sense her smile, which was a disturbing thought.

"I didn't say that." She probably should stop looking at him.

"Sam was Blake's dog." Geneva, not seeming to

161

notice the byplay, bent to ruffle Sam's ears. His tail thudded against the Oriental rug. "He still misses him, don't you, Sammy?"

The dog didn't respond. But Trey's muscles tightened so much that Jessica didn't have to be looking at him to feel his tension. Wishing she hadn't mentioned the dog, she sought for a change of subject.

"I take it you didn't make much progress with the young people you interviewed today," Leo said, coming to the rescue.

"Not much." The reminder was discouraging. "It was the teenage wall of silence. No one would admit to anything more than seeing Thomas and Cherry at the party. No one saw anyone slip the drug to Thomas, or knows anything about any drugs, or will even admit to seeing them leave, either separately or together."

"Kids watch too much television," Leo said. "They know they don't have to talk to you."

"You'll have better luck tomorrow night with the Amish kids." Geneva was the eternal optimist. "If Bishop Amos told them to talk, they'll talk."

"I just hope somebody at that party was sober enough to notice something." She stared down into the cup of coffee that Geneva assured her was decaf. "The trial date is coming on fast, and right now we have nothing."

"Something will turn up." Geneva closed the

newspaper and tossed it aside. "Honestly, I'm going to cancel my subscription to that paper if they don't stop printing all that garbage about Thomas."

"It might make more of an impression if you canceled your advertising," Leo said. "The Morgan name means something around here."

"That's a good idea." Geneva brightened. "Trey, that's just what we should do. I'll call tomorrow and cancel our advertising. And when they ask why, I'll tell them."

Trey sat up marginally straighter. "We can't do that. We need them as much as they need us."

"Advertising?" Jessica blinked, the comment taking her off-guard. "What do you advertise?"

"Morgan Lumberyard, Morgan Real Estate, MRB Construction, Morgan's Tractor Parts . . ." Trey stopped, frowning. "Anything else we're running ads for right now, Mom?"

"The feed mill," Geneva said. "And I really feel we ought to do more about the general store. I know you think it's old-fashioned, but tourists find it quaint."

"You own all those businesses?"

Trey had mentioned something about businesses and rental property in relation to Morgan Enterprises, but she'd assumed . . . well, she wasn't sure what she'd assumed. Still, he'd made it clear that he was taking time away from work to help with the case.

"Anyway, I will not pay advertising dollars to a paper that prints innuendo as news." Geneva's cheeks flushed. "Imagine, hinting that Thomas was using drugs."

Leo looked a little startled at the response to what had been an offhand comment. "I really didn't mean you should rush into anything, Geneva. Why don't I call the publisher tomorrow and see if that does any good?"

Geneva looked reluctant to give up on the idea of taking on the newspaper. "I feel as if I'm not doing a thing useful. As least if I did cancel our advertising, I'd be making a statement."

"Let's see how they respond to Leo first, Mom." Trey's voice soothed, but his eyebrows had drawn together. "And you're doing plenty. It encourages Thomas to know you're behind him. Really." He turned to Jessica. "By the way, I have to go to Harrisburg tomorrow to attend a couple of meetings with state legislators about the proposal to turn the interstate into a toll road, but I'll be back in plenty of time to pick you up. The kids won't be gathering until it's getting dark—probably nine or so."

She recognized the appeal in his look. Get his mother off the subject of mounting a campaign against the newspaper, it said. "That's fine. I have some other things to do during the day anyway. I want to interview Cherry's employer and her coworkers."

Leo stirred. "I read through their statements to the police. Not much there."

"What do you think they'll tell you that they didn't tell the police?" Trey's eyebrows lifted, as if to question her use of her time.

"Maybe nothing." She was a little nettled. What did he know about preparing a case? "But I need to see for myself. I don't believe in taking things for granted."

"Always want to do it yourself," he said, his voice deceptively lazy.

She straightened. "That's right. I want to track down Charles Fulton, as well. Leo, you said he worked at a local garage?"

"Chip Fulton?" Trey's voice cut across Leo's answer. "What does he have to do with this?"

"He and Cherry apparently had a relationship, and he has a history of violence. The police didn't bother to do more than a cursory interview with him."

"Thought they already had their killer gift wrapped," Leo murmured.

"Maybe Chip should be interviewed," Trey said. "But you can't do it."

She gave him a chilly look. "I beg your pardon?"

"I mean, you shouldn't do it. Not alone."

"I'm perfectly capable of taking a statement from the man." Trey had a nerve implying that she liked to do everything for herself. His protectiveness was far worse. "I've never required a bodyguard before, and I don't now."

Trey sat bolt upright in the chair, any pretense of relaxation dropped. "I'm telling you, Chip is nobody to fool around with. He's got a nasty temper, and if he thinks you're hinting that he killed Cherry . . ."

"That's ridiculous." Her own temper wasn't helped by the fact that Geneva and Leo were watching them with identical expressions of amusement. "First of all, I'm not going to hint anything of the kind. And secondly, I might need your help in communicating with the Amish, but the Chip Fultons of the world I can handle on my own. I spent three years as an A.D.A. in Philadelphia, and I doubt very much that Chip can match what I dealt with there."

Trey's mouth tightened. "I still say—"

She stood. "Thank you so much for dinner, Geneva. I really think I'd better get back to the motel."

"Don't rush off just because Trey is being bossy," Geneva said, for all the world as if Jessica were ending a playdate because of a childish spat. "He can't help it. He was born that way. You can have another sliver of pie, can't you?"

"Not possibly." She didn't dare look at Trey to see how he reacted to his mother's comments. "It's not anything Trey said. I have some work I have to get through before I quit for the night."

"Well, if you're sure." Geneva looked doubtful.

"I'm sure." She bent to pick up her bag. "Good night, Geneva. Leo."

"I'll walk you out." Trey shoved himself from his chair before she could say that wasn't necessary.

When she turned to precede Trey out the door, Sam lumbered to his feet and followed them.

"Time for a little walk, old boy?" Trey's voice relaxed when he spoke to the dog. "Come on, then."

They stepped out into the night, the dog at their heels. Once they were beyond the yellow glow of the porch light, she paused to let her eyes grow accustomed to the dimness.

Trey took her arm, his hand large and warm against her skin. "Look, about Chip—"

"Don't start," she warned. "I can take care of myself."

"Right." He didn't sound convinced, but at least he didn't continue to argue. "I'll give you a call when I get back tomorrow."

"Fine." She couldn't deny that she needed his help just to find the Amish teens' party, let alone to talk to them.

She reached for the car door, but Trey beat her to it, opening the driver's side door. "My mother might be watching. You don't want . . ." His voice died out.

She followed the direction of his gaze. On the

front seat of the car, clearly visible now that the dome light was on, was another warning note.

Trey picked it up, holding it by one corner. His breath hissed out.

It was a photo of her, taken outside the jail. Across her figure, someone had drawn a thick, red X. The line trailed down, looking just like drops of blood.

CHAPTER TEN

"Come on." Trey grabbed Jessica's arm and hustled her toward the house. The idea that someone was out there, in the dark, maybe watching them—

Get Jessica inside, then he'd go looking for the person who'd come onto his property, threatened his guest.

"Trey, you're overreacting."

He ignored her efforts to pull away from him. Of course she would. If he'd met a more stubbornly independent woman, he didn't remember it. "Maybe so." They reached the door, and he shoved her inside. "But I'd rather be safe than sorry."

Leo and his mother hurried toward them from the family room. Sam, probably alerted by his tone, let out a deep bark, turning to look toward the woods.

"What's going on?" Leo glanced at Jessica but looked at him for an answer.

"Somebody's been here. Left a threatening note in Jessica's car." He gave Jessica a gentle push toward his mother. "Mom, please keep Jessica inside while we search the grounds."

She didn't argue, just put her arm around Jessica's waist and picked up the phone with her other hand. "I'll call Adam Byler. You two be careful out there."

He nodded, jerking open the closet door to grab a couple of flashlights from the shelf. He tossed one to Leo. "You okay to take a look around?"

"You're not leaving me behind." Leo's face set. He switched on the flashlight and followed Trey out. The sound of Jessica's voice, asking who Adam Byler was, faded with the closing door. "Don't worry. Your mother won't let her come out," Leo said. "How long will it take the township police to get here?"

"Depends upon where they are. Ten to twenty minutes, I'd guess." Someone—Mom, he supposed—had switched on all the outside lights. He stepped beyond their reach and paused, swinging his flashlight in a wide swath. The grass, cut only yesterday, wasn't long enough to reveal any footsteps.

"He'd have come from the road, most likely." Leo aimed his flashlight toward the woods that shielded the house from the road.

"Sam barked at something out that way. Let's have a look." Trey started toward the stand of pines, scanning the ground for any sign of the intruder.

"If he's smart, he wouldn't hang around," Leo said. Trey felt his gaze on him. "How bad was the note?"

"It was a photo of Jessica. With an X across her image." His stomach tightened at the thought. "I'd call that a threat, wouldn't you?"

"Nasty. But I don't think it will scare Jessica off."

Did Leo think he was overreacting, too? Probably. He couldn't explain it to himself, but the revulsion he'd felt when he'd seen that threat, known someone had come that close to her . . .

Well, maybe it was better if he didn't explore those feelings too closely.

They'd reached the trees, and Trey moved cautiously, searching the ground with his flashlight. But the smooth, thick carpet of pine needles didn't yield any clues.

"If he came through here, he didn't leave any sign," he said, reluctant to give up with nothing to show for it. "Out by the road—"

A siren wailed in the distance.

"Sounds as if the township boys weren't too far off," Leo said. "Maybe we should walk over to the drive and meet them."

"You don't want me playing detective?" Trey tried to keep his tone light.

"Let's give Adam Byler a chance. I'm sure he'd like something more interesting than speeders and Saturday-night drunks once in a while."

They emerged onto the lawn and reached the gravel just as the township police car came shrieking into the drive, siren wailing. He raised his hand, and the car skidded to a halt, sending up a spray of gravel.

He leaned on the window that lowered at his approach. "You boys in a hurry?"

"Turn off that siren, you idiot." Adam Byler glared at the young patrolman who was behind the wheel. "You take a turn like that again, and it'll be the last time you drive the patrol car. You think the township has an unlimited supply of tires?"

"No, sir." The kid gulped, probably flushing and grateful for the dark.

Adam swung around to face Trey. "You caught the prowler for us?"

"Just taking a look around," Trey said. He realized suddenly that his hands were closed into fists, and he forced them to relax. "We wouldn't want to rob you of the most excitement you've had in a month."

"As a taxpayer, you ought to be glad we keep things so quiet. So, what's going on here tonight?"

Adam got out as he spoke, standing next to the car and looming over it. Adam had been a lineman, back when they'd played high-school football. Unlike some, he'd never let himself run to fat. Six feet of solid muscle, but it wasn't muscle between his ears.

"Leo was here for supper, along with Jessica Langdon, the attorney who's acting for Thomas Esch. Someone got into her car and left a threatening message for her."

Put into a bald recital of facts, it didn't sound quite so bad. Not bad enough, at any rate, to account for the anger that pumped through him.

"You find any sign of the prowler?" Adam's

impassive face didn't give anything away. If he thought this a fool's errand, no one would know.

Trey shook his head. "We figure he must have parked along the road and walked in, maybe from the woods. All the outside lights weren't on then. He could easily have gotten to the car without being seen and left the same way."

"Let's have a look at the vehicle." Adam bent to put his head in the car window. "Jarvis, take your flashlight and scout along the road near the driveway. You're looking for any sign someone was parked there and walked toward the house."

"Yessir." The kid was out of the police car almost before Adam finished speaking. "I'll get right on it." He trotted back down the lane toward the road, flashlight swinging.

"He won't find anything," Adam said dispassionately. "Wouldn't spot a stolen car unless it drove right over him."

"He's enthusiastic," Leo observed as they started toward the house.

"Yeah." Adam didn't sound as if he thought that made up for the kid's shortcomings. "The rule is, if I get a kid who's any good on the township force, he'll go on to something bigger and better as soon as I've got him trained. If he has no talent at all, he'll be with me forever."

It sounded as if he thought Jarvis fit into the latter category.

"So," he went on, "is Ms. Langdon a friend of

yours, or is the rumor true that you're funding the Esch kid's defense?"

"Both." No point in trying to put Adam off. He knew everything that went on in the township. "It's too bad you weren't in on that case."

Adam shrugged. "Didn't happen in Spring Township. And I don't know as I'd have done things any differently."

They reached the drive, and Adam went directly to Jessica's car, obviously knowing which was hers. He flashed his torch inside. "Did Ms. Langdon lock the car?"

"I don't think so. I doubt it." She shouldn't have to lock her car when it was parked outside his house. This ought to be safe.

Adam gave him a searching look. "This is really bugging you."

Tough to hide your feelings from someone you'd known most of your life. "I don't like the idea of some cretin coming onto my property. Threatening a guest in my house. That's all."

"Uh-huh." Adam's raised eyebrow expressed doubt. "Let me get the note secure, and then I'd better have a word with your . . . guest."

He pressed his lips together to keep from snarling. Adam hadn't even met Jessica and he was jumping to conclusions about their relationship. It was laughable.

Except that his own anger was revealing just how much he'd begun to care about Jessica.

• • •

"A PIECE OF PAPER CAN'T hurt me," Jessica said for what seemed like the tenth or twentieth time. She shoved away the photocopy Trey had made before his cop friend took away the original threat.

She shouldn't have been surprised to learn that he knew the township police chief well, or that they had played high-school football together. They'd had the easy, ragging banter that betrayed their closeness, even with a serious undertone.

She, Trey, Leo and Geneva were sitting around Geneva's kitchen table, mugs of hot cocoa in front of them, Geneva having insisted they needed something soothing after the excitement. Adam had tried to be encouraging. Leaving a threatening note was a criminal act, and he took it seriously, but since no one had seen anything . . .

"I don't understand how the prowler got away so quickly, without our seeing or hearing anything." Trey looked anything but relaxed now. His big hands clenched the mug.

"Isn't it odd that the dog didn't hear him?" Jessica was making a determined effort to sound as if this sort of thing happened to her every day, but she couldn't stop shivering inside.

As if he sensed what she didn't say, Trey put his hand over hers in a brief, hard grip before taking it away. "Poor old Sam doesn't have much hearing left. He's fine if you're in the room with him, but

I doubt that he could pick anything up from that far away."

"I should have had the motion-detector lights on." Guilt wrinkled Geneva's brow. "Trey always says that, but I hate to turn them on because it frightens away the animals, and now look what's happened."

"It's not your fault," Jessica said quickly. "If someone was determined to do this to the extent of following me here, he'd have found some other way."

"That determination is what bothers me the most." Trey touched her fingers again, almost absently, before wrapping his hand around his mug. "The idea that someone is so obsessed with this case that he'd go to this length—" His jaw tightened. "He came onto our property."

He came close to Geneva—she was sure that was what Trey was really thinking. No matter what Trey did, the ugliness grew nearer to his mother.

"There's a lot of nasty feeling out there," Leo said. "Haven't you been reading the Call-In Column of the paper?"

"I avoid it whenever possible," Trey said. Seeming to notice Jessica's confusion, he smiled slightly. "You don't want to see it. People can call the newspaper anonymously. All the nutcases in the county get to see their libelous rants in print without having to put their names or e-mail addresses to their words. Cowardly."

"Not libelous, though," Leo said with his lawyer's exactitude. "The newspaper does stop short of that. But it does display all the worst in human nature. Seriously, Trey, you ought to look at the column. There have been a number of comments about the big-city lawyer trying to get a killer off. It's not surprising that someone with marginal intelligence and less common sense would attempt to frighten Jessica away."

"Not that little intelligence," she found herself saying. "Someone had enough imagination to think of taking a photo of me and drawing an X over it."

"Probably saw it on a television crime show," Leo muttered. "Nothing but gory crimes on TV these days."

"You're right about that." Geneva gave a fastidious shudder. "I'd rather watch an old movie. Some of the classics from the forties . . ."

"Let's try to stick to the point." Trey wore the harassed look he so often did when he talked to his mother. "I agree with Jessica. Someone had to find the photo—"

"Take the photo," she said. She tapped the paper. "That picture was taken today, when I was leaving the jail."

"It wasn't a copy from the newspaper?" Trey shot the question at Leo, who shook his head.

"No. I've been watching the papers carefully, in case we need to file a change-of-venue motion."

"What is this little drawing at the bottom of the page?" Jessica pointed to the tiny figure in the corner of the page . . . black lines, entwined in a pattern.

"I had a look at it through the magnifying glass," Trey said. "It resembles a hex sign, but I've never seen one exactly like it."

"Hex sign?" Her mind scrambled for an association with the words. "Isn't that some sort of folk art?"

"Pennsylvania Dutch," Geneva said. "They commonly use symbols resembling flowers and birds. You'll see them painted on barns and furniture. My husband collected them—there's a wall full of them in his den."

Jessica peered more closely at the tiny design. "I thought a hex was kind of a curse."

"Some people believe they're a protection, but if you ask any Pennsylvania Dutchman, he'll insist they're 'just for pretty.'" Geneva shrugged. "They're an old tradition. Most people have probably forgotten why they put them up."

"Why put it on an anonymous threat?" Leo frowned. "I don't like any of this." He peered at the copy again. "Hex signs sometimes feature distelfinks and bluebirds, but I've never seen one that resembled a raven."

A raven. Her face must have given something away, because Trey turned to her.

"Jessica? What is it?"

"Probably nothing."

His fingers closed over hers, compelling an answer. "Tell me."

They were all looking at her. She'd have to tell it, whether it sounded foolish or not.

"Last night I heard someone walking past my room. He or she paused by my window for what seemed like a long time." She tried to smile. "It was probably only seconds. Anyway, eventually the person moved on. I opened the drapes a bit to see if I could spot him, when something hit the window."

Geneva made a soft exclamation, and Trey's hand was hard on hers.

"I called the night manager, of course. When he came, we found a dead bird beneath the window. He said it was a raven. He thought it had killed itself smashing into the window." She took a breath. "But I touched it. It was cold and stiff. Someone had thrown it."

"You . . ." Trey seemed at a loss for words. "You should have called me. Or the police. Why didn't you say anything?"

She shrugged. "What could anyone do?" Somehow it didn't seem as intimidating now that she'd told them about it. "I was afraid that if it got into the papers, it would just encourage more of the same."

"It looks as if we've still gotten more of the same," Leo said, his voice dry.

Geneva reached across the table to clasp

Jessica's hand in hers. "We've put you in a terrible position, bringing you here. My dear, I never dreamed it would be this bad for you." Her eyes swam with tears. "Maybe you should give this up. I don't want you to be hurt, but poor Thomas . . ."

Jessica squeezed her hand firmly, her heart touched by the obvious caring in the older woman's expression. "I wouldn't think of giving up on Thomas. I'm not going to be scared off by a few nasty notes."

And a few slashed tires, her mind added. To say nothing of that person in the parking lot. And the dead bird.

"Well, you can't continue to stay at that dreadful motel by yourself," Geneva said. "You must move in here with us, where you'll be safe and we can look after you."

"Jessica may not think this place is all that safe." Trey's jaw was tight, but a tiny muscle twitched as if to testify to the enormous effort it took to control his anger. Ugliness and danger had come right to the very doorstep of the Morgan family's peaceful enclave. No doubt he thought that was his responsibility, too.

"It's not that," Jessica answered his emotion as much as his words. "We're all upset right now. Let's talk about this tomorrow."

"Jessica's right," Leo said. "We're not in any shape to make decisions now."

"Besides, maybe Chief Byler will find something," Jessica added. "He seemed very competent."

"Adam's a good guy. Smart. He can't touch the original crime, but this was in his jurisdiction, and he won't take it lightly." Trey's tension seemed to ease. "Maybe you have a point. We can talk all these through once we've had a decent night's sleep." He turned to her. "If you want to stay here tonight—"

It took all her determination to make her stand. Smile. Look braver than she felt. "No, thanks. I'll head back to the motel. Again."

"I'll follow you there." Trey's tone didn't allow for any argument.

Once again Jessica said her good-nights, once again she and Trey walked outside together. He waited while she got in and started the car, and she didn't miss his glance into the backseat, as if to assure himself there were no unwelcome surprises. Only when she'd locked the door did he walk to his pickup and climb in.

She'd expected to have some reaction once she was finally alone, but she didn't, perhaps because she wasn't really alone. Trey was there, in the reflection of his lights, shining and steady in her rearview mirror.

By the time she pulled up to the motel, she was yawning. Maybe she'd actually sleep tonight. This time the space directly in front of her unit was free, and she pulled in with only the faintest inward quiver.

Still, she was cautious enough not to open the door until Trey had drawn up beside her. He got out, leaving the truck's motor running.

She slid from the seat before he could open the door for her, grabbing her laptop. "Thanks so much for the bodyguard duty. I'll be fine now."

He managed a smile, but his strong-boned face looked stern in the dim light. "My mother always told me I should walk a lady to her door."

"That sounds a little old-fashioned for Geneva." She fell into step with him. "Are you sure you're not making that up?"

He gave her a look of mock astonishment. "My mother might look like a flower child from time to time, but she was brought up in the strictest Main Line tradition. We learned to write thank-you notes before most kids learned their ABCs."

"We?"

"My brother and sister and I."

She stopped at the door, fishing in her bag for her key. "I saw a picture in the family room. They're younger than you, aren't they?" She hadn't had any trouble picking out Trey's face in the family photo—he hadn't really changed all that much from his younger self.

"Link and Libby. Twins, two years younger than I am." His mouth twitched. "It's a good thing they're not here, or they'd be in this thing up to their necks."

"And then you'd have someone else to protect."

She looked up in his face as he took the key card and opened the door for her. "Don't you ever get tired of being in charge?"

If his face changed at that, she couldn't be sure. The door opened, letting out a soft glow from the lamp she'd left on. She tried to smile, tried to find something casual to say.

"I'll . . ."

He touched her cheek, and whatever she'd intended to say was lost in the warmth that emanated from that touch. Her breath caught as his palm cradled her face, tipping it up to his.

His lips found hers, tentatively at first, and then more surely. His hand trailed down her neck, and she felt the pulse there pound against his palm. Warmth flooded through her.

He pulled away, finally, looking as startled and bemused as she must have looked. His fingers trailed down her cheek, leaving heat in their wake.

"Good night." His voice was husky. "Lock the door."

He waited until she was inside, until the dead bolt clicked. And she waited until she heard his footsteps recede and the truck drive away. Even then, her breath still came quickly.

Something had happened, something more than just a kiss. She didn't know exactly what it meant, but she knew that their relationship had changed. Irrevocably.

CHAPTER ELEVEN

BY THE TIME TREY reached the house, reality had set in. He couldn't begin a relationship with Jessica when they were in the midst of something that could change lives forever. All their attention had to be focused on finding the truth.

Was that what Jessica wanted? Or would she be content with anything that cleared her client? He didn't know. He'd stumbled into caring about her without even considering whether she shared his values.

He put the truck away and walked into the house, where he was met by Sam, tail waving gently. "Good boy." He patted the silky head.

A light shone down the hallway—the light in his father's study. He followed it, uneasy. Mom seldom went in there these days, although she'd practically lived there in the weeks after Dad's death.

He paused in the doorway. His mother sat in the leather armchair that had been Dad's, her eyes closed.

"Mom? Anything wrong?"

She shook her head, but when she opened her eyes, he saw that they had filled with tears. He strode to her, sitting on the leather hassock and taking her hands in his. "What is it?"

Sam whined a little, maybe at the tone of his

voice. He padded across the room and put his head in Mom's lap.

She gave a watery chuckle. "You two are just alike. Too worried about me. I'm fine."

"If you were fine, you wouldn't be sitting here crying." He tried to keep his voice even, but it did strange things to his insides to see his mother cry.

"I'm just being a bit foolish." She wiped her eyes with both palms. "I started wondering what your father would think about all of this, and the next thing I knew, I was sitting here crying."

"I'm sorry." He felt about as awkward as a man could feel. "I know how much you miss him."

"He was my rock." Her lips curved. "Not that we always agreed on everything, mind you. But he was solid, all the way through."

"I know." He did know. His father had defined integrity.

"I've never understood, you know. I think I've accepted what . . . what he did, but I don't understand."

He didn't either, but he didn't suppose it would do any good to say so. "Maybe he didn't want to put us through it. If he was convinced he wasn't going to get well—"

"But he had a chance." Her fingers bit into his hands. "The oncologist was encouraging. He said that even if Blake could never get entirely well, he could have lived with the cancer for a while, at least. We'd have had that time together."

If Dad wanted to spare Mom seeing him go through that final decline, maybe Trey could understand that, at least a little, but his mother wouldn't want to hear that.

She sat up a little straighter and patted his hands. "Well, it's foolish to keep going over it." She paused, seeming to stare past him, maybe into the past. "Trey, did you ever feel as if your father had something else on his mind those last weeks?"

"Something else?" He drew back, his gaze instinctively going to the framed photograph on the end table next to the chair—a family camping trip, with Dad grinning and pulling a protesting Libby into the circle of his arm, Trey and Link behind him, leaning on his shoulders. He'd been about thirteen, the twins eleven that summer.

His mother nodded. "I could never quite put my finger on it. Sometimes I convince myself I'm mistaken about it, but then I see his face again. Worrying. And that was before he got the news from the doctor."

Trey tried to think through those weeks, only to discover that they'd been completely obliterated by the twin shocks they'd endured—learning about the cancer, then Dad's suicide.

"I don't know, Mom. I don't think I noticed anything. He might have been preoccupied with business. Or maybe he guessed there was something wrong with his health but wasn't ready to admit it yet."

"That could be. I don't suppose we'll ever know." The words sounded lost. Then she shook her head. "All this worry about Thomas has made me morbid. And now these threats against Jessica. The world seems turned upside down."

"Just pieces of it. We'll find the answers." We have to.

"There's another thing." Mom shoved Sam's head gently off her lap and stood. "I thought of it when we were talking about your dad's collection of hex signs."

Trey glanced toward the wall opposite his father's desk. The rows of brightly colored wooden hex signs covered most of it with geometric shapes, flowers, stylized birds. "What about it?"

"I remembered seeing this." She took something from the desk and laid it on his palm. A miniature hex sign, but not like the ones that lined the walls. This one was different. A raven, done all in black—it was the symbol that marked the threatening note.

His fingers closed over it, the wood cutting into them. "Where did this come from?"

"I don't know. I saw your father looking at it once. When I asked, he said someone had given it to him. Then he put it in his desk drawer, closed the drawer and started talking about something else." Her face clouded. "Trey, I don't understand. What does it mean?"

He couldn't answer. He didn't understand either. But the cold prickle down his spine suggested that it wasn't anything good.

BY THE TIME JESSICA arrived at the Springville Inn the next afternoon to talk to Cherry's employer and fellow workers, she had accepted the fact that she wasn't going to be able to forget what had happened with Trey last night. Just letting her thoughts stray in that direction made her cheeks warm and her lips tingle. The best she could do was suppress the memory long enough to get her work done.

The parking lot at the inn was sparsely populated. Apparently she'd guessed right, timing her visit for well after the lunch rush. With any luck, Owen Barclay, the inn's manager, would be available to talk with her and would be willing to steer her to any particular friends Cherry had among her coworkers.

At least this couldn't be any less fruitful than the two visits she'd already made today. The first, to the jail to talk with Thomas yet again, had been discouraging. The boy had been pale, his eyes huge in a drawn face. This relatively short time in jail must seem like an eternity to him.

If he were sentenced to state prison . . . her stomach twisted rebelliously at the thought. Could he even survive that? She doubted it, which made her task all the more crucial. She had to find something—anything—on which to build a defense.

So far this day hadn't produced much. She'd thought to start off with Chip Fulton, despite Trey's determination to keep her from doing just that. However, fate had done what Trey hadn't been able to. She'd called the garage where Chip worked, but his irate employer said Chip hadn't been in for days.

She frowned, walking around the brick-and-frame inn to the front door. That was odd, now that she thought about it. Did the police realize Chip had been absent from his workplace all week? It was certainly worth following up.

She rounded a clump of rhododendron and the Springville Inn spread out in front of her. The graceful Federal building stretched welcoming wings out on both sides of a core that surely dated back to pre-Revolutionary days. It was everything that a country inn should be; everything that her motel was not. She could just imagine what the officer manager's reaction would be if she turned in an expense voucher for a place like this.

A glass-paneled door opened into a center hallway with a lofty ceiling, wainscoted walls and an arched entrance to what was obviously the dining room where Cherry had worked. She'd like to walk straight in there and start interviewing Cherry's coworkers, who surely were the people most likely to have understood her, but protocol demanded she speak with the manager first.

The graying, motherly type behind the reception desk nodded pleasantly, heard her name with only a hint of undue curiosity and departed to fetch the manager.

"Ms. Langdon." Owen Barclay advanced on her with an outstretched hand. "Leo Frost told us you'd be coming by. Welcome to the Springville Inn. How can I help you?"

Jessica shook hands, ticking over her impressions of the man. The welcome seemed a bit overdone, but for all she knew, he could be a friend of the Morgan family, or at least eager to please them. As for the rest, Barclay was somewhere in his forties, with a trim figure showing just a hint of flab under the well-tailored suit jacket, dark hair artistically touched with gray at the temples and hands so well kept that he must surely visit a manicurist on a regular basis. He had a politician's smile that didn't quite warm watchful dark eyes.

"It's kind of you to make time for me." She said the expected words. "As you know, we're representing Thomas Esch, and I hoped I might speak with you about Cherry Wilson."

"Of course. Come and sit down." He piloted her to a cluster of upholstered furniture in the lobby, his hand a little too familiar on her elbow. She took an upright chair rather than the sofa he tried to steer her to. He sat down opposite her.

"Yes, yes, a sad business." His face registered appropriate sorrow. "Such a tragedy, to see two young lives ruined because of drugs and alcohol."

"I take it you're assuming Thomas is guilty."

"Oh, well, innocent until proven guilty and all that. One would hate to think an Amish youth would do such a thing. They're solid citizens, important to the local economy."

They brought in all the tourists who stayed at the inn, in other words. "Can you tell me a little about Cherry?"

"I can't say I knew her all that well. Not outside work, that is. She was a good server, popular with the patrons, got along with her coworkers, always pleasant and cooperative."

She began to think that a lengthy conversation with Owen Barclay might give her whiplash, watching him leap from one side to the other of every issue. At least Trey was uncompromisingly blunt.

And what was Trey doing, sneaking into her thoughts that way?

Clearly she wasn't going to get anything from Barclay but platitudes. "I'd like to speak with some of Cherry's coworkers. Was there anyone with whom she was particularly good friends?"

"I don't know . . . well, I suppose." He rose. "You might try Milly Cotter or Kristin McGowan."

"Thank you, Mr. Barclay. You've been most helpful."

"My pleasure." He pressed her hand a little too long. "Come and see us anytime."

Freeing her hand, she escaped toward the dining room. It was empty, with the round tables obviously in the midst of being relaid for the dinner service, but a woman came through the swinging door from the kitchen, stopping when she saw Jessica.

"Sorry, we don't start serving again until five." She straightened the mobcap that sat atop curly brown hair. The outfit, with its white apron and square-yoked dress, was obviously meant to suggest colonial days. "You could try the Village Soda Shop. They're open now."

"That's all right. I'm not looking for something to eat. In fact, I think I'm looking for you, if you're Milly." She nodded toward the young woman's name badge.

"That's me." The pert face sobered. "If you're a reporter—"

"My name is Jessica Langdon. I'm an attorney, working on the Thomas Esch case. Would you be willing to talk with me?"

"I don't think—" She darted a glance toward the reception desk.

"Mr. Barclay said it was all right. He suggested I talk with you and Kristin McGowan."

The young woman shrugged. "Well, I guess

that's okay. Kristin's not on today, though." She pulled out a chair. "We might as well sit. I'll be on my feet enough later."

"I know what you mean." Jessica sat down across the table from her. "I waited tables in college. I used to go home and soak my feet while I counted my tips."

A smile dissolved the wary look on Milly's face. "That's me, too. I'm a junior at Gettysburg College. Believe me, I don't want to wait tables all my life."

"Did Cherry feel that way?" Maybe she'd finally get something to make the woman more than just a figure in a crime-scene photo.

She got a doubtful look in return. "Cherry wasn't interested in college, if that's what you mean. She said it was okay if you didn't have anything better to do, but not for her."

"So, did she have something better to do?"

"Not unless partying is your only goal in life." Milly's mobile face broke into a grin. "Come to think of it, she'd have fit right in with the party animals at school."

"Did you know her well?"

Milly shrugged. "We talked. You can't help doing that when you work with someone."

"Did Cherry have a boyfriend?"

"Not so's you could notice. She dated some guy who worked in a garage, but I always had the feeling she was looking for something better."

That would be Chip, no doubt. This didn't seem to be adding much to what she already knew. "Did she ever talk about Thomas Esch?"

"I don't think so. I mean, she used to laugh about how wild a few of the Amish kids got at parties, but she never mentioned him in particular."

"What about anyone else she might have dated? A guy she dumped, or someone who had a grudge against her?"

"She used to drive the chef wild by saying his soup needed more salt, but you don't kill someone for that. She was always one for a joke, y'know? It seemed like she could find the one thing that would drive someone wild and pick on that."

That was an interesting sidelight on Cherry's personality, but Jessica didn't see that it got her much further. "Nobody she turned down? Someone who wanted to date her?"

"Well, not other than . . ." She sent a wary glance toward the reception area.

"Barclay, you mean?" She wasn't surprised. "Were they an item?"

"I shouldn't say anything." Milly leaned toward her, lowering her voice. "He tried, but she wasn't having any of it. He's married, though you wouldn't know it to listen to him around here. Not that Cherry would have let his being married bother her, but she said it couldn't lead anywhere, and when it was over, like as not she'd be the one out of a job and with nothing to show for it. Always had an eye out for what was in it for her—that was Cherry."

A line of speculation opened up in Jessica's mind. Cherry was a party girl—everyone who knew her agreed on that. Maybe she'd partied with the wrong person, or refused to party with someone who didn't take rejection well. There could be any number of possibilities other than Thomas, including, perhaps, Owen Barclay.

NEITHER HE NOR JESSICA had said much since he picked her up to track down the Amish kids' party, but he was way too aware of her presence in the truck cab. The faint aroma of her perfume touched his senses. Trey clenched the steering wheel, trying to think of something that would get them back to normal.

Or, at the very least, back to where they had been before he'd been so foolish as to kiss her last night. His lips tingled at the memory. Foolish maybe, but also intriguing.

Stop that, he ordered his straying imagination. This situation was difficult enough without adding in an emotional attachment between them. Jessica wasn't remotely his type, and he wasn't even sure that he trusted her. So what was he doing thinking about holding her in his arms again?

"Did something go wrong on your business trip today?" Jessica broke the silence, not him.

"No." He glanced toward her, trying to make out her expression in the fading light. The sun had already slipped behind the hills, and the teenagers would be gathering at the Miller barn. "What makes you say that?"

"You seemed lost in thought. I thought maybe you were worried about something related to your visit to Harrisburg."

"Just talking to a few legislators about some bills that are coming up soon, especially this idea of putting tolls on the interstate. With the current budget crisis, there's talk of cutbacks in programs that will hurt a lot of people, and the toll idea would hurt small farmers and manufacturers who have to get their goods to market."

She blinked, looking at him in what seemed to be amazement. "I didn't know you were involved in politics. Are you a lobbyist?"

"Heaven forbid," he said quickly. "But that doesn't mean I can ignore what goes on in Harrisburg. None of us in rural areas can afford to do that. Too many people think of Pennsylvania as Philadelphia and Pittsburgh and ignore everything in between."

"And you have influence on your state legislators?"

He could feel her eyes on him, and he shrugged. "I don't know that I'd say that, exactly. I know our local representative and state senator pretty well. My grandfather was involved in politics at the state level, and people seem to think the family still has influence. It's okay if they think that, as long as it makes them listen to common sense."

Her expression said she was trying to adjust what she knew about him in light of this new information. "And here I thought you were just . . ."

"Just what?" he asked, when she didn't finish. "What do you think about me, Jessica?"

"Well, how would I know what to think? You always seem to have plenty of time to follow me around, which makes me think heading up Morgan Enterprises isn't exactly a full-time job."

He didn't know whether to be amused or annoyed. "As it happens, it's more than full-time. I'm not exactly Donald Trump, but I do run the twenty-some businesses the family owns in the county, as well as take care of all the rental properties and land development."

He was beginning to sound rather heated by the time he got to the end of that. Maybe he'd better shut up. What difference did it make if Jessica thought him some kind of slacker?

"Right. The feed mill and the lumberyard and so forth. I'm sorry. I didn't mean to offend you."

"You didn't." But the fact that he snapped the words gave him away.

"Maybe we'd better stick to business, since everything else seems to lead to an argument."

He darted a look at her. "Isn't that what lawyers do best? Argue?"

"No. At least, not me. But if you intend to pick on me because I'm an attorney, don't bother with the lawyer jokes. Believe me, I've heard them all."

He grinned, the tension between them collapsing like a spent balloon. "Too bad."

"Isn't it, though? Anyway, maybe you'd better tell me about this Amish teen party we're headed for."

He slowed down, watching for the turnoff. "It's not exactly a teen party—or at least, not what you'd think of in those terms. This is a singing, held under parental supervision to some extent. If you're picturing a mob of drunken Amish kids, get that image out of your head."

"A singing. You mean, actual singing?"

He grinned. "Actual singing, although to be fair, most of the kids have other things on their minds. Each other, for instance." He flipped the turn signal and made a right into a farm lane, following a string of Amish buggies. "Some probably have boom boxes in their buggies and maybe a few cans of beer tucked away, but for the most part, this will be pretty clean."

"Thomas didn't link up with Cherry at a party like this, then."

"Not a chance." He frowned. "There are always kids who push the boundaries. Most of them have a few English friends and get invited to wilder parties. That must be where he ran into Cherry."

"So we need to find someone who knows about that, who maybe even went with him."

"That's right." He pulled the truck to a stop under a drooping willow tree. All around them kids in Amish dress streamed toward the barn, glowing with light from a dozen lanterns. "The bishop told them to talk to us. We'll just have to hope they take that seriously."

He slid out, and she joined him before he could go around and open her door. He'd told her to dress casually, and he'd been relieved to see that she wore khaki slacks and a turquoise knit top instead of her usual suit. As she joined him, she pulled on a tan windbreaker.

"Ready?" He lifted an eyebrow at her.

She nodded. "Where do we start?"

"Let's see if we can find Jacob Stoltzfus. He's Thomas's best friend. If anyone knows something, it will be Jacob."

He touched her arm to guide her onto the gravel lane leading toward the barn. He'd agreed that they ought to stick to business. But somehow it seemed natural to let his fingers slide down her sleeve and entwine with hers, just as it seemed natural for her to return the pressure of his hand.

This wasn't withdrawing from the feelings between them, he reminded himself. But at the moment, he didn't seem to care.

CHAPTER TWELVE

THE ODDITY OF THE scene hit Jessica forcibly as she walked down the lane with Trey. All around them were young people in sober Amish dress, all moving in the same direction. If it had not been for the noise, she'd have found it almost frightening.

But the noise—that was familiar. It was like being in a crowd of kids on their way to a high-school football game. They chattered, they called out to friends, they laughed and teased each other just like any group of teens.

Trey took her arm protectively when she stumbled over a rough patch in the lane. "Easy. You don't want to take a header on the gravel."

"I'm not used to the dark." She tilted her head back. "You never see the stars like this in the city."

"One of the benefits of doing without electric light," he said. "You can actually see the sky."

"You'll be able to see better now." They neared the barn, and Trey loosened his grip. "Tiki torches. I'll bet that's not something you associate with the Amish."

"I have to confess, it never crossed my mind."

Several torches lit the scene, helped by the glow of a bonfire. A group of kids played volleyball at one side of the barn, although it must be getting hard to see the ball. Others clustered around a table spread with chips, dip, nachos, brownies, even pizza.

Apparently Amish teens liked their junk food just as much as any other kids did. Boys nudged each other in greeting, girls giggled, heads together, glancing at the boys out of the corners of their eyes.

"Looks like any teen party anywhere, other than the clothes."

He nodded, scanning the crowd. "They'll go into the barn to start the singing before long. We should try to catch Jacob first."

"Trey. Bishop Amos told us you would come by tonight." The man who approached was no teenager—his beard nearly touched his chest. "Not that you wouldn't have been welcome, even without the bishop's blessing."

Trey shook hands, grinning. "Denke, Jonas. Jessica, this is Jonas Miller, our host. It's hard to believe his little Becky is old enough for rumspringa already."

"Ach, the years pass quickly." Jonas turned to her, eyes curious. "This would be Ms. Langdon, ja?"

"Jessica," she said. "Thank you for helping us."

He inclined his head, the movement grave. "The bishop has told the young people to speak with you. I think they will all cooperate."

She met his gaze. "Does that mean some are opposed to what I'm doing?"

"There are those . . ." He paused. "All of us dislike the publicity, but most, I hope, know that you are doing what must be done to protect Thomas." He glanced at Trey. "Trey is an old friend, ain't so? You'll stay for the singing and the food, ja?"

"Sounds good," Trey said. "Let's see how it goes. We'd like to have a word with Jacob Stoltzfus first, if he's here."

Jonas nodded. He walked to the volleyball court and tapped one of the players on the shoulder.

The boy turned, and Jessica saw his Adam's apple bob and his eyes widen as he looked at them. She half expected him to dart away, but instead he came toward them.

Brown eyes in a round face surveyed them with some anxiety. Like Thomas, he looked younger than she knew he must be. He seemed stricken with speechlessness.

"We just want to talk for a minute," Trey said, his tone reassuring. "This is Jessica Langdon. She's Thomas's lawyer."

"Ja. I . . . I know." He gulped.

She hadn't imagined she was that intimidating. "You want to help Thomas, don't you, Jacob?"

He nodded.

"You can help him by telling me what you know. His father said he was going to meet you that night. Is that right?" She'd started to say the night Cherry was killed, but she thought that might spook him entirely. And he surely knew what night she meant.

He glanced around, as if searching for a way to escape. "Ja," he whispered.

"Were you going to the party together?"

He ducked his head in a nod. "Ja."

This was an uphill battle. "How did you hear about the party?"

"Some Englisch kid told Thomas about it. Said we could come."

"What English kid?" Trey said quickly.

He shrugged. "Thomas didn't say."

She couldn't be sure whether he knew or not. She glanced at Trey, his expression saying that he thought just what she did. The invitation could have been set up between Thomas and Cherry.

"Did Thomas talk about seeing Cherry there?" She pressed on, trying not to let discouragement show.

"No."

Clearly she wasn't going to get anywhere with this boy. Maybe Jacob would open up to someone, but not to her. She made a final try. "Is there anyone else here who was at that party?"

For the first time, some animation came into the boy's face. "Ja. Peggy. Peggy Byler was there. Shall I get her for you?"

"Tell her we'd like to talk with her."

Jacob spurted off almost before she'd finished speaking. She glanced at Trey. "Byler. She's surely not related to the police chief?"

"Everybody is related around here, if you go back far enough, especially if they have a German name."

"I can't tell if Jacob doesn't know anything or was stonewalling a nosy adult."

"I don't think it's that. Maybe just a little shy of talking to a woman lawyer." Trey's voice warmed. "You'll have better luck with Peggy. She works at the bakery in town, so she's in contact with English all the time."

When Jacob came back with the young woman, Jessica saw that he was right. Peggy had a pert smile and a confident manner that seemed to say she could fend for herself.

"You understand what we want, Peggy," she said, once the introductions were made. "Anything you know about Thomas's relationship with Cherry Wilson, anything you saw or heard that night at the party."

Peggy nodded. "The first part's easy," she said. "He didn't have a relationship with her at all. In his dreams, maybe. Oh, she smiled at him sometimes, teased him a little bit, but she did that with all the boys. I think she liked to see them get all ferhoodled and embarrassed-like."

"It sounds as if you didn't like her much."

She got a guarded look for that. "I didn't know

her. She wasn't interested in being friends with girls."

"So that night—did she get Thomas um . . . ferhoodled?" Interesting word, that.

"Ja." Peggy frowned. "It seemed like she was paying a lot of attention to Thomas. She kept giving him drinks."

"Was he drunk?"

"Getting there, I think."

"Nobody interfered?" Trey asked.

"Jacob and I tried, but Thomas wouldn't pay us any mind. He was all wrapped up in Cherry." She shrugged, but there was an edge of hurt in her voice, making Jessica wonder what her feelings were for Thomas. "So we figured he was old enough to know what he was getting into."

"Did you talk to him again that evening? See him?"

"Not talk to him, no." Peggy's face lost some of its confidence, making her look younger. "I saw him going outside. Staggering so he could hardly walk. I started after him, thinking he needed help. But when I got to the door, I saw that Cherry was with him. Had her arm around him, practically dragging him to her car. So I figured he didn't need my help." She looked suddenly lost. "I should have done something, shouldn't I?"

Her expression went straight to Jessica's heart. "I don't know what you could have done then, Peggy. But you can do something now. We might want you to testify at the trial. Can you do that?" She had second thoughts, not sure if an Amish person was permitted to do such a thing.

"Ja, I will," Peggy said instantly. "Anything for Thomas. And Bishop Amos says if we are asked, we must obey."

"Good." She clasped the girl's hand. "Thank you, Peggy."

"A little progress," Trey said after Peggy rejoined her friends.

She nodded, feeling the smallest ray of optimism. "From what she said, Thomas was already pretty far under the influence when he left the party. That makes it less likely he'd be able to stage an attack."

"Yes." Trey frowned. "A lot depends on when he was given the drug. What does your expert say?"

"We don't have an answer from him yet. Leo's going to call him again tomorrow."

"If you get . . ." Trey's voice trailed off as there was a movement of the kids around them.

The girls had formed a line and headed into the barn, falling silent as they went through the door. The boys shuffled around, seemingly reluctant to follow, but then a few brave souls started after them.

"The singing is about to begin." Trey held out his hand. "Want to stay for a while?"

"That sounds good." Besides, she told her skeptical side, she might come across someone else who knew something if she stayed. She took his hand and they walked into the barn together.

Inside, the girls sat on benches along one side of a long row of tables. The boys, shuffling and nudging one another, jockeyed for position opposite them.

Jonas Miller, surveying the proceedings from a post near the door, turned to give them a welcoming smile. "Komm, wilcom. The singing will begin in a moment." His eyes twinkled. "As soon as someone is brave enough to start."

He moved off in answer to a question from someone, and Trey tugged at her hand. "I'll show you the best place to watch."

He led her to a sturdy wooden ladder—one of several that led up to the loft that surrounded the barn floor. "Up you go."

She looked at it doubtfully. "You first."

"It's perfectly safe." He climbed up quickly then held out his hand to her, smiling, his face intriguing from the inverted angle. "Come on."

Glad she'd worn slacks and sneakers, Jessica clambered up the ladder and onto the floor of the loft.

"Over here." Trey lowered his voice as it grew quieter below them. He led her between bales of hay to a spot about midway along then sat on the edge of the loft and drew her down next to him.

She sat cross-legged. Stacks of hay bales surrounded them, forming a little alcove in which they could sit overlooking the scene below without being too noticeable. The only light was from lanterns, and the loft behind them was dark. The barn grew silent. How could that number of teenagers possibly be so quiet?

A boy's voice lifted in the first notes of a song. Immediately the others joined in, their pure young voices rising in unison, unaccompanied. Jessica's breath caught. It was beautiful. Bare and untrained, the voices nevertheless touched her heart, even though she didn't understand a word they sang.

"They'll sing familiar church songs." Trey's lips were so close to her ear that his breath ruffled her hair. "At least, familiar to them. Later, they'll probably branch out into some old folk tunes. Some congregations don't allow that, but Bishop Amos doesn't mind."

She nodded, caught in the web of the music and his closeness. *Inappropriate,* the little voice at the back of her mind commented, but she didn't seem to care.

The voices continued, moving easily from one song to another as someone started each one, seemingly at random. She imagined the notes of music rising to the roof of the barn and beyond, to the silent stars.

Jessica wasn't sure how long they sat motionless, entranced by the music, but at last movement below caught her attention. Jonas

Miller and a woman who was probably his wife carried jugs of what looked like cider and pitchers of water to a table against the wall.

As if that was a signal, no one started a new song. Instead, the young people got up, stretching, talking, some of them pairing off as they headed to the table for a drink.

"Is it over?" She could hear the reluctance in her voice. She didn't want it to end.

"Just recess for a drink." Trey stood, stooping under a slanting beam. "Stay put. I'll go down and get us something."

She tilted her head back to look up at him. "How do you propose to carry glasses up the ladder?"

"Don't underestimate me," he said, smiling. He was gone before she could scramble to her feet and follow him.

She watched his long, lithe figure move easily down the ladder. No, she wasn't making the mistake of underestimating Trey, not on any count. He was too sure of himself and his place in the world for that, to say nothing of having far too much influence on her feelings.

She shouldn't let that happen. She had to keep in mind that their goals weren't necessarily the same, just because they coincided for the moment.

She watched the young people milling around below her. This was obviously the Amish equivalent of date night . . . a time for young people to pair off, to move toward a relationship that, for them, would end in marriage and family and a continuation of their culture.

Simplistic, she supposed. Old-fashioned. But for a moment she was aware of the appeal. It seemed both simpler and surer than the courtship rituals of her urban society.

The sound of a footstep had her turning toward the ladder again. Surely Trey hadn't gotten up without her noticing. No, that was his tall figure still in the crowd, seemingly deep in conversation with Jonas Miller.

She leaned forward a bit, watching him from her secluded spot. He'd draw any woman's eye. So why was he still unmarried, still living at home with his mother? He certainly wasn't a mama's boy, by anyone's definition.

Another sound, as if something rustled in the loose hay that had filtered from the bales. An animal? She looked around, apprehension rising, but there was nothing to be seen.

Disturbed now from the fascination that had held her in place, she put her hand out to the nearest beam and started to rise. She'd go help Trey with that cider.

There was a sense of movement behind her. She turned, hand out for balance, and her breath caught in her throat. The stack of hay bales tumbled toward her.

No time to cry out, no time to grab anything. A blow to her shoulder threw her toward the edge.

She flailed with her hand, catching hold of the upright beam, but her grip was sliding . . .

For an instant she hung over the edge, aware of cries below her, rushing feet. Then her grip failed, and she plummeted, helpless, toward the floor below.

TREY RUSHED FORWARD, impeded by all the others who hurried to help. None of them could reach Jessica before she hit the floor. Heart pounding, he dropped to his knees beside the crumpled figure.

"Jess . . ."

Jonas caught his hand when he would have reached for her. "Careful."

He tried to wrench away, but Jonas's grip turned to iron.

"Your cell phone, Trey. We must call the rescue squad."

He was right, of course. Trey's mind seemed to have stopped working. He pulled the phone from his pocket, flipped it open, handed it to Jonas.

Sarah, Jonas's wife, bent over Jessica. Her hands moved, gentle and competent, over the limp form, and she talked softly all the while, as if Jessica would be comforted by her voice.

Trey sucked in a breath. She was unconscious. That had to be bad. He clasped one hand in his, trying to warm it. "Jess, it's going to be all right."

"Ja, it will." Jonas put a big hand on his

shoulder. "Let my Sarah tend to her. She's seen more bumps and bruises and broken bones than most with our kids. She knows what to do better than us, ain't so?"

He managed a nod. Sarah was undoubtedly more skilled than he was. Even now one of the girls came running with a blanket, which she tucked around Jessica.

Jonas gave a quick order, and several boys rushed out, grabbing lanterns as they went. "They will run down to the road, show the rescue squad where to turn. We'd best make sure there's plenty of space for them to bring the ambulance right into the barn."

"Ja." Peggy Byler took care of the kids, directing some to move the tables back, others to move any buggies that might block the way.

Even as the kids scattered, Trey heard the wail of a siren in the distance growing steadily louder. He willed it to move faster, his heart twisting painfully in his chest. Jessica would be all right. She had to be.

Half an hour later he waited impatiently in the emergency room waiting area. He paced across the room and stopped at the window. With the darkness outside and the bright lights within, it formed a mirror, reflecting the empty chairs along the wall and the reception desk, beyond which were the double doors into the treatment area. Jessica was back there, somewhere.

His jaw tensed. That moment when he'd seen her fall—he didn't think he would ever get that image out of his head.

He forced his fists to unclench. The paramedics had been reassuring. Jessica herself, coming to just about the time they arrived, had insisted she was fine.

He hadn't believed her. Her white face, the pain that darkened her eyes . . . no, he hadn't believed she was all right. If he hadn't stopped to talk to Jonas—

The outer doors swished open. Leo, his hair ruffled and his tie askew, rushed in, coming to grasp his sleeve.

"Trey. Your mother called with some garbled story about Jessica being hurt."

Trey shook his head. "Not so garbled. But how did my mother find out about it? I didn't want her to worry."

"You should know by now that Geneva learns everything, sooner or later."

"Usually sooner." Trey rubbed the back of his neck. "They're treating Jessica now. The paramedics didn't seem to think it was too serious, but she hit her head when she fell, lost consciousness for several minutes."

Some of the anxiety faded from Leo's eyes. "She'll be all right?"

"I think so." He prayed so. "My mother—"

"Is on her way right now," Leo finished for him.

"I couldn't dissuade her, but at least I got her to agree to have Bobby drive her. She sounded so upset I didn't think she should be behind the wheel."

"Thanks." His hand rested for a moment on the older man's shoulder. "That was good of you."

Leo shrugged the words off. "What exactly happened? You were at Miller's tonight, weren't you?"

"We were sitting in the loft, watching the singing." It seemed days ago now. "I went down to get something to drink, and she . . . fell."

Fell. He wasn't sure he wanted to speak the suspicion that filled his mind.

Running footsteps, and the door whished again. His mother rushed across the room to envelop him in a warm embrace. "Is Jessica all right? What do the doctors say?"

He hugged her back. "Mom, there was no need for you to come. I can take care of everything."

Bobby approached. "How is Jessica? Did someone . . . How did she get hurt?"

He'd almost said what Trey had been thinking. Did someone? "She fell from the barn loft. She was conscious when the paramedics got there, so I don't think it's too serious."

"That's a relief. I'd hate to think of anything happening to her. I'll stay and take Geneva home—"

"That's okay." They didn't need any more

people hanging around. "Thanks, Bobby, for bringing her. I'll see that my mother gets home. Even though she shouldn't be here."

Bobby nodded, fading out the door as his mother turned a stern look on him.

"Nonsense." Her brisk tone belied the worry that drew her brows together. "If a woman is hurt, she wants another woman around. Now, where is she?"

"Back in the treatment area. But you can't . . ."

She was already marching toward the reception desk. Whatever she said, it must have worked, because a moment later they were being ushered back through the double doors.

Leo put a hand on his arm to slow his pace. "What really happened?"

"I'm not sure." Trey shook his head in frustration. "A stack of hay bales fell, knocking her off the edge of the loft."

Leo considered. "It could happen."

"It could, I guess. But I don't think I'd ever see the day that Jonas Miller would stack bales so clumsily that they'd topple over."

Leo's frown deepened, the corners of his lips compressing. "Who would do that? You didn't see anyone?"

"No. So unless—"

Ahead of them, his mother disappeared into a curtained cubicle. He hurried his steps, letting the rest of that thought slip away.

He was holding his breath as he brushed the white curtain aside. Jessica sat on the edge of a bed, her left arm in a sling. She looked at him and smiled, and he expelled the breath in a relieved sigh.

"Are you okay?"

"Of course she's not okay." Mom was scolding, as she did when she was worried. "Goodness, just look at her. What a thing to happen."

"It's not serious," Jessica said, patting her hand as if Mom were the one who needed to be comforted. "One sprained wrist, a nice assortment of bruises and a mild concussion. I'd say I got off pretty lightly."

He didn't shift his gaze from hers. "You gave us quite a scare."

She attempted another smile, but it seemed to tremble on her lips. "I imagine this is one singing the kids won't soon forget."

"Or me." He wasn't touching her, and the words were as casual as they could be. But a world of emotion was sizzling between them, so strong he was surprised no one else in the room could feel it.

"One thing's certain," his mother declared. "You're not going back to that motel tonight. You're coming home with us, where I can take care of you."

"You don't need to . . ." Jessica began, but Trey shook his head at her.

"Don't argue this one, Counselor. You'll lose."

"Well, now, I'd suggest that I drive Geneva to the motel to pick up whatever Jessica might need," Leo said. "That way Trey can take her straight to the farm and get her comfortable."

"Good idea. I'll go pull the truck around whenever they're ready to release you." His gaze still clung to hers. "Right?" If she argued, he just might pick her up and carry her to the truck.

She touched the side of her head gingerly. "Right."

CHAPTER THIRTEEN

ALL TREY COULD THINK, when he jogged out to the truck and pulled up at the emergency room entrance, was that he had to get Jessica someplace safe. Home. Once she was there, once he knew nothing else could happen to her, he could think this whole thing through.

The light over the E.R. door made a bright pool of illumination, surrounded by shadows. And he was jumping at those shadows, scanning the shrubbery as if someone lurked there.

The doors slid silently open, and he jumped out of the truck as a nurse pushed a wheelchair through. Jessica, pale in the artificial light, looked as if it took an effort to hold her head up. His mother and Leo emerged behind them, Mom still talking. Nerves, probably. She'd always been a pillar of strength when any of them damaged themselves, saving her reaction for afterward.

"You go along to the motel, Mom. We'll see you back at the house."

Leo, meeting his eyes for an instant, took her by the arm. "Come on, Geneva. Jessica will want her things so she can get settled comfortably for the night."

Jessica rose, the nurse steadying her. "I can—"

Before she could insist that she could climb into the cab by herself, he picked her up, sliding her into the passenger seat without a word. He pulled the seat belt down and watched as she fastened it, then he closed the door and called out his thanks to the nurse, who was already headed back inside.

Once in the truck, he took a careful look at her. "Ready?"

She managed a faint smile. "I'm well enough to sit here. Honest."

"I know your head must be pounding." He drove carefully down the hospital drive. "I'll take it easy."

"Actually, thanks to the medication, it's down to a dull roar." She touched her head with cautious fingers. "I don't know what it was, but I think it'll make me sleep tonight." She leaned her head back against the headrest and closed her eyes, her lashes making dark crescents against her cheeks.

The urge to talk about what had happened was strong, but he managed to beat it down. "Let yourself drift off, if you want. I'll wake you when we get to the house."

Jessica was obviously in no shape to go over the accident again tonight. Besides, what could she add to what he knew himself?

The hay bales had toppled over. Despite his doubts, he had to admit that it could have happened accidentally. Vibrations, maybe, caused by the number of people going in and out of the barn. Or she'd leaned on it, somehow dislodging a bale.

Trouble was, he didn't believe any of that. If someone had been up there in the loft, watching them, biding his time until Jessica was alone . . .

He glanced toward her. He didn't like thinking that way, but they couldn't ignore the warning notes she'd received. Someone wanted Jessica off the case. How far would they go to make that happen?

He sensed, rather than saw, her move. "Are you okay? Am I going too fast?"

"You're fine. I'm just feeling guilty, coming in on your mother like this."

"There's nothing my mother likes better than company. And at least—"

"At least what?" she asked, when he didn't finish the thought.

"At least while someone's there with her, she won't be as apt to do something foolish."

"Your mother doesn't strike me as a foolish person." Jessica's voice stiffened.

"My mother is one of the sanest people I know," he said. "But she imagines she can do almost anything she thinks of. A month ago I found her up on a ladder, trying to move a bird's nest from the eaves. Sam was at the bottom of the ladder, trying to follow her up. It's a wonder they didn't both break their necks."

He said it lightly, but he couldn't forget the

panic he'd felt when he rounded the house and saw her. He'd already lost his father too early. He didn't intend to lose his mother.

"That does sound a little rash. But if there was no one else to do it . . ."

"There were a dozen people within a mile radius who'd have run over to help her. She just didn't want to ask."

"I can understand that, I think." Jessica's voice was drowsy. "She doesn't want to be a burden."

"She could never be a burden." He almost snapped the words. Jessica was the last person in the world he should expect would be on his side. She was as independent as his mother, and probably twice as stubborn.

She fell silent, and he thought she did doze a little. When he pulled up at the front door, she stirred. "There already?"

He nodded. "Don't move. I'll come around and help you down."

Predictably, she already had the door open and was starting to slide out when he reached her. He caught her around the waist and lowered her gently to the pavement.

"How do you think that would feel when your feet hit the ground?" he scolded.

"Not too great," she admitted. She steadied herself, holding on to his arms. "I can walk."

"Stubborn," he muttered, and she looked up and smiled at him.

"Just a little."

With his arm around her waist, they made short work of the distance to the door. As he put his key in the lock, Sam greeted them with a single, full-throated bark.

"Good boy," he said as they went in. He guided Jessica down the hallway to the family room. "Let's settle you on the sofa in the family room until Mom arrives. She'll insist on fussing over you. Take my advice and let her. It's easier than arguing about it."

"Right." She sank down on the sofa with a little sigh, and she didn't object when he guided her to lean against a pillow and lifted her legs to the sofa.

He pulled the knitted afghan off the back of the sofa and tucked it over her. "Do you want anything? Some tea, maybe?"

"I'll wait and let your mother fix it."

"Now you've got the idea," he said approvingly. He pulled the hassock over so that he could sit down next to her. "I'm sure your mother would be the same way. It comes with the territory."

"I don't know." Her gaze slid away from his. "My mother died when I was two."

"I'm sorry." He couldn't help it—he put his hand over hers where it lay on the covering. Maybe that explained the instant bond she'd seemed to form with his mother. "You must miss her."

"I don't have many memories." She frowned.

"Sometimes I think I can remember her face, but I'm never sure if it's real or a photo."

"Who took care of you then?"

"I had a nanny. An honest-to-goodness proper English nanny, like Mary Poppins."

"Did she dance on the rooftops and fly with her umbrella?"

Her eyes warmed when she smiled. "Not quite, but I always half expected her to. Nanny Grace was a wonderful woman—hugged me, comforted me, scolded me, trotted me off to Sunday school, went to all the mother-daughter affairs."

"She sounds ideal. I'll bet you're still close."

A shadow crossed her face. "I . . . we lost touch. When I was about eight, my father decided I'd be better off at boarding school."

"That seems young to go away to school." He was responding to the feeling under the words, and he discovered that he knew exactly what those feelings were. Loss. Loneliness. Abandonment.

"It was." Her mouth moved as if she made an effort to smile and couldn't quite manage it. "Well, anyway. Enough about the past. Just cherish your mother."

"I do." He brushed a lock of hair back from her face with a gentle finger. It flowed through his hand like silk. "It sounds as if you got the short end of the stick when it came to parents. I'm sorry."

She could have responded with a tale of a

223

wonderful relationship with her father, but he wasn't surprised when she didn't. Any man who would send a small child away from the only security she knew couldn't be much of a father.

She settled a bit deeper into the pillow. "I did all right." There was an edge of defensiveness in her voice. "Everybody doesn't have the picture-perfect American family like you do."

Before he could react, her eyes flew open. "I'm sorry. I didn't mean . . . I forgot."

"No wonder. You're half-asleep from those pills they gave you." He stroked her hair. "It's okay. I guess everybody has something rough in their family to deal with. At least I had my dad for a lot of years." Time to form a lot of good memories, unlike Jessica's situation with her mother.

"And your mother . . ."

Whatever else she was going to say seemed to drift away. More than half-asleep, he decided. Ninety percent of the way, maybe.

He stroked her hair. "Just rest." Obeying an impulse, he bent to touch her lips gently with his.

It was meant to be nothing—a comforting gesture, nothing more. But she woke at his touch, her lips warming, coming alive under his. He slid his arms around her, feeling her touch as her unbandaged hand stoked the back of his neck, drawing him even closer. He was falling into the embrace, they both were, and where—

The front door swung open, and Sam gave a welcoming bark. "Trey, Jessica, we're here," his mother called unnecessarily.

He pulled back. Jessica's cheeks were flushed, her eyes wide and dark.

"Trey . . ." She whispered his name.

THEY HAD ALL GANGED UP on Jessica the next day, insisting she spend it being coddled by Geneva instead of working. Geneva had fixed her favorite things to eat and smoothed the covers over her in the four-poster bed in the cozy guest room. Rather guiltily, she'd enjoyed it.

But by midafternoon, Jessica's mind had begun churning over the facts of the case. She had a little more ammunition now, thanks to the drug tests and to Peggy's willingness to testify, but was it enough to convince a jury?

Leaving the bedroom behind, she wandered into the family room, sunny and pleasant with its white wicker and flowered cretonne slipcovers. The television set in the corner was turned on to a game show, the sound muted.

Jessica sat down at the desk, trying to organize her thoughts. There were avenues yet to explore, if only she could ignore the throbbing in her head long enough to make a list.

"Jessica, what are you doing out here?" Geneva hurried into the room, her tone scolding. "I thought you were resting."

"I'm rested out." That sounded too blunt, and she patted Geneva's hand in apology. "I can't stop thinking about the case. Usually I can compartmentalize business, but not this time."

Geneva nodded, pulling over a bentwood rocker and sitting down. "I know. I do understand. Some things are just so consuming you can't get your mind off them." Her eyes misted, and she rubbed the smooth surface of the chair arms. "After my husband's death, I couldn't think of anything else. People tried to take me out, distract me, as if that would make me forget."

For a moment Jessica couldn't speak. Then she put her hand over Geneva's. "I'm sure you never could."

"No." Geneva sighed. "The police say he killed himself. I couldn't believe Blake would do that. It haunted me. It still does, but I've learned to accept what can't be changed."

"I'm so sorry." The words were inadequate. She hadn't expected such a confidence. Geneva was giving her the gift of being open with her, and she sought for a response. Probably the only fitting one was to be open in return. "My mother died when I was very small. I don't really remember her, but I still feel her absence, if you know what I mean."

Geneva nodded, her grip tightening on Jessica's hand. "I know."

"But you . . . you've accepted your loss." She

was trying to grope her way to an understanding of something she rarely allowed herself to think about. "How have you done that?"

"Turned it over to God," Geneva said. "Each time the burden seemed too heavy, or I didn't think I could go another step without Blake, I just reached out for His hand. It was always there."

"That must be very comforting, to know you have someone to lean on."

Geneva sighed again. "It's harder for some people, I think. Trey, for instance. He's so determined to be the strong one that he can't admit he needs help, but he does."

Trey would hate it if he thought she'd discussed him with his mother. Even though Geneva had brought it up, there wasn't a doubt in her mind that he'd blame it on her.

"Trey seems to feel it's his duty to take care of everyone else," she said carefully. "Right now, he's torn between wanting to protect you from involvement in the case and wanting to protect me by having me here, which is a really good reason for me to go back to the motel."

"I won't hear of it," Geneva said instantly. "How on earth does Trey think he can keep me away from the case? I'm committed to seeing Thomas exonerated. That's what's right."

"Unfortunately, being right isn't enough in a court of law. We have to be able to prove it." She gestured toward the television set in the corner. The noon news had come on, and Thomas's face flashed on the screen.

Geneva lifted the remote to turn up the sound. The reporter, having nothing new to report, rehashed the case, sitting in front of a picture of Cherry Wilson, head thrown back, laughing.

"It's disgraceful," she muttered. "They take it for granted he is guilty."

"The reporting hasn't crossed the line, but each time people hear something like that, they become more convinced that Thomas is guilty. If we can't find some way to counter the bad publicity, I'm afraid we'll never find an impartial jury."

"If . . ." Geneva stared at the television screen, her face curiously blank.

"Geneva? Is something wrong?"

Her usual smile erased the impression. "No, not at all. You just reminded me of something."

The telephone rang. Geneva reached across the desk to answer and then handed the receiver to Jessica. "It's someone from the courthouse."

She took the phone. She listened, made the appropriate response and hung up, pressing her fingers against her throbbing temples.

"What is it?" Geneva reached out, as if prepared to comfort.

She shook her head slowly. "They've finalized a trial date. It's only a month away."

A month. She repeated the words in her mind.

She'd expected to have until the next term of court, at least.

A month. Four weeks to find a way to prove that Thomas was innocent, or he could face spending the rest of his life in the state penitentiary.

TREY DIDN'T RETURN TO THE house until well after supper. Because he didn't want to spend time with her? Jessica didn't know. But she suspected that he was as blindsided by the feelings between them as she was.

He came into the study, where she'd been working on her laptop, giving her a frowning gaze. "I understand the trial date is set."

She nodded. "Just a month. Although I'm not sure having more time would help."

Trey sat in the chair next to her. She could feel his gaze on her face, so intense that he might as well be touching her skin.

"Where were you today?" She didn't mean that to sound accusing. She just wanted to get him talking so that she could dismiss the intimacy of the moment.

"I had some work to do. Then I went over to Jonas's place and had a look around the barn."

The words startled her. "But I didn't tell you—" She stopped, not sure she wanted to say the rest of it.

"Didn't tell me what?" He clasped her hand in his. "What, Jessica? You can trust me."

"I know." Her smile flickered. "I just didn't want to sound paranoid."

His gaze met hers steadily for a long moment. "You don't think it was an accident."

She shrugged, not sure she wanted to go that far. "I heard . . . thought I heard . . . someone in the loft just before the bales fell over."

"You didn't see anyone?" His words came quick and hard.

"No. I can't even be sure of what I heard. Maybe it was just a natural sound. The floorboards settling or something."

"But someone might have been there. Someone might have given those bales a shove."

"How could that happen?" She'd been over this in her own mind a hundred times today. "Wouldn't he or she have been spotted?"

He frowned, turning her hand idly in his. "Not necessarily. Probably no one was looking at the loft. The kids were all intent on each other, and the few adults probably had their minds on their own chores. Besides, it was dark enough looking up there from below that a person might not have been visible."

A shiver went through her. She'd much rather think it had been an accident, pure and simple. "How would he get up there? And get away?"

"Easier than you might think. There are several ladders that lead down to the barn floor." He snagged a pen and tablet from the desk and paused, looked at the image she had doodled earlier that day—the odd little hex symbol that had been on the threatening note. "Is this worrying you?"

"Only because I don't know what it means, if anything."

He shook his head slowly, frowning, and she had the sense that he didn't say what he thought.

"Well, about the barn." He flipped the page over and drew a rough sketch. "Here, here and here there are ladders." He pointed. "Somebody could come down while everyone was intent on you. There's also another ladder over here at the far end. It leads into the equipment area, so if he came and went that way, he didn't have to go into the main part of the barn at all."

She looked at him, raising her eyebrows. "Someone in Amish dress wouldn't have been noticed."

"That's ridiculous." His words slashed back at her. "They wouldn't do such a thing."

"They . . . he . . . might not have intended to do much harm. If I hadn't been getting to my feet when the bales fell, I doubt that I'd have been hurt. Startled, maybe. Scared."

"What reason could any Amish person have for trying to scare you away? They want Thomas to be found innocent."

"I don't know." Her hand twisted involuntarily, and he smoothed his fingers over it, as if he calmed a child. "But you can't deny that some have been opposed to my involvement. And you must have been suspicious, or you wouldn't have been out there looking over the barn today."

"I suppose I was," he admitted. "Jonas is a good friend, and I could see that he wasn't satisfied, as well."

"Did he think it was deliberate?"

"He didn't say that, but I could tell it was in his mind." He shook his head. "I can't make any sense out of it. I suppose an outsider could have followed us, but how would they know you were in the loft? How would they know how to get up there without being seen?"

"That brings us back to accident," she said.

"I guess." He enclosed her hand in both of his. "Maybe I'm just spooked, worrying about you."

She was suddenly breathless. "You . . . you shouldn't. I'm used to looking out for myself."

"And I'm used to looking out for the people I care about." His voice deepened on the words, and her breath caught. She ought to look away from the intensity of his gaze, but she couldn't. She seemed to be drowning in it. He leaned toward her—

"There you are, Trey." Geneva hurried into the room, and Trey jerked back in his chair as if he'd been shot.

"Mom, we were talking."

"Were you, dear? That's nice." She gave them a

bright-eyed look and then switched on the television. "I won't disturb you for long, but there's something on the local news at seven that I want you to see."

Jessica retrieved her hand. Lucky Geneva had come in when she had. An interruption was all that would have kept them from kissing again. From getting more entangled in a relationship she was afraid couldn't go anywhere.

The television newscaster was giving a report on a three-car pileup. Jessica looked from Trey to his mother, but judging from Geneva's expression, this wasn't the news tidbit she was interested in.

A brief close-up of the reporter—the same one who'd waylaid her outside the jail and again at the Esch farm. The woman turned, and Jessica realized who she was interviewing.

Geneva. Geneva, big as life, smiling at the camera and telling the world that she believed in Thomas's innocence, and that she was happy to be paying for his defense.

"There you have it, ladies and gentlemen, a TV 10 exclusive with Geneva Morgan, local business owner, revealing that she is providing representation for Thomas Esch, accused in the brutal murder of Cherry Wilson. A request for comment from Esch's family and other local Amish was refused."

The interview was short—that was the only bright spot Jessica could find. It ended, and

Geneva switched the set off and turned to Trey with a smile identical to the one she'd worn on camera.

"There. Wasn't that excellent?"

"Mom . . ." Trey often sounded frustrated when he talked with his mother, but for the first time since she'd known him, he seemed to feel helpless. "Why did you do that? What on earth possessed you?"

"The community needs to know that some of us believe Thomas is innocent. Now they do." She beamed. "I'm so pleased about it, and it's all thanks to Jessica. She gave me the idea."

Jessica felt her mouth drop open. "I didn't . . ."

Trey was looking at her with rage burning in the eyes that had been so warm only a few minutes ago. "Why would you do that? You know I don't want my mother exposed to that sort of publicity."

"I didn't." She was angry right back at him, but underneath the anger was pain. He judged her so quickly. "Geneva, for pity's sake, I didn't suggest that you do any such thing."

Geneva finally seemed to wake up to just how angry her son was. "No, dear, of course you didn't suggest it. Trey, stop looking like a thundercloud. We were talking about all the bad publicity, and Jessica said it was a shame there wasn't anyone giving the other side."

"I didn't say that, exactly. Just that I'd like to find a way to counter the bad publicity." She experienced the helplessness Trey seemed to feel so often with his mother. "Geneva, I certainly didn't want you to do anything."

"Well, it worked, didn't it?" Geneva beamed, unrepentant. "I showed the community that we support Thomas."

"Yes. You did." Trey looked weighted down with the responsibility he took so seriously. "I just hope you don't have cause to regret it."

CHAPTER FOURTEEN

BY MONDAY MORNING, Jessica couldn't stay in the house any longer. She told herself it was because she had to get back to work, but she knew the truth. She really wanted to get away from reminders of the complicated situation with Trey.

Apparently Trey felt the same. He'd left the house even earlier than she had.

She sighed, pushing herself back from the desk in Leo's office, and flexed her fingers. At least it was her left wrist, not her right. The doctor had given her a wrist support, saying it ought to allow her to use her left hand to some extent. He hadn't mentioned how much that would hurt.

Leo, standing at the floor-to-ceiling bookshelves to consult a reference, peered at her over the top of his wire-rimmed glasses. "How do you feel about getting a psychiatric exam for Thomas?"

She brushed her hair back from her face, generating an instant memory of Trey doing the same thing, Trey's fingers lingering against her cheek . . .

She forced herself to concentrate. "If we bring in a psychiatric defense, that means we're admitting he's guilty. I don't believe that."

"I don't either." Leo put the heavy tome down on his desk. "But—"

"But I suppose we shouldn't miss any

possibilities." She finished the thought for him. "Do you know anyone?"

He nodded. "Leave it to me."

It was the right thing, wasn't it? "What has happened in other local trials involving the Amish?"

Leo stared at her blankly for a moment. "There haven't been any—well, at least not of this nature. The Amish are far more likely to be victims. A couple of Amish young men were arrested on drug charges a few years ago."

"What was the public reaction to that?"

"Mixed." He sat on the corner of his desk. "The fact that they were Amish caused a bit of sensationalism, but most local people understood that they were unbaptized teens who probably were in the process of leaving the church anyway."

She nodded. "I've had an attorney friend looking into cases nationwide. She hasn't been able to find anything helpful. Other than causes like having their own schools and the recent issues with the state's attempt to outlaw lay midwives, the Amish simply don't appear in connection with the law."

"Even in the case of the drug dealing, there wasn't the kind of outcry there's been in this case."

"Our favorite television reporter has been responsible for a lot of that."

"To say nothing of the district attorney. He held another news conference." Leo tossed the book he held on the desk, and it landed on the blotter with a dull thud. "He's riding the publicity for all its worth."

Jessica pushed back from the desk, dissatisfied. She hadn't followed up every other possibility, and she had to. The trial date was coming at them like a freight train. Or maybe like a train wreck.

She stood. "I'm going out for a while. I'll check back later."

"Do you want me to drive you?"

"No, thanks." If Leo knew where she was going, he might react the way Trey had, and she didn't need any protective males following her around.

As soon as she was out of the office, she called for a taxi. Twenty minutes later, she was getting out at the garage where Chip Fulton worked.

The bay doors stood open, so she walked inside. A burly man leaning over a car's motor straightened, gesturing toward the door. "Boss is in the office."

She spotted the name embroidered on his striped coveralls. "Are you Chip?

"That's right." Tall, heavyset, he had the look of someone who'd once been an athlete but had lost the battle to stay in shape. "I'm Chip." His gaze drifted over her body, and he smiled. "What can I do for you?"

"I have a few questions I hope you can answer."

His gaze sharpened on her face, and his smile disappeared. "Hey, you're her. That lawyer trying to get Cherry's killer off." His beefy hand closed over a wrench. "You got a nerve, coming in here."

Her pulse quickened, but she kept her voice even. "Thomas is innocent until proved guilty, you know."

"He's guilty as sin, that's what I know." His face reddened, and a vein throbbed in his temple. "You'd better get out. Go back where you belong, and leave us alone."

It was an unpleasant echo of the notes. She took a step toward him, anger overcoming caution. "It was you, wasn't it? You slashed my tires. You sent me those notes. Did you push me, too?"

He raised the wrench. "I didn't do nothing. You can't blame stuff on me."

He was only feet from her. The empty garage echoed with the sound of his voice. Her stomach twisted, and she gripped her bag, hefting it. Not much of a weapon, but all she had. If he . . .

"Fulton!" The man who strode out of the office area was slight and graying, but his voice carried a note of authority. "What do you think you're doing? Get away from that lady."

Chip took a step back. "I wasn't doing nothing. She's the one, coming in here, accusing me of stuff I didn't do."

The older man turned to Jessica, a mix of apology and curiosity on his face. "If you have a beef with Fulton's work, you'd better take it up with me. This is my shop."

"It's nothing to do with his work, Mr. Walbeck." Like Chip, he wore his name on his coveralls. "My name is Jessica Langdon. I'm an attorney representing Thomas Esch." She probably didn't need to say more, as much publicity as the case had had. "I'm sorry to interrupt his work, but I'd like to ask Chip a few questions about Cherry Wilson."

He could tell her to get out, but she hoped he wouldn't. He paused a moment, studying her face. Then he gave a short nod and turned to Chip.

"Answer the lady's questions and be done with it, Fulton. You haven't got anything to hide, do you?"

"No, sir," he said quickly. "I didn't do nothing."

"Then answer the questions and get back to work." He turned abruptly and stalked toward the office.

He didn't go inside, though, Jessica noticed. He stopped at a board covered with pegs from which sets of keys were hanging. He might be looking for something, but she had the feeling he wanted to hear what was going on. Or maybe he was being protective.

"Go ahead, ask." Chip tossed the wrench into a toolbox, where it landed with a metallic thud. "I got nothing to hide."

She took a breath, reorganizing her thoughts. This was about Cherry Wilson, not about notes and slashed tires. "I heard that you and Cherry dated."

He shrugged massive shoulders. "Sometimes. Not serious. We knew each other a long time, see? Since third grade, maybe. We'd go out, talk, have a few drinks, a few laughs, but I knew she'd never get serious about me."

"Why not? If you were old friends—"

"Cherry wouldn't settle for a mechanic. She wanted better for herself."

She raised her eyebrows. "How would an Amish farm kid fit into that?"

"He wouldn't." Chip's face tightened and his hands clenched, but he didn't make a move toward her. "No way Cherry would ever get serious about a kid like that. She might party with him, just for laughs, but that's all. He got mad when she turned him down. He killed her."

"We don't know that. It could have been someone else."

"He was the one was there," Chip said stubbornly. It was unanswerable. It might also be the view a jury would take.

"Was she dating anyone else?"

"Hey, I didn't follow her around. She didn't tell me everything. She coulda been. Like I say, she wanted better. Always had. She wasn't gonna end up living in a trailer, trying to feed six kids, like her mother did. That's why she worked at the inn. Said she met a better class of guys there."

"Anybody in particular?" Like the manager, for instance?

He half turned toward the car. "Don't know. I got work to do. You want to know anything more about Cherry, you better ask someone else." His head came up, and something malicious sparked in his eyes. "Ask Trey Morgan. Seems like you two are thick as thieves. Ask him."

It was like a dash of cold water in her face. "Why would Trey Morgan know anything about Cherry?"

"Cherry always said he was her favorite customer. Used to go in there for lunch all the time, talked to her. Gave her big tips." He turned his back entirely. "Maybe he wanted something in return, y'know?"

She didn't know. But the sick feeling in her stomach said she'd have to find out.

GENEVA WAS INTENT ON getting everyone together to talk about the case that evening, as if they were a committee planning a new playground for the school. Jessica suppressed the impatience that roiled through her and took a chair in the conversational corner of Geneva's pleasant living room. She'd have to get through this, and then she could make an opportunity to talk to Trey about Chip's accusation.

Just the thought of how he might respond, let alone how she would bring it up, was enough to give her a queasy feeling in the pit of her stomach. Geneva had admitted to receiving a few unpleasant calls in the wake of her television appearance. That couldn't help but make Trey even more resentful and less inclined to talk about his association with Cherry.

Maybe this council of war of Geneva's was a good thing. It gave her a little more time to think, at any rate.

She glanced across at Trey. He was handing out coffee cups at Geneva's direction, his expression as calm as ever, but she had the distinct impression of something under that placid surface—of strong emotion suppressed for the moment but ready to spring forth at the first excuse.

An excuse like a gesture of comfort turning into a kiss that had seared her heart. She backed away from that subject hurriedly.

Leo settled on the sofa next to Geneva, and Bobby perched on a straight chair he'd pulled over.

It was an unconventional group, that was certain. Jessica pulled a file from her briefcase. Back in the office, she might consult with another attorney, a legal assistant, maybe an investigator. Not a nearly retired lawyer, a crusading housewife and a. . . .

She stopped there, unable to think how to classify Trey. Not a client, though she supposed the money that paid for the defense came from him, as well as his mother. Not an investigator, although he'd been playing that role. If Chip had been speaking the truth, Trey was withholding information. He—

Trey looked at her, as suddenly as if he'd read her thoughts. Her breath caught, and she slapped the folder onto the table with hands that weren't quite steady. A sheet of paper slid out.

"What's this?" Leo picked it up.

"A copy of one of the notes. Sorry." She reached out for it. "I thought I should hang on to it."

Leo nodded, sliding his glasses into place to look closely at the note. "Did you ever figure out what this is at the bottom?"

Trey came to lean over his shoulder. "A hex sign, very stylized. Mom did find one very similar in Dad's collection."

"Did he tell you anything about it?" Leo asked. "I don't recall ever seeing one like this."

Geneva shook her head. "I think he said someone gave it to him, but he didn't say who."

"You didn't mention that when we were talking about the symbol." What else are you keeping from me, Trey?

He shrugged, moving back to his chair. "I was distracted." He met her gaze, as if to say that they both knew what had distracted him.

"Is the hex sign an Amish thing?" She put the question hurriedly, trying not to look at Trey but finding it impossible.

"Not Amish." Leo answered for him. "I'd call the hex sign a Pennsylvania Dutch heritage symbol. Supposedly early settlers brought the idea with them from Germany. You'll see the same symbols painted on furniture and carved into dower chests." He turned back to the paper in his hand. "But this . . ." His frown deepened. "It reminds me of something, but I can't quite put my finger on it."

Bobby cleared his throat. "I was thinking . . ." His voice died out when everyone looked at him.

"Yes, Bobby?" Geneva said, her tone encouraging.

"Chip Fulton," he said. "He works on my car, so it wouldn't be hard to strike up a conversation with him about Cherry. I mean, if you want to follow up on him. He might say more to another guy than he would to you." His eyes fixed on Jessica.

"That's probably true." She'd trust Bobby to be more tactful in that situation than Trey would be.

"I will, then." He seemed to slide back as if into the wall, effacing himself. Maybe he felt awkward being drawn into this situation, but after all, he'd been involved from the beginning. The Morgan family clearly trusted him to be discreet.

"I'll look into the symbol," Leo said. "If that's

all right with everyone. Geneva, might I borrow the hex sign from Blake's collection?"

"Of course. I'll get it for you." Geneva started to rise, but Jessica held up a hand to delay her.

"One other thing I thought you might help me with. I'd like to find an informal setting to talk with Elizabeth Esch, Thomas's sister. I had a feeling she knew something she wasn't willing to say in front of her parents."

"I'd love to do that." Geneva beamed at the idea of something useful. "I'll tell her we're making strawberry jam. We can do a lot of chatting over a batch of jam."

Jessica half expected a protest from Trey at that, but none came. Maybe, after Geneva's adventure with the television reporter, he'd given up trying to keep her out of Thomas's defense.

"I need to speak with one of Cherry's coworkers," she said. "I'll try to set that up for tomorrow."

"I'll drive you," Trey said immediately.

"That's not necessary." Being alone in a car with Trey, the echo of Chip's hints sounding between them . . . no, she didn't want that. "I'm sure by tomorrow I'll be able to drive myself."

His jaw tightened. "I'll drive you," he repeated, in a voice that didn't brook argument.

"Is there anything we're missing?" Leo said, with an air of shoving himself between two combatants. "Geneva, have you had any more unpleasantness after your interview?" He sounded just as disapproving as Trey had, although not so hot under the collar.

Geneva's cheeks grew pink. "Not what I'd call unpleasant. I mean, if people are childish enough to say they don't want to serve on a committee with me because of my principles, I can't help that."

"Who told you that?" Trey snapped the words. He obviously hadn't heard about this.

Geneva's friends were turning on her. That was one of the things Trey had feared. Geneva might say she wasn't bothered, but it had to hurt.

"It doesn't matter in the least," she said. "Now, is there anything else I can do, besides arranging a talk with Elizabeth?"

"Not that I can think of." If she could keep Geneva out of things, she would, but Geneva had a mind of her own.

"Strawberry-rhubarb cobbler for dessert," Geneva said. "I'll bring it in now. Leo, do you want to help me? And Bobby, there's a fresh pot of coffee on the stove."

Leo followed her toward the kitchen, and Bobby trailed along after them. Trey stood, hand on the back of his chair. She didn't need to look at him to know that he was still frowning.

"Maybe I should help—" she began, but Trey stopped her with a look.

"What's going on?" His voice was a furious

undertone. "Why don't you want me to drive you to see this coworker of Cherry's?"

Because Chip hinted that you might have been involved with her. Because Cherry's coworker might be in a position to confirm that, and she'd hardly do it with you standing there.

No, she couldn't say any of that. Any more than she could come right out and tell him what Chip had said while they were sitting in his house, with his mother likely to come back into the room at any moment.

"She may talk more freely to another woman. In private," she added.

She could feel his gaze on her face, probing.

"I'll wait in the truck." His tone didn't allow argument. "Are you sure that's all?"

"What else could there be?" She stared at him, needing to see his face when she asked the question.

"Nothing," he said, but again she had that sense of emotion moving behind the word. "Nothing."

"HOW WELL DID YOU KNOW Cherry Wilson?" Jessica tried to keep the question from sounding accusatory. But accusing or not, it wasn't fair to anyone to avoid the subject because she was afraid of what she might hear.

She gave a cautious glance across the front seat of the pickup at Trey as they drove toward the mobile-home park where Kristin McGowan lived.

He didn't look particularly bothered by the question.

Trey shrugged. "As well as you know anyone in a small town. I was several years ahead of her in school. She'd have been peddling Girl Scout cookies when I was playing football."

Sidetracked, she raised her eyebrows. "Let me guess. You were the quarterback."

"I was. But how did you know that? Has my mother been showing you her family album?"

"Bobby mentioned something about high school." But now that she thought about it, she'd love to see the Morgan family photo album. "He seems to have a pretty big sense of obligation to you."

"I wish he'd forget all that." Trey's hands moved on the steering wheel. "Maybe I kept him from being stuffed into a locker a time or two. That's no big deal."

"It might to the one being stuffed." That wouldn't have happened to Trey, she felt sure. He would always have been the Big Man on Campus. "But about Cherry—"

"What about Cherry? We'll be at her friend's house in a minute. She probably knows more about Cherry than I do."

"It would help me to know what to ask if I had a better sense of what she was like," she improvised. "As it is, she's a body in a crime-scene photo to me."

The lines in his face deepened, and his hands moved again on the leather-padded wheel. "That wouldn't give you much of an impression, I guess. But I still don't see what I can tell you."

"You went to the inn for lunch sometimes, didn't you?"

"Sure. Once a week, at least."

"Just tell me the impression she'd make on a customer."

"That depends."

"On what?"

"On whether the customer was a man or a woman. She always flirted with the men. Maybe she thought it brought her bigger tips."

"Did it?"

"How would I know?" Now he did sound irritated. "What's this all about, Jessica? Why this sudden interest in what I thought of her?"

She could evade the question, but that would be the same as lying, and she didn't want a lie between them. "It was something Chip said, about how you were one of Cherry's favorite customers. About how well you always tipped her."

The look he gave her set a distance between them. "I didn't hit on her, if that's what you mean." He dropped the words like ice cubes. "If I tipped her better than most—well, I do that, for the most part. I try not to forget that I have it easy compared with a lot of people."

His lips clamped shut on the words, and he turned into the mobile-home park. He leaned forward, not speaking, obviously checking the numbers for the one she wanted.

She'd succeeded in making him angry with her, and to no good end, as far as she could see. The car stopped, and Trey gestured to a mobile home on the right.

"That's it. I'll wait here."

"Thank you." She slid out quickly, glad to get away from the frigid atmosphere. "I don't know how long I'll be."

He shrugged, picking up the newspaper that he'd stuffed into the door pocket. "No hurry."

Kristin McGowan was a very different type from Milly Cotter, the college student who waited tables to help pay the bills. Kristin stood back to let her enter the crowded living room of the trailer, pausing to switch off the television, and led her to a seat on the cracked-vinyl sofa.

"Sorry about the mess." She waved a vague hand at the clutter of toys, magazines and newspapers that seemed to cover every inch of the floor. She yawned broadly. "My mom's watching the kids so I can get a little sleep. I hafta be at work at four, so maybe we can make this short. Don't see what I can tell you, anyway."

Nobody ever did. "I'm interested in Cherry, and I understand you were one of her closest friends. Tell me about her."

Kristin shrugged. "Close—well, yeah, I guess. Cherry wasn't the type to make friends with women, y'know? But we knew each other since middle school, and there we were working at the same place."

"So you'd talk. It's only natural you would, when things got quiet at the restaurant."

"Mostly Cherry talked. She wasn't interested in hearing anything about my kids, that's for sure." She ran her hand back through shaggy blond hair, yawning again. "Cherry liked to talk about Cherry, period."

"So I suppose you knew all about her boyfriends. Like Chip."

"Chip." Kristin tossed Chip aside with a wave of her hand. "He was just somebody she went to school with. Like I said, she didn't have women friends, so he was somebody to talk to. Tell her troubles to, I s'pose."

"Did she have a lot of troubles?"

"Well, men." She gave an expressive gesture that seemed to say men were always trouble. "Milly said she told you about Mr. Perfect."

"Your boss? She said he wanted to go out with Cherry but she wasn't having any of it."

Kristin snorted. "That's all innocent little Milly knows. Cherry went out with him a couple of times. But she figured out he wasn't going to give up his wife or his job for her, so she put a stop to it."

It was a little different from the story Milly told, but it still didn't reflect very favorably on either Cherry or her boss. "Anybody else she dated? Anyone she met at the restaurant, maybe?"

"Cherry didn't go out with customers. At least, that's what she said." Kristin's voice expressed doubt. "She did hint around about a guy— somebody she said was a cut above anybody else she'd dated. Kept saying as how he was crazy about her, and he was worth a lot of money, and she wouldn't be waiting tables at that place forever."

"Really? Did you ever see him?"

"Nah. She was pretty cagey about it. I thought maybe she was just making it up to have someone to brag about, 'cause of Milly getting engaged and showing her ring all over the place."

"So you think there wasn't really any secret boyfriend?" The faint hope went glimmering away.

"Well, I thought that at first, but then she showed me . . ." Kristin stopped, giving Jessica a sidelong look that hinted at more.

"What did she show you, Ms. McGowan?"

"Wasn't anything that looked that special to me. Just a funny-looking piece of old jewelry. But Cherry insisted it was worth a lot." Kristin studied her fingernails with a casualness that was a little overdone. "She . . . um, she gave it to me to keep for her. Said nobody would look here for it."

"So you have it."

Kristin dropped the pose and leaned forward. "If it's important, seems like I ought to get something for it."

"I won't know that until I've seen it, will I?" This might be a wild-goose chase, but it was the first tangible thing she'd run across, and she couldn't let it go. "Tell you what. You let me get an expert opinion on it, and if it's something that is useful to the defense case, I promise a reward. How's that?"

"If I was to take it to the district attorney . . ."

"Then all you'd get was his thanks for being a good citizen," she said crisply. "Seems to me you're better off dealing with me."

Kristin stared at her for a moment, as if considering. Then she shrugged, rose and waded through toys to the television cabinet. She reached behind the DVD player and brought out a plastic sandwich bag. Opening it, she shook its contents into her palm. She hesitated and then handed the object to Jessica. "I'm trusting you to play fair."

"You won't regret it." Jessica stared at the object on her palm, and a shiver seemed to curl through her. It was a small tile, probably two inches square, with a hole drilled in it, probably to allow it to be hung from a cord or chain. It looked old, scratched and worn, with the black lines dim and faded.

But she could still make out the design. It was the same as the symbol of that threatening note— the hex sign.

CHAPTER FIFTEEN

WHAT JESSICA WANTED to do was research the pendant, if that's what it was. However, Geneva had asked Elizabeth to help her make strawberry jam, giving Jessica a chance for an informal chat. So she headed back to the house.

The powerful scent of fresh strawberries and sugar nearly knocked her over when she entered the kitchen. Geneva, flushed, stood mixing something in a kettle on the stove while Elizabeth cleaned strawberries at the sink with swift, practiced motions.

"Hi. Looks pretty busy in here." She'd taken the precaution of changing to jeans and a casual shirt. Good thing. Geneva was liberally spattered with pink splotches.

"Come and join us." Geneva waved a wooden spoon, adding a few more pink drops. "We can use all the help we can get, can't we, Elizabeth?"

The girl just smiled, apparently used to Geneva. The long sleeves of her dress were pushed back to the elbows, but her blue dress and its matching apron were spotless. With her hair pulled straight back from its center part in a knot under her kapp, she might have been the model for a centuries-old painting.

Jessica approached the sink. "What you're

doing looks a bit safer for someone like me. I'm not much of a cook."

"You're a lawyer, ja? You have other things to do."

Elizabeth hadn't said more important things. Just other things. Was that a reflection of how the Amish viewed the world?

"How can I help?"

Elizabeth gave her an appraising look, apparently to be sure she was serious. "If you'd like to, you can wash and stem the berries. That way I can get on with mashing them. If you want," she added.

"Sounds good." She moved into Elizabeth's spot. Simple enough. Wash and stem the berries. "They smell wonderful."

That got her a shy smile from Elizabeth. "My mamm always says if one looks specially gut, go ahead and eat it. They always taste best fresh-picked."

With some idea of establishing rapport, Jessica picked out a berry and popped it in her mouth. The flavor seemed to explode. "I've never tasted better."

"That's because the ones you've eaten before have been picked days or weeks ago," Geneva said, beginning to ladle the rich red liquid into jars. "They're even better picked right from the plant and popped in your mouth still warm from the sun. Ain't so, Elizabeth?" Geneva used the Amish phrase easily.

"Ja." Elizabeth wielded what seemed to be an old-fashioned potato masher in a large yellow mixing bowl. "My little brothers picked these this morning, soon as the plants dried off, so they'd be just right for you."

Jessica didn't miss the affection in the girl's voice. Not surprising. She hadn't met anyone yet who didn't succumb to Geneva's warmth. "How many little brothers do you have?"

"Three." Elizabeth's face clouded. "And one big brother." Her hands stilled on the bowl. "Daadi says we must accept that whatever happens is God's will. But—you will help Thomas, won't you?"

"I'm doing my best." She tried to keep her gaze on the berries, so that she wouldn't put too much emphasis on this and frighten the girl off. "You know, you could help, too, Elizabeth."

"I could?" There was no doubt about her reaction to that. The sun seemed to come up in Elizabeth's face. "I would do anything for Thomas, I would."

"Good. I was sure you'd feel that way. You can answer some questions for me, then."

"Ja, for sure. If I know the answers," she added.

Jessica hesitated. But there was no way to ask but directly. "Did you know about Thomas and Cherry Wilson?"

She sensed the girl's withdrawal. "I don't think—"

"Elizabeth, please." She caught Elizabeth's hand impulsively. "You said you'd do anything to help Thomas. You can tell me. I won't use it against him."

"Ach, I know that." She still looked troubled.

"She won't say anything to your daadi, either," Geneva said.

Of course that would be what troubled the girl. She should have seen that.

Elizabeth nodded. "Daadi wouldn't like it. But Thomas told me that there was an Englisch girl that liked him. He said he met her at a party."

"What else did he say about her?" Jessica prompted.

A frown settled on Elizabeth's face. "She was the one who invited him to that party. He told me so. Said she told him to come, and she'd meet him there."

That was what Jessica'd begun to suspect, but it was good to have it verified. Cherry had been taking the initiative with Thomas. But why? Just out of a malicious wish to embarrass an Amish kid?

"Had she ever done that before?"

"I don't think so." Elizabeth began mashing berries again, the juice squirting up between the metal tines. "He hadn't known her very long. Just met her at a couple parties, and she invited him to the next one."

Jessica tried to make that add up to something

but couldn't. "Did your brother have many girlfriends?" He certainly didn't look like a player, but what did she know about Amish teens?

"Ach, no." Elizabeth grinned at that. "He always got red when a girl even talked to him. I'll tell you who liked him, though. Peggy Byler."

"I met Peggy." And she'd suspected something of the kind. "Were they going together?" Would Elizabeth understand the phrase? "I mean—"

"Ja, I know what it means." Blue eyes twinkled. "Sometimes I babysit for an Englisch family. They have television."

"I guess you'd know, then. So, were they?"

"Peggy would like for Thomas to be her special come-calling friend. I think Thomas liked her, but one of his friends liked her, too. So it was hard."

An Amish teenage love triangle? She couldn't make that fit, either. But she had an idea she knew who the friend was. "This friend . . . was it Jacob Stoltzfus?"

Elizabeth looked relieved that she already knew. "Ja, that's so. Thomas wouldn't want to cause trouble for a friend."

No, he wouldn't. But Peggy had impressed her as a young woman who knew her own mind and would make it up without any regard for male egos.

It was a sidelight that complicated matters. But how it fit into Thomas alone in a barn with a murdered woman, she couldn't imagine.

• • •

BY EVENING, TREY HAD battled his way to the conclusion that he was being unreasonable. It didn't come easily—he was ruefully aware of that. Was he really so accustomed to everyone's good opinion of him that he couldn't tolerate anything else? That was a humbling thought.

And as if that wasn't enough, his mother informed him, rather accusingly, that Jessica was talking about moving back to the motel in the morning. Clearly Mom thought that was his fault.

He found Jessica sitting in the corner of the sofa in the family room, intent on her laptop screen.

"Still working?"

She looked up at his words, face startled. She glanced at her watch. "I guess it is getting late. I was trying to find something about this." She touched, with one finger, the object that lay on the end table next to her—that odd little tile she'd gotten from Cherry's friend.

"Any luck?" He leaned on the back of the sofa, close enough to smell the faint fragrance of her hair, and tried to focus on the screen.

"Nothing." She stretched, the movement bringing her even closer, so that her hair brushed his fingers. "I hope Leo has better luck."

"He will," he assured her, hoping he was right. "Leo's forgotten more about the history and folklore of this region than most people ever knew. He'll track it down."

"It's not familiar to you? I mean, other than from your father's collection?" She tilted her head back to look at him, her eyes more green than blue in this light, like a pond in summer with the trees reflecting in it.

It took him a moment to wrench his gaze away and look at the tile instead. He frowned at it.

"It seems vaguely familiar, that's all I can say." A memory teased at the corners of his mind, like something slithering out of the shadows, and was gone again. "Leo will know." He shoved the subject aside to focus on her face. "What's this I hear about you moving out?"

Her gaze slid away from his. "I just think it's time I got back on my own." She flexed her hand. "My wrist is well enough that I can drive again, so there's no reason to impose."

"It wouldn't, by any chance, be because I acted like an idiot today?"

"No, of course not." Her denial was too quick. "I mean, did you?"

He grinned, coming around to sit down next to her. "Too late. You know I did."

"You thought I was accusing you of something." She said the words carefully. "I was only—"

"You were doing your job," he finished for her. "I'm too used to people's good opinion of me, maybe. It stung, that you considered I might have been running around with Cherry and keeping it quiet."

"Because Blake Morgan the Third wouldn't do that."

"It sounds a little pompous when you put it like that."

"You're not pompous." She closed the laptop and set it aside. "Just sure of yourself. Sure of your place here."

She said that almost wistfully, as if she envied him that. Maybe she did. Given what she'd said to him about her early life, shipped off to boarding schools and camps, there probably hadn't been much sense of a solid place to cling to.

"I've always known where I belonged. What my future held." He said it slowly, feeling his way. "Maybe it sounds hopelessly old-fashioned, but Morgans are important to this community. My father . . . I never wanted more than to be the kind of man my father was." His throat tightened on the words.

"His suicide hurt you," she said softly. "I'm sorry."

"I didn't understand it. I still don't. Mom says he was troubled about something else. I didn't see that." His voice thickened. He didn't talk about this, not to anyone. But Jessica wasn't just anyone. He knew that as surely as he knew anything.

"You're not blaming yourself, are you? If your father didn't talk about it to your mother, he wouldn't have to you, would he?"

"Probably not." He stared absently at the braided rug. "And what could have pushed him to suicide, other than his illness?" He shifted his gaze to her. "If you heard about a suicide like that, not knowing anyone involved, what would you think?"

Her eyes showed so clearly that she didn't want to say anything. Didn't want to risk hurting him. "I don't know. Debts, I suppose. Or depression, mental illness. Or some scandal that was about to be revealed."

"That's the list I've come up with, too. But any of those things would have come out." He shook his head, trying to shake off the feelings that clung like cobwebs. "Anyway, I just have to carry on, but there's a hole where something sure and solid used to be. Like stepping through a familiar doorway and finding yourself falling into a well."

It was a relief to say the words. He hadn't been able to, not to anyone else. He'd had to take his father's place, to be the rock everyone could depend on.

"I'm sorry." Jessica's voice was very soft. She touched his cheek, turning his face toward hers. "I've never known anything like your relationship with your father, so I can't claim to understand. But when I was sent away, on my own, all my security was gone. It was like I was walking a tightrope without a safety net." Tears glimmered in her eyes, like rain on still water. "I do understand the feeling."

He put his hand over hers where it lay against his cheek, feeling the warmth and comfort that flowed from her. He turned his face slightly, so that her palm was over his lips, and he kissed it. There was a pulse beating in her wrist, and it seemed to be beating in him, as well.

He turned, drawing her into his arms, and kissed her. The familiar lamplit room receded, the sounds of the old house faded. His responsibilities, her duty . . . they'd be waiting, but for now there was nothing beyond the two of them.

PREDICTABLY, TREY WAS still arguing with Jessica when he followed her down the hall to Leo's office the next day.

"There is no reason for you to move back to the motel." It was probably the thirtieth time he'd said that, with an increased edge of irritation to his voice with each repetition. "Especially now." His fingers closed over hers warmly.

She returned the pressure of his hand, feeling warmth and caring flooding through her. "Maybe because of that." She paused, her hand on the door, knowing there was something she had to say before she lost the will. "Trey, we've moved a long way in a very short time."

"Yes." He brushed her face, a featherlight touch,

his eyes darkening. "Too far? Is that what you're trying to say?"

She shook her head. Impossible to deny her feelings. "Just that I have a job to do now. I have to concentrate on that. Afterward . . ."

"Afterward." There was a promise in his gaze. "But you're wrong about one thing."

"What?"

"*We* have a job to do. Not just you." He pulled the door open. "We're all involved. Especially me."

Not alone, in other words. She didn't have to do this alone.

A flicker of excitement lit Leo's face when he saw them. "Guess what I've found." He held up a slim book—an old one, judging by the faded, stained cloth cover. She could just make out the title, *Legends and Lore of Old Pennsylvania.*

"Something about the hex sign," Trey said. "I figured you'd get so caught up in the research that you wouldn't quit until you'd found it."

"Guess I am a bit predictable." Leo didn't look as if that bothered him. "I knew it was familiar to me."

He flipped open the book. Jessica stowed her wet umbrella safely out of the way before she looked. The illustration was of something that looked like a woodcut—a raven, identical to the one on the threatening note.

"What does it mean?" She dropped her bag on

her chair and came to look over Leo's shoulder at the book. Closer examination didn't help. She still felt the revulsion she'd had the first time she'd seen it.

"Sign of the raven," Leo said, satisfaction in his voice. "The so-called hex signs have been part of Pennsylvania Dutch folk art for hundreds of years. Most of them are used over and over—painted on barns and pottery, carved or stenciled on furniture, even inked onto documents. This particular symbol is rare, though. It's almost never seen, except . . ." He paused.

Trey nudged him. "Quit trying to build up suspense. Just tell us."

Leo gave him a mock affronted look. "I am telling you." His face warmed with a smile. "I can't help getting excited. How often do my antiquarian and legal interests coincide? Anyway, back in the 1700s, this—" he tapped the image on the page "—was the sign of a secret society so powerful it controlled virtually the whole area."

"Secret society?" Was he making a joke? "That sounds like something out of a comic book, Leo. You're not serious."

"It was serious business all right." Leo pushed his glasses up with the tip of his finger, and his voice had taken on a lecturing tone. "Secret societies were rampant in Europe and the colonies in the seventeenth and eighteenth centuries. It made a certain amount of sense in an era when rulers could control the lives of their subjects. Banded together, committed to the group by its secret signs and rituals, people had more power than anyone could individually."

"You're serious." She found it hard to believe. "This group really had significance?"

"Very much so. Supposedly they became so large and so powerful that they controlled most of the business and political life of the area. Undercover, of course. It was one of those things everyone knew and no one talked about."

Trey stirred. "So what happened to them?"

"A number of the secret societies became perfectly respectable and well-known, like the Masons and other fraternal orders. Others, including the Brotherhood of the Raven, faded from view." Leo frowned. "It's odd, actually, that the brotherhood disappeared. I suppose, in all the turmoil of the American Revolution, things like that came to seem unimportant."

"Sheds a new light on the things our forefathers got up to, doesn't it?" Trey obviously took it lightly. "So what does that tell us? That the person who wrote that threatening note to Jessica was a history buff?"

"Or that he saw the symbol someplace and decided to copy it," she said, trying to chase away the unpleasant feeling in the pit of her stomach. "He thought it would add a creepy tone to his threats."

"Could be. Must be," Trey said, but she could see that he was troubled. "It can't be anything else. Still, I don't like the premeditation and the violence implied in wringing the neck of that bird and throwing it at your window."

Leo glanced at her face and then, warningly, at Trey.

"I'm not going to go into hysterics at the idea that this joker is prone to violence," she said, irritated. "So you two can stop trying to protect me from facing facts. Anyway, it may have nothing to do with proving Thomas's innocence."

"Maybe not, but Cherry had that piece of jewelry, and the raven reappeared as a motif in the threats against you. That can't be coincidence," Leo said.

"It may just mean that Cherry's secret lover doesn't want the person he sees as her killer to get off," Trey said briskly. "Anything else we should know about this raven thing, Leo?"

"The Brotherhood of the Raven crumbled to dust a long time ago. Still, it's odd that it should recur in such a context. Among other things, the brotherhood supposedly controlled the legal system. Just a glimpse of the symbol would be enough to keep witnesses from testifying and sway juries to deliver the verdict the brotherhood wanted. So using it to scare away an attorney would fit right in."

Trey plucked the book from Leo's hand and

closed it with a slap. "Like I said. Interesting, but as Jessica said, it doesn't necessarily have anything to do with defending Thomas."

Jessica's grip tightened on the back of the chair as Trey's words set up an echoing response in her mind. There was something—some reason why the sign affected her as it did, some connection she hadn't yet made.

She turned, images clicking together in her mind like tiles. She picked up her briefcase, found the file she wanted and dumped its contents onto Leo's desk.

"Jessica?" There was a question in Trey's voice. He and Leo were looking at her with identical expressions of concern. "What is it?"

She shuffled through the crime-scene photos. There it was, the picture showing the area around the body. She pointed to an object in the picture— an object she hadn't consciously remembered until now. It was a necklace, a thin gold chain that had apparently been ripped from Cherry's neck in her final struggle. It lay next to her body on the rough wooden floor of the barn.

She pointed. "Tell me I'm not seeing what I think I'm seeing."

But now that she studied it, she knew. The chain hadn't just been tossed aside. It had been arranged—its fine gold links formed into an exact replica of the symbol of the raven.

CHAPTER SIXTEEN

HIS MIND STILL preoccupied with the image of the crime-scene photo, Trey barely noticed when his cell phone rang. He answered automatically, but the sound of Bishop Amos's voice startled him to attention. His frown deepened as he heard what the bishop had to say, and when he hung up, he realized that Jessica and Leo were both staring at him.

"Bishop Amos, calling from an English neighbor's house. He wants us to meet him at the Stoltzfus farm as soon as possible."

"The Stoltzfus farm," Jessica echoed. "Why?"

"It seems there's something Jacob has to tell us."

She lifted the photo in a protesting gesture. "Can't it wait? We really need to discuss this."

"If Bishop Amos calls, it has to be serious. Maybe Jacob has remembered something important. Or decided to tell us something he's been hiding. I think we should go now." He nodded toward the photo, its image of the dead woman's necklace repellent. "We can talk that over later."

"That's right." Leo weighed in on his side. "I agree that the symbol is significant, but I can do a little more digging while you're out."

Jessica looked as if she thought they were

ganging up on her, but then she shrugged and reached for her bag. "All right. Let's go."

It took them twenty minutes to get clear of town and reach the Stoltzfus farm—twenty minutes during which he tried to keep Jessica talking and tried to keep himself from thinking about that crime-scene photo. Each time the thought intruded, he pushed it away.

Concentrate on the problems of the moment. That was enough to deal with.

"That's Bishop Amos's buggy," he said, pulling the car to a stop in the driveway. "Let's hope Jacob has something helpful to say."

"We could use a bit of concrete evidence." Jessica walked around the car to join him. "The recurrence of the raven symbol may seem significant to us, but I'm not sure I could explain it in a convincing manner to a jury."

"Right."

They crossed the lawn. Bishop Amos waited for them at the door, looking unusually serious. "Trey. Jessica." He inclined his head gravely. "It is kind of you to komm."

He ushered them into the living room. Jacob sat between his parents, his hands dangling between his knees. None of them looked very happy at whatever was going on.

"Now." Bishop Amos's voice must have sounded like the crack of doom to Jacob. He jumped, the whites of his eyes showing. "Jacob, you muscht say the truth to Trey and Ms. Langdon."

Jacob's father intervened, speaking in Pennsylvania Dutch, apparently in the hope that they wouldn't understand. Jacob would confess to the church. Was it necessary that he also confess to these Englischers?

"Jacob has done wrong." There was no give to the bishop's tone. "He must make amends to the ones he has wronged."

His father looked as if he would say more, but Jacob jerked to his feet like a puppet yanked by its strings.

"I never meant anyone to be hurt. I didn't. I didn't."

Trey's breath caught. Was the boy going to confess to the murder?

"What did you do?" Jessica put the question as calmly as if she were in a courtroom. "Who didn't you want to hurt?"

Jacob stared at her, eyes wide. "You," he said. "I didn't want to hurt you."

Jessica paled, and he took an instinctive step closer to her. "You?" Her voice held disbelief. "You slashed my tires and followed me to my motel? You left those notes for me?"

"No, no, no." Jacob shook his head and went on shaking it as if he couldn't stop. "I did none of those things. I only . . . I . . ." He swallowed, his Adam's apple moving. "I knocked over the hay bales."

His mother made a small, pained sound. He shot her a look of apology. Of pleading.

"I'm sorry. I didn't mean to hurt you. I didn't mean any harm to anybody. I chust—" He stopped, clamping his mouth shut.

"Didn't mean any harm?" Trey's fists clenched, nails biting into his palms. "You could have killed her."

"No!" It was an anguished cry.

"No." Surprisingly, Jessica echoed him. "If I hadn't started to get up just then, I wouldn't have fallen at all."

Tears spilled over onto the boy's cheeks. "I didn't know. I couldn't see you for the hay bales. I didn't know you were getting up. I was chust trying to get close to talk to you, but when I leaned against the bales, they fell, and then you screamed, and everyone was shouting." He clutched his head with his hands. "I couldn't think . . . I didn't know what to do. I ran. I am so ashamed. Please forgive me."

Jessica was moved by his words. Trey could see that. But he wasn't so easily satisfied, not where her safety was concerned.

"You could have talked to us outside, Jacob. Why did you sneak up into the loft when Ms. Langdon was alone if you didn't mean to hurt her?"

"I . . . I . . ." Jacob sent a glance toward the bishop, but Bishop Amos stood, arms folded, watching. "It was because of Peggy." Jacob hung his head, his cheeks reddening.

"Peggy Byler? What about her?"

"I think I know," Jessica said. "You like Peggy, don't you, Jacob?"

The flush reached his ears. "Ja."

"But your friend Thomas liked her, too. Did you think maybe Peggy liked him better?"

"It . . . it wasn't that." Jacob stumbled over the words, and maybe no one in the room believed him. "I heard what you said to her. She would go into an Englisch court. It's not proper. Not fitting for her to do that."

"It is if it helps save Thomas's life." Jessica stepped toward him and grasped his arm. "Look at me, Jacob. You climbed up into the back of the loft so no one would see you. You wanted to convince me not to bring Peggy into court. Is that the truth?"

"Ja." He rubbed at his tears with his hands, like a little kid. "That's it. That's all I did. I am ashamed."

"You will confess in church that you caused Ms. Langdon's accident," Bishop Amos said. "You will accept the punishment the brothers and sisters agree upon."

"Ja," he whispered.

"Gut." Bishop Amos turned from his erring parishioner to Jessica. "Are you satisfied with what the boy has said?"

"Yes. Thank you, Bishop Amos. It is helpful to have this much cleared up."

He nodded gravely. "You have gone through troubles to help one of us. We will not forget it."

Trey walked back to the car beside Jessica, frowning a little. He stopped her before she could open the door, his hand on her arm. "Did you really believe all Jacob wanted to do was talk to you?"

She considered for a moment. "Talk to me. Scare me, maybe. Judging by the father's expression, he's one of those who resent my involvement in Thomas's case, don't you think?"

"Probably." That fit with what the man had said about Jacob confessing to Englischers. "What does that have to do with it?"

"Just that Jacob might have picked up on that disapproval from his father and thought it wouldn't be all that bad if I had a bit of a scare. Maybe even enough to make me think twice about the case, although I suspect Jacob is more concerned about his love life than anything else."

"Possible, but—"

"Look, whatever he intended, he seems genuinely sorry. Nasty notes I can handle, as long as physical violence is off the table." She pulled the door open. "Let's get back to the office and see if Leo has found anything."

Jessica could be right. He hoped so. But he found he couldn't quite believe it.

BY EVENING, THEY HAD discussed the discovery of the raven symbol at the scene of the murder so much that Jessica's head was spinning. Geneva, predictably, was over-the-top excited. She was convinced that this was the key to securing Thomas's release. In fact, she didn't understand why they didn't immediately rush to the police, show them the images and demand they let Thomas go.

Jessica had turned to Trey to enlist his support in explaining the situation to his mother, to find him oddly withdrawn. It was almost as if he hadn't been paying attention to the discussion. Bobby and Leo had pitched in, helping her to convince Geneva that they still had a long way to go.

Finally Leo and Bobby had left, ducking under umbrellas to escape the rain that still pelted down. Leo promised to continue to search for any hint that the symbol of the raven had appeared in recent years, and Bobby insisted he'd track down where Cherry had obtained the raven pendant. Trey, muttering something about calls to make, disappeared into his home office.

Geneva looked after him, a perplexed frown on her face. "What's wrong with Trey?" She turned to Jessica as if she should have the answer.

"I don't know that anything's wrong. He's just busy with something else, I suppose. He's taken a lot of time from the business to help me." Trey's reaction disturbed her, too, but she wasn't about to discuss it with his mother.

Geneva's gaze held a certain amount of doubt, but she didn't argue the point. Instead, she began gathering up coffee cups. "It seems to me . . . well, we've already been through that."

Jessica rose. "I'm going to head back to the motel now. There are some things I should pick up." Geneva had talked her into staying at the house another night, but the pretrial hearing with the judge was tomorrow, and she'd need her power suit for that, which was still at the motel room.

Geneva put the cups down with a clatter. "But it's already dark out, and raining besides. I'm sure Trey wouldn't want you to go alone. Let me get him."

"No, don't." She caught Geneva's hand to stop her instinctive movement. "Honestly, Geneva, I can certainly drive a few miles alone. Now that we know Jacob was responsible for the accident, I'm not worried." She was about to add that she'd spend the night at the motel, but Geneva looked distressed enough already. "I'll be back before you know I'm gone." She squeezed the hand she held. "Really, I'll be fine."

She had to repeat the words several times before Geneva was convinced, and even then she stood looking after Jessica with a worried expression.

She hurried to the car, eager to get away before

Geneva brought Trey's wrath down upon her. She could stand to have a few minutes, at least, free of Trey's presence. When she was with him, her mind had a deplorable tendency to flicker off to his thoughts, his feelings, the slightest change in his eyes. The fact that they warmed every time they rested on her did wonders for her emotions, but nothing at all for her powers of legal reasoning.

The dark shadows of the pines swallowed up her headlight beams as she pulled onto the road. She and Leo were agreed that they needed considerably more than they had in the way of a link between the note left for her and Cherry's death, but at least now there was reason to hope. The thought filled her with energy. She had ammunition, and she was determined to dot every *i* and cross every *t*. No one would be able to claim that she'd been negligent in preparing this case.

Her stomach clenched, as always, when she thought of that accusation. She hadn't been negligent, and Henderson Junior knew it. He was the one who'd failed to follow through on the papers she'd put in his hand, documents that would have saved the firm's client a tidy sum in damages from a disgruntled former employee. But Henderson had looked on blandly while she took the brunt of the blame, secure in his position as the son of the firm's founder.

Trey would never let anyone else take the blame

for his mistake. Instead, he'd very likely jump into the breach, accepting responsibility even for something that wasn't his fault. A decent, honorable man . . . one a woman could count on. She hadn't thought to find someone like him, had certainly never expected to trust her heart to anyone. But Trey—

Lights flashed in her rearview mirror, nearly blinding her. She blinked, moving her head a bit, trying to escape the glare. Where had that idiot come from? And why didn't he have sense enough to switch to low beams? Didn't he realize she couldn't see with that high-powered light in her eyes?

She slowed instinctively, trying to concentrate on the road ahead. There was nothing at all in sight. Plenty of room to pass. He could—

The vehicle behind her hit her bumper hard enough to snap her head back. Her stomach clenched, adrenaline racing along her nerves. She couldn't think, could only react. He slammed into her again, metal shrieking. Her car swerved toward the edge of the road and the darkness beyond.

She fought the wheel for control, heart pumping, pain shooting though her injured wrist. This wasn't an accident; this was deliberate. He wanted to make her crash. She had to get away.

The instant her wheels straightened she stepped on the gas. Stupid, stupid. She'd been distracted, her thoughts wrapped up in Trey, not paying attention to the road. She didn't know how far she was from the edge of town and safety. If she could just get far enough ahead of him—

She rocketed down the narrow road, seeing nothing but the reflection of pavement in front of her and the intense glare of the headlights behind her. Nothing at the side of the road, nothing but darkness. She vaguely remembered pastures and cornfields on either side, a ditch running along the road. No lit farmhouses, no place to seek help.

The pursuer smashed her bumper again, jolting her down to her toes. Her car spun, out of control on the rain-slicked road. Headlights glanced crazily off a road sign, a kaleidoscope of images, and then she was off the road entirely, wheels bumping for a moment before she went nose-down into a ditch, the air bag exploding in her face.

Brakes screeched behind her. She fought to shake herself free of the blackness that threatened to overcome her. She had to keep her eyes open, had to move, get out of the car, call for help . . . She reached, fumbling, trying to find her handbag and her cell phone in the smothering folds of the air bag.

Something bumped against the side of the car, sending a fresh spurt of terror through her. Someone was coming, climbing down into the ditch on the driver's side.

But not to help. She knew that instinctively. He'd forced her car off the road. Now he was coming to finish the job.

A clang against the side of the car—metal on metal. A tire iron? Panic surged through her, clearing her head. She had to get out, get away, but she couldn't even find the release for the seat belt through the muffling folds of the air bag.

Closer—in another step he'd yank open the door. She'd be trapped. Helpless. Her fingers touched the smooth surface of the seat-belt latch. Fumbled, pressed the button.

Release. She shoved at the air bag, diving for the passenger seat, pulling herself over, toward the door, toward safety, but she couldn't make it, there wasn't enough time . . .

Dear God, if you're there, if you care, help me.

Metal clanged. He was reaching for the handle, he . . .

And then he was gone, scrambling up the bank. She pulled herself around, trying to see who it was, but he was nothing but a dark figure melting into the shadows.

Then she realized why he'd run. Headlights, coming fast down the road from the direction she'd come. A car door slammed. The assailant was gone, speeding toward town without lights.

The oncoming car . . . no, truck . . . stopped with a scream of brakes. The inside light came on as Trey leaped from the seat, leaving the door hanging open, the motor running as he rushed to her.

Thank you, she breathed. *Thank you.*

He was there in a second, pulling the door open, calling her name. "Jessica. Are you all right?"

"I . . . I think so." She hadn't had time to decide that, intent only on getting away. Now she flexed muscles, moved arms and legs, tried to assess damages. "Bruised. I think that's all." She gave a shaky laugh that ended on a sob. "Thank goodness for air bags."

"Thank goodness I decided to come after you when Mom told me you'd gone off alone." His voice roughened with emotion.

She moved, trying to get out, but her legs seemed to have turned to rubber. Trey leaned in, his hands gentle as he disentangled her from the air bag and lifted her from the car.

Once she was on her feet, leaning against the car, he let his breath out in a whoosh of air.

"He could have killed you." Anger threaded through the concern in his voice. "What possessed you to leave the house alone at night?"

"I thought . . ." Her voice sounded too weak. She stopped, started again, stronger. "Did you see him?"

"Not to identify." The words sounded as if he bit them. "This is crazy. Why is he after you? It doesn't make any sense."

"None of it makes sense." She touched her face,

wincing a little. Brush burns, it felt like, and she was probably going to have a black eye tomorrow. "If he thinks I know something, he's wrong."

"Come on." He put his arm around her. "The E.R.—"

"No, not again." She stiffened. "I'm all right. Just take me home." Her voice broke on the words. Home. How could she think of Geneva's house as home?

Trey made a sound deep in his throat. Then he pulled her into his arms and held her close, his heart beating strong and sure against her cheek.

"DO YOU REALLY WANT to do this?" Leo peered at Jessica anxiously, his bushy white eyebrows drawing down in a frown. "Maybe you ought to wait a bit longer before speaking to the press."

"I've waited as long as I dare to. The trial date is coming up too fast, and so far we don't have enough to mount a convincing defense."

It had been two days since they'd discovered the connection between the note she'd received and Cherry's death, and despite what seemed a definite link, they had nothing to take to court. She had, finally, taken the photo and the note to the district attorney, where she'd been met with polite disbelief.

The D.A. had gone so far as to offer a plea bargain, but it had been so stiff as to amount to an insult. Apparently he felt confident in his ability to explain away the drug in Thomas's system. As for the photo . . . he'd implied that a jury would laugh that out of court.

Leo hadn't found out anything more about a resurgence of the brotherhood; Bobby had been unsuccessful in tracing the pendant.

As for Trey—after the promise that seemed implicit in the way he'd held her the night she'd been hurled off the road, he'd withdrawn. From her, from the case, everything. A wall had come up between them, a wall she had no idea how to breach.

"The only possibility I can come up with is to go public with the sign of the raven. Maybe it will mean something to someone."

She glanced into the mirror of her compact, aware of the murmur of voices in Leo's outer office. The press had arrived, and she was about to appear before television cameras looking as if she'd been in a prize fight. The black eye was spectacular, to say the least, and all the makeup in the world wouldn't hide it.

"Well, if you're sure." Doubt laced Leo's voice.

"I'm not, but I'm going to do it anyway." She spared a brief thought for Henderson, Dawes and Henderson, who undoubtedly would not approve. Henderson Senior had been on the phone to her only yesterday, wondering why she hadn't persuaded her client to accept the D.A.'s offer.

She couldn't let that matter to her. Her

obligation was to her client, no one else. She took a deep breath, seized the doorknob and stepped into the lion's den.

It wasn't quite as bad as she anticipated, maybe because of that black eye. The reporters stared at it with ill-concealed curiosity, obviously just waiting until her prepared statement was over to ask about it.

Until she showed the enlargements she'd made of the note she received and the necklace from the crime scene. Cameras flashed, questions erupted and the television reporter thrust a microphone in her face.

"Are you seriously suggesting that a secret society is responsible for Cherry Wilson's death?" Disdain was clear in her tone.

"No, of course not." Jessica had to raise her voice to be heard over the babble of questions. "I am suggesting that this symbol of the raven meant enough to the killer that he replicated it. And since it appeared on a note left for me after Thomas Esch was arrested, Thomas clearly didn't write it. That has to mean something."

"Ms. Langdon, you want to tell us where you got that shiner?" One of the print reporters this time.

"My car was run off the road two nights ago," she said, keeping her voice noncommittal.

"You think that's related to this threat you supposedly received?"

Her lips tightened. "The threat was real, as was the vandalism to my car." No point belaboring the point. They'd believe what they wanted to. The important thing was to get her message out.

She looked straight at the television camera. "I'm making a plea for information. If anyone out there knows anything about this symbol, anything at all, we hope that you'll call us." She gave the number of Leo's office.

She managed a smile for the rest of the reporters. "I think that's all. Thank you for your attention." She escaped into the inner office while they clamored for one more answer.

Shutting the door, she leaned against it, looking at Leo. "What do you think?"

He gave her a hug. "Good job, Jessica. Good job."

"Let's just hope it *does* some good. If not . . ." If not, what had she risked by making that plea? She wasn't sure.

The noise from the outer office died away. It had barely faded when the door was yanked open behind her, nearly sending her toppling.

"Why on earth did you do that?" Trey's anger spurted out, fury coloring his voice. "Are you crazy?"

CHAPTER SEVENTEEN

TREY FOUGHT THE MIXED emotions that battered at him. This wasn't him. He didn't lose control. He always kept it together. But when he'd heard what Jessica intended to do—

He took a breath, halting the words that pressed on his lips. Leo was peering over his glasses, as if studying a curiosity. And Jessica . . . Jessica stared at him, looking at once startled and vulnerable.

He wanted to tell her. He wanted to make her understand why he'd been afraid . . . a bone-chilling, paralyzing fear . . . ever since she'd pointed out the sign of the raven next to Cherry's body.

"Trey, I had to." Jessica, overcoming her surprise at his impetuous entrance, came toward him. "Don't you understand? If we can just find someone who knows what the sign means, maybe we can unravel this."

That was exactly what he had to prevent. He had to protect his mother. His father's suicide had devastated her. If she had to withstand another blow about the man she'd loved, Trey wasn't sure how she'd survive.

"Trey?"

He'd been silent too long. "I'm sorry, Jessica." Her expression shook him—caring. Loving. "I'm afraid for you. You're setting yourself up as a target." That was true enough, at least, even if it wasn't the whole story.

"I've been a target, remember? At least now that the business about the symbol is out in the open, the killer has no reason to go after me."

"She's probably right, you know." Leo stood. "But I think I'd better let the two of you argue it out." He went quickly to the outer office, closing the door firmly behind him.

Trey ran a hand through his hair. "Maybe I'm overreacting, but when my mother told me what you planned to do, it scared me. I can't help but think . . ." He stopped, because she was shaking her head.

"No, Trey. That's not what's going on. You've been pulling away since the moment we made the connection with the symbol."

"No."

"Yes." She put her hand on his wrist, gripping him urgently. "Trey, what is it? What does that symbol mean to you?"

"Nothing." He shook his head, knowing he was giving himself away with every breath.

"Don't shut me out." Her lips compressed. "Tell me, whatever it is. Help me understand how you could tell me we were in this together one minute and then pull away from me the next."

That punched him right in the heart. "I didn't intend to do that. I meant everything I said to you."

"Did you?"

"Yes." He caught both her hands in his. "I'm sorry. I just—"

He turned away, walked blindly until he reached a filing cabinet and braced his hands against it. This was no good. He had to tell her. He sucked in a breath.

"Okay. You're right. When you showed us that picture of the chain in the shape of a bird . . . it was familiar to me. When I found my father's body, his tie was lying on the table—twisted into the same shape."

Silence, so dense he could hear the thudding of his own heart. And then she moved next to him. Put her hand over his.

"I'm sorry." Her voice choked a little. "Trey, I'm sorry. I never imagined."

"No. I didn't either." He let out another breath. "My father was the most honorable man I ever knew. He couldn't have been involved in anything wrong. But that symbol—" He shook his head, sure of only one thing. "My mother can't know about this. His suicide was devastating enough. I can't let her be hurt again."

"Trey, you're not thinking straight. There could be some innocent explanation."

"Like what? If Dad was involved with this society, if his name comes up in connection with Cherry's death, don't you see how that would hurt her?"

She drew back a little. "You're underestimating your mother. She's a lot stronger than you think."

"You think I'm overprotective, is that it?" A distance seemed to have opened between them, and he stared at her across it.

She stiffened. "Yes. I do. I know how much you love your mother, but you're treating her as if she were a child."

"You don't know anything about it." He snapped the words and was instantly sorry, realizing how that must sound. "Jessica, I didn't mean that."

She took a careful step away. "It doesn't really matter, does it? You have to put your mother first. I have to put my client first. That's the way it is."

He wanted to say something, anything, that would bridge the chasm that had opened between them, but he had a feeling anything he said would just make matters worse. His jaw clenched. Then he turned and walked out of the office.

JESSICA DIDN'T HAVE TIME to vent. Leo came back in almost immediately after Trey left. Well, it was his office, after all. He probably wanted to get on with the sorting and packing he was doing as he prepared for his retirement.

Leo glanced at her, seeming to register the fact that something was wrong. But he refrained from comment, sitting down and pulling over the file box he was sorting.

It was an effort to keep a calm facade when what she wanted to do was crawl into a corner. But what she'd said to Trey was true. From the moment they'd met, the same barrier had stood between them. His loyalty was to his mother and hers to her client, and that seemed destined to put them on a collision course.

How could a relationship between them ever have worked? Trey had to control everyone in his orbit. Oh, he probably didn't think of it that way. He thought he was protecting, thought he was doing what was best.

But she'd learned the hard way that the only person she could rely on was herself. She couldn't ever be the kind of woman Trey needed, even if she had turned to him for support.

No, it was better this way. But it would be a long time before she stopped hurting. Before she stopped thinking of what might have been.

Somewhat to her surprise, calls began to come into the office as soon as the noon news had aired. Apparently a number of people had opinions on the symbol, none of which seemed very helpful.

And, of course, there were the requisite number of crank calls. After the third suggestion that the symbol was a message from outer space, she looked across at Leo and lifted her eyebrows.

"Was I crazy to do this?"

"Not crazy," he assured her. "But you did bring the crazies out of the woodwork. And we should weed through all of the calls, just in case."

"Except the outer space ones," she amended. "I draw the line there."

The smile lingered on her face when her cell phone rang. It disappeared when she saw that the caller was Mr. Henderson. Taking a deep breath, she answered.

Henderson didn't waste time on pleasantries. He was furious, as furious as Trey had been, but where Trey was hot, Henderson was cold.

"You are making a spectacle of yourself. More important, of this firm."

"Sir, I—"

"You were given a simple task, one any first-year law student should have been able to handle. Make a deal with the district attorney, do the best you can for the client and get out. What is so difficult about that?"

Anger began to stir under the intimidation. "Nothing, except for one small fact. I believe my client is innocent."

"Innocent. And do you have any evidence to back that up, other than this fairy tale about a secret society?" He sounded as if the words tasted sour on his tongue.

"Not evidence, exactly—"

"Then stop this nonsense. You're not doing the client any good, and you're holding the firm up to ridicule. Talk to the district attorney—no, better yet, just come back to the city. I'll send someone else to make a deal."

Her heart seemed to stop for a moment. "You can't do that."

"This is my firm." His voice froze. "I will do as I see fit."

"The client will never agree." She hoped. How long would Thomas stand up against a lawyer determined to make him plead guilty?

"Then you'd better find a way to make him agree. Do that, now, or your association with Henderson, Dawes and Henderson is at an end. Do you understand me?"

She closed her eyes, seeing her father's face against the blackness. Disappointed. But then, when had he not been disappointed in her?

She couldn't kid herself. If Henderson let her go under a cloud, she wouldn't find another firm eager to accept her. The career she'd always wanted could be at an end.

"No." The word was out before she'd even thought it through, but she knew it was right.

"No? What do you mean?"

"I will not let my client down for the sake of sparing the firm embarrassment," she said, her voice surprisingly clear.

"Then your association with us is ended as of now," he said promptly. "As for your client—feel free to take him with you. Just make sure that everyone knows that you are no longer acting as a member of this firm."

"Very well." If he said anything about her father, she'd . . . she wasn't sure what she'd do.

But he didn't. Apparently he was just as eager to end the call as she was. He clicked off, no doubt to begin spreading the word that her embarrassing conduct did not represent Henderson, Dawes and Henderson.

She tossed the cell phone onto her desk, not sure what she felt. She glanced at Leo. He'd obviously heard enough to understand what happened.

"I'm sorry." He hesitated. "But if you'll forgive my saying so, I never did think you were a good match with them."

"Maybe not." It was too bad that her father would never share that opinion.

"Are you all right?"

She considered. She'd just lost the man she thought she loved and been fired by her firm. She ought to feel miserable.

"I think so," she said slowly. Deep inside, the conviction was growing. She had done the right thing. No matter what anyone else said or thought, no matter what it cost, she'd done the right thing.

JESSICA STAYED ON AT the office after Leo left that afternoon. He was bound for home and grumbling about the rest his doctor insisted upon, muttering that he was being treated like a two-year-old.

She didn't really have a reason to stay. The phone calls trickled off. The truth was that she couldn't bear the thought of going back to Geneva's house.

She'd have to go through with her plans to move out. That was the only possible thing to do, and now even Trey would agree to that. But her stomach tightened into a knot at the thought of trying to explain her reasons to Geneva. She couldn't tell Geneva the truth, and the woman had an uncanny knack of knowing all the things a person wasn't telling her.

The telephone rang. Since Leo's secretary had left when he did, she picked up. To her surprise, it was Bobby Stephens.

"I hope I'm not disturbing you," he seemed tentative, as always. "But there's something I need to talk with you about."

"That's fine, Bobby." She found herself sounding a little overly reassuring. Bobby's hangdog air seemed to bring that out in her. "I have time to talk now."

"Not over the phone," he said, rushing the words as if he thought someone might be listening in.

She suppressed a sigh. "Maybe at Geneva's—"

"No, no, I can't talk about this there. Once I tell you, you'll understand. Why don't we meet in the restaurant at the inn? It'll be quiet this time of day."

At least that had the virtue of keeping her from sitting here feeling sorry for herself. And it delayed the time when she'd have to return to the house.

"That's fine." She glanced at her watch. "I can be there in about fifteen minutes."

"I'll see you then." He hung up before she could ask him again what this was all about.

She shut down her laptop and slipped it into the case. Bobby had offered to track down the origins of Cherry's pendant. She hadn't thought it much more than busywork, but was it possible that he'd actually found something?

A thread of excitement ran through her as she headed for the car. Maybe she'd catch a break at last in this case.

She walked into the inn's dining room in a little less than the fifteen minutes she'd allowed, but Bobby was there before her. He stood as she approached the table. As he'd said, they had the place to themselves.

He held out her chair as solicitously as if she were ninety-five. "Thank you so much for coming, Jessica. I hate to burden you with this, but I honestly didn't know who else to talk to."

"You have my curiosity going now." She smiled as he sat down opposite her at the small round table. "Have you found something?"

He glanced at the waitress who was approaching the table. "We'd better wait until we won't be disturbed."

Milly Cotter smiled at Jessica in recognition. "Good afternoon, folks. What can I get for you today?"

"Just an iced tea," Jessica said, eager to get on with this.

"Coffee for me." Bobby looked troubled. "But are you sure you won't have something else? A piece of pie, maybe? Or a sandwich?"

"Nothing else, thanks."

"Coming right up." Milly scurried away.

Jessica studied Bobby's face. Behind the thick glasses, his eyes held a sort of troubled excitement. Apprehension snaked down her spine. He had the air of one who'd gone looking for a mouse and found a boa constrictor.

"Won't you tell me . . ." She let that die off, because Milly was approaching with their drinks.

It was only when the server had disappeared through the doors to the kitchen that Bobby stopped fiddling with his teaspoon.

"That's better. Now we can talk."

"Why all the secrecy? Have you actually found something relevant to Thomas's case?"

"In a way." He was maddeningly evasive. "I guess you could say that, though I don't know that it's actually going to help."

She took a firm hold on her patience. "Why don't you tell me and let me decide?"

"Well, you remember I said I'd try to trace that raven symbol—the pendant—that you got from Cherry's friend?"

He made it a question, and she nodded.

"I thought it might turn up on the Web. You know, most dealers use the Internet these days. So that's where I started. You'd be surprised at the number of people who are interested in hex signs. And memorabilia from secret societies."

"I can imagine. People collect all kinds of things." And when was he going to get to the point?

"So, anyway, finally I hit pay dirt. I found a dealer in Pittsburgh who sold that pendant, or one just like it, about two years ago."

"Pittsburgh." Not that far away, but not right around the corner, either. "Did he still have records on it? Did he remember who bought it?"

Bobby shrugged, looking down at his coffee. "He remembered. I got the idea that his business is more of a hobby, and that piece was unusual enough to make an impression. He said he could have sold it a couple of times over."

He was stalling. She tried to shake off the apprehension that gripped her.

"Who bought it?"

He met her gaze then. Sympathy, maybe pity, filled his face. Something was coming, something bad, and she braced herself to hear it.

He glanced around, apparently making sure they were alone before he would speak. "It was paid for with a company credit card that belonged to Trey's father."

She sucked in a breath, unable even to think for a moment. If Trey's father bought the piece, if he had given it to Cherry—

"No." The denial was almost automatic. "That doesn't have to mean the obvious. It doesn't have to indicate that he gave it to Cherry. He could have sold it to someone else."

Bobby shrugged. "Maybe. But it's odd that neither Trey nor Geneva knew anything about it."

Her fingers tightened around the glass. Bobby had a point, and at the moment she was too shaken to think of any but the most obvious conclusion—that if Trey's father had given the pendant to Cherry, that implied a relationship between them.

"I can't believe that. I never knew the man, but the way Trey talks about him, the way Geneva obviously felt . . ."

"Geneva can't know about this." Bobby looked horrified at the thought. "It would kill her if she thought that her husband . . ." He stopped, unwilling to say it. "Well, she can't know, that's all. That's why I brought it to you. I didn't know what else to do." He shook his head. "There has to be some other explanation. Mr. Morgan was devoted to Geneva. Someone else must have given it to Cherry. After he died, his things would have been gone through . . ."

He let that fade away, but they both knew who would have been the one to do that. Trey. If Trey found the pendant—

He couldn't have. He couldn't have, because that would mean that he'd been lying all along.

Jessica shoved her chair back, hardly aware of what she was doing. "I . . . I have to think about this." She grabbed her bag and stood, knowing she had to get away. She couldn't sit here and discuss Trey with him.

He nodded. "I'm sorry." He was looking down, and she couldn't see his expression. Maybe that was just as well, because that meant he couldn't see hers, and she was afraid of what she might be revealing.

It was only when she'd lost Trey that she'd realized how much she loved him. That was bad enough, losing him because of an honest difference of values. But to lose him because he wasn't the man she'd thought he was at all—she didn't think she could bear that.

CHAPTER EIGHTEEN

JESSICA FOLDED A SILK shell and put it into her suitcase, trying to concentrate on the mechanical movements of packing. Trying not to think of what Bobby had told her.

It was no use. She couldn't prevent her mind from playing and replaying that conversation. If what Bobby's source said was true, the conclusion seemed inescapable. Either Trey or his father must have given the pendant to Cherry.

"Jessica, what are you doing?"

Jessica spun, a suit jacket slipping from her fingers. Geneva stood in the bedroom doorway, her gaze wide as she looked at the suitcase lying open on the bed. "You're not leaving."

"I'm sorry—I was going to tell you as soon as I'd finished here."

And how would she explain it? She could hardly tell Geneva what had happened between her and Trey. Or tell her what Bobby had learned, with its implication that she could be compromising Thomas's interests just by being here.

"My dear, I thought you were happy here." The sorrow in Geneva's face reproached her. "I'm sure you're safer here . . ."

That, at least, gave her an opening. "I'm sure I'll be fine. Now that the business about the symbol is out in the open, the person who threatened me has no reason to come after me."

"It's not just that." Geneva crossed the room to clasp Jessica's hands in hers. "I've so enjoyed having you here. It's been like having my daughter home again. Really, won't you reconsider? You can't be comfortable at that motel."

She had to smile at the words. Geneva made it sound as if the motel was some sort of flophouse. "Actually, I've decided to move to the inn." Now that she didn't have to account to Henderson's secretary for her expenses, she could suit herself. "I . . . I should probably tell you that Mr. Henderson has terminated my employment. He feels that I should have made a deal for Thomas—"

"That's outrageous." Geneva flushed. "Besides, I wouldn't hear of such a thing. You are still going to defend Thomas, aren't you?"

"I won't let him down. I just wish I had a little more ammunition."

Like the pendant. If she tried to use it, she'd be casting suspicion on the Morgan family. But if she didn't, she could be harming her client.

"But you will as soon as we find out how the symbol fits in." Geneva was pursuing her own line of thought, but it ran parallel to Jessica's. "I trust you with Thomas's defense. And I trust God to use you to see that justice is done."

The complete faith in Geneva's words floored her for a moment. When she could speak, she said, "That's a pretty heavy burden, don't you think?"

"Not at all." Geneva patted her hand. "If there's one thing I've learned, it's that when God gives us a job to do, He also gives us the ability to do it. We just have to rely on Him."

"I'm afraid I'm not very good at relying on others."

Geneva touched her cheek. It was a featherlight caress, one that a mother might give to a daughter. Pain gripped Jessica's heart at the thought.

"That's coming between you and Trey, isn't it? No, don't answer," she added quickly. "I shouldn't have said that. I always promise myself I'm not going to interfere, and then my mouth runs ahead of my intentions."

"I think it's your heart, not your mouth." Surprising herself, Jessica hugged her. "I appreciate your concern. It's just . . ."

"You don't want to talk about it, not to Trey's mother, of all people." Geneva sighed, shaking her head. "He means well, bless him. He just doesn't understand yet that there can be a balance between protecting someone you love and trusting them to handle things on their own. Oh, there I go again."

She pressed her cheek against Jessica's. "Just you remember that you're always welcome here, no matter what. All right?"

"All right." It was the easiest thing to say, the simplest way out of the situation.

Unfortunately she knew it wasn't true. If her defense of Thomas involved casting doubt on Geneva's husband or her son, that was the one thing she'd never be able to forgive.

HER ROOM AT THE INN would be delightful, if she were in the mood to be delighted by anything like that. Two rooms, actually—a small sitting room and a bedroom, each furnished with solid Pennsylvania Dutch furniture. She traced the tulip design on the coffee table with one finger, unpleasantly reminded of the use to which one twisted mind had put a simple bit of folk art.

She leaned back on the love seat, too tired to do anything else. A rap at the door shook her out of her lethargy. Must be the soup and salad she'd ordered for supper.

"One second," she called and pulled the door open. And stared.

"Dad." Her father. Here in Pennsylvania instead of his Beacon Hill flat, wearing one of the signature gray suits that matched his silver hair.

"Well, Jessica? Must I continue to stand in the hallway, or will you invite me in?"

She scrambled after what was left of her wits and stepped back. "Please, come in. I'm surprised to see you."

Surprised didn't do justice to the feeling. She

didn't know what would. Her father had never visited her in Philadelphia, assuming that if she wanted to see him, she'd come to Boston. And yet here he was in Springville.

He stalked into the small sitting room, glancing around with a dismissive stare, and turned to face her.

"Won't you sit down?" She didn't attempt to hug him in greeting, knowing how much he disliked that. For just a second Geneva flitted through her mind, with her quick hugs and gentle touches.

"What I have to say won't take that long."

She'd learned to excuse his curtness long ago. He was a busy man, important people depended upon him, he didn't like seeing her because she reminded him painfully of her mother. The familiar excuses were just that—feeble excuses that didn't amount to a thing.

Still, she'd never challenged him. Maybe it was time she did. "You came all the way from Boston to see me, and you can't take the time to sit down?"

He blinked. Then he pulled out the straight chair from the desk and sat. Trying to quiet the butterflies dancing in her stomach, she took the end of the love seat opposite him.

"I'm on my way to Baltimore on business. It wasn't that much out of the way to stop in Philadelphia and see Henderson."

See Henderson. Not to see her. "I take it you know that my employment has been terminated."

His lips thinned, and his aristocratic nose wrinkled slightly, as if in reaction to an unpleasant odor.

"Henderson was perfectly amiable. He regretted having to take the steps he did. He is still willing to forget your unfortunate behavior and reinstate you." He glanced at the understated gold watch he wore. "It's too late to call him now. You'll get in touch first thing tomorrow. Apologize. You'll find him eager to move on."

In other words, her father had brought pressure to bear. She would give in all along the line, and life would return to normal. Thomas's frightened young face filled her mind.

"No."

A faint tic appeared in her father's jaw. She watched it, fascinated. She'd never openly defied him before.

"What did you say?" The words were lowering, ominous as an approaching storm.

"No. I'm sorry you've had this trip for nothing, but I don't intend to return to Henderson, Dawes and Henderson." Just saying the words was freeing. "I happen to believe my client's welfare comes before the risk of embarrassing the firm."

"How is your client served by his attorney making a spectacle of herself, appearing on television like that?" He gestured toward her battered face.

"I didn't give myself a black eye." The mildness of her tone surprised her. Didn't she care what her father thought?

Maybe the answer was there, in his words and actions. She'd spent her life trying to please him, to wring one word of approval from him, and he didn't care. Sorrow came with the thought, but something that had been tight inside her started to relax. If nothing she did could please him, she could stop trying.

"I can see it's no use trying to talk sense to you." He planted his palms on the arms of the desk chair. "Henderson was right. You are willful and incapable of being a team player." He thrust himself to his feet. "I trust you'll enjoy this case, since it may be the last one you ever try. Without my backing . . ."

She couldn't let it go like this. "I appreciated your help in getting the position with Henderson. Surely you must see that we're not a good fit." She was quoting Leo, she realized. "There's far more to this case than Henderson has been willing to hear. If you'd care to listen—"

"I've heard enough." He towered over her, face set in rigid lines.

She stood, too, with a sense of finality. "I'm sorry you feel that way."

"Any rational attorney would feel the same." He stalked toward the door.

"What about any father?"

Her words stopped him, his hand on the knob. At least she'd given him pause. Maybe . . .

But when he glanced at her, there was no feeling at all in his face. "I see no reason to prolong this conversation. When you've come to your senses, you may contact me."

He went out. The door closed with a muffled slam, as if to put a period to one part of her life.

SHE WEPT, OF COURSE. But there was a sense of relief in the tears. She'd burned all the bridges now. There was no place to go but forward.

Still, she couldn't help a flare of hope when she heard a rap on the door an hour later. If her father had come back . . .

"Who is it?"

"Trey. Open the door, Jessica. We have to talk."

Given the impatience in his voice, it seemed likely that if she refused to let him in, he'd stand there and knock until the entire floor had heard him. The Springville Inn seemed a bit limited in its security when first her father and then Trey could arrive at her door without warning.

She may as well face him, although it didn't seem likely they had anything left to say to each other. She turned the knob then stepped back as he entered.

"What is it, Trey? It's late." *And I've been through enough emotion for one night.*

"Sorry." He didn't sound sorry. "I had things to do. By the time I went back to the house, you were gone." He hesitated for a moment. "That wasn't necessary, you know."

"It seemed best." Only the firmest control kept her face noncommittal.

"Something's wrong." He reached out a hand toward her and then let it drop. "What's happened?"

She suppressed an insane desire to laugh. What wasn't wrong? If she told him what Bobby had found out about the pendant—but how could she do that?

"My father was here earlier," she said finally. "It was a . . . difficult conversation."

"I'm sorry." The sympathy that filled his voice sounded genuine, and it touched something deep inside her, something that wanted to respond to him.

But she couldn't. She had to stand on her own in that, as in everything else. "It's all right. What was it you wanted to talk about?"

He ran his hand through his hair. "Look, what I told you about my father's suicide today . . . I want your word that you won't make that public. I should never have said it."

"How can I promise that? For heaven's sake, Trey, it fits in with the idea that more is going on in Cherry's murder than a lover's quarrel that went too far. I have to protect my client any way I can."

His face hardened. "Don't you mean your career?"

"Career?" Once again that crazy need to laugh swept through her. "What career? Obviously you haven't talked to your mother or Leo. Henderson gave me an ultimatum this afternoon—either settle the case quietly with a plea bargain or forfeit my position."

He stared at her for a long moment. "You gave up your job for Thomas."

"What else could I do? I wasn't going to sacrifice his life for the dignity of Henderson, Dawes and Henderson. That's what it would be, we both know that. He wouldn't survive in prison . . . certainly not emotionally, maybe not physically, either."

"Is that why your father was upset with you?"

She didn't want to look at his face. The subject of fathers was too loaded for both of them. "He took it as a personal affront. I let him down."

"I'm sorry." He did touch her then, the lightest of strokes on her hand. "That must have hurt."

"It doesn't matter." She had to believe that. "The only thing that matters now is the truth."

He looked at her steadily for a long moment. "Do you really believe that?"

"Yes."

Three vertical lines appeared between his brows as they drew together. "Then tell me the truth."

She blinked. "About what?"

"About whatever it is that you're hiding, whatever is bothering you so much I can sense it. What aren't you telling me, Jess?"

He'd called her that once or twice, in moments of stress. No one else ever had except Sara. The intimacy of it twisted her heart. She couldn't lie to him. But how could she tell him the truth?

"I can't." She choked on the words.

"Just tell me. It has to do with my family, doesn't it? That's the only thing I can think of that you'd feel you had to keep from me."

She took a breath, released it. Her heart seemed to reach out in a silent plea for guidance.

The uncertainty drained away. Telling him would widen the barrier between them, but she couldn't help that.

"Bobby traced the ownership of the pendant." She didn't want to see his expression, but she forced herself to meet his gaze. "It was bought from a dealer in Pittsburgh two years ago. By your father."

He stared at her, his eyes unreadable. "That's impossible. You must have misunderstood."

"I didn't misunderstand. That is what Bobby found. It was purchased with a company credit card belonging to your father." She had to ask. "You didn't see it? He never mentioned buying such a thing?"

He shook his head, frowning and baffled. "Never. I suppose . . . well, he might have bought it, just as a curiosity for his collection. But he'd have shown it to me. And he'd never have given it to Cherry. He barely knew her."

"Are you sure of that?" She hated to ask, but—

"Of course I'm sure!" The words exploded from him.

"He bought it. She had it. If he didn't . . ." She stopped, unable to finish the thought.

"If he didn't, then I must have?" He said it for her, acid lacing the words. "Nice to know you think so highly of me." He spun and walked to the door, purpose in every determined line of his body.

"What are you going to do?" Her heart throbbed with apprehension. Pain. Doubt.

He paused, hand on the knob, and gave her a dark look. "I'm going to find Bobby. I'm going to look at this so-called evidence. And I'm going to find out the truth."

CHAPTER NINETEEN

TREY LEANED BACK IN the desk chair that had been his father's and rubbed his eyes. Had he slept at all last night? It seemed unlikely, unless he'd dozed off in the chair while searching through Dad's credit-card records.

He'd been trying to reach Bobby since he'd left Jessica last night, with no success. Anger surged. Bobby should have come to him with this information, not Jessica. And where was he? By this time he ought to be in his office, but he wasn't answering there, just as he hadn't answered his cell or responded to the messages Trey had left.

Trey clipped receipts together and returned them to a file folder. The anger he'd felt at Jessica had dwindled in the long hours of the night to sorrow and pain. Given Jessica's background, it was already difficult for her to trust anyone, and he'd certainly given her no reason to believe she could rely on him. If he felt anger at anyone, it had to be himself. He'd handled this whole situation badly, and he didn't see any way it was going to right itself without a lot of people getting hurt.

The truth, Jessica had said. The only thing to do was find the truth. He rubbed the back of his neck, trying to ease the tension. Well, he'd spent the night looking for truth, and he hadn't found anything even remotely suspicious anywhere in Dad's records.

Of course, Bobby would be the one with access to the business end of things. Bobby's scrupulous care of financial records was an asset, since that sort of thing bored Trey to tears. If the vendor said the charge was on Dad's card, Bobby would have checked the records. But there had to be an explanation.

The tile pendant had been in the locked drawer of the desk since the night they'd talked about it. He took out the pendant and held it in his hand. Such an insignificant thing to be the cause of so much trouble.

The phone rang, and he dropped the tile on the desk to snatch up the receiver. "Bobby?"

An open line crackled, and then Bobby's voice, sounding as if he was in a well. ". . . didn't get back to you . . . couldn't . . ."

"You're fading out. Where are you?"

". . . back from Pittsburgh . . . decided to talk to the dealer . . ."

Excitement rippled through him. He pressed the receiver hard against his ear, as if that would make Bobby's voice clearer. "What did you find out?"

". . . not what . . . meet me at the cabin . . ."

"Did you say the cabin?" His voice was sharp. "Why?"

". . . almost there . . . something . . ." The

connection faded away to nothing. Frustrated, he hung up, then tried Bobby's cell again. Nothing.

He shoved his chair back and stood. Bobby had sounded excited, and they couldn't afford to ignore anything that might help to clear up this mess. Snatching his keys, he headed for the door.

He reached it to find his mother coming in, the dog at her heels. He tried to arrange his face in an expression that wouldn't arouse her instinct for trouble.

"It's a beautiful day." She kissed his cheek. "The kind of day when anything seems possible."

That was certainly the kind of day he needed. "I have to go out for a while, Mom."

"Without your breakfast?" Her hand on his arm stopped him. "Surely you have time—"

"I'll grab something later. I'm running out to the cabin to meet Bobby. He claims to have found something that might help Thomas's case."

"He has? That's wonderful." Hope bloomed in her eyes. "What is it?"

"I won't know that until I get there." He detached her hand. "I have to go."

"Take Sam with you." At the sound of his name, Sam stood, tail waving. "You know how he loves to ride in the truck."

As always with his mother, it was faster to agree than to argue. He patted his leg. "Come on, Sammy boy."

The dog trotted alongside him, giving an excited woof when he saw they were headed for the truck. Trey had to help him up to the high seat, but there he settled happily, head out the window, breeze ruffling his fur.

Trey swung onto the main road with a squeal of the tires. This was probably a wild-goose chase, but it was better than concentrating on his regrets. He'd have plenty of time to do that.

No matter how this turned out, Jessica would go away, eager to see the last of him. He couldn't blame her for that. He just wished . . . well, he didn't know what he wished. No point in longing for the impossible, was there?

Twenty minutes later he pulled into the narrow lane that led to the cabin. Branches brushed the sides of the truck, and Sam drew his head in, looking at Trey reproachfully.

"You can do it on the way back," Trey assured him.

The brush thinned out, and there was the cabin, with Bobby's car backed up to the porch. Trey pulled up next to it and forestalled Sam's move to get out with a hand motion.

"Stay, boy. Stay." No point in letting the poor old guy go through the ordeal of getting down and up again.

The cabin was quiet. Too quiet. Why hadn't Bobby come out to meet him? He must have heard the truck.

The porch boards creaked as he stepped on them. He moved toward the door, apprehension lifting the hairs on the back of his neck.

"Bobby?" He opened the door. "You here?"

He stepped inside. Something moved, beside and behind him. Before he could turn, pain crashed into the side of his head, exploding in a display of sparks. Blackness.

"JESSICA, WHAT IS IT?" Leo stood when she walked into the office, concern filling his face. "You look as if you've lost your last friend."

She felt as if she had, but that was neither here nor there at the moment. "I've just come from seeing Thomas." She touched the still-tender bruise around her eye. "I thought I looked bad, but Thomas is ten times worse. One of the other prisoners got at him."

Leo let out a wordless exclamation. "Is he all right? How could that happen?"

"He's been seen by a doctor, and they've moved him into a cell away from the other prisoners. They say they're taking every precaution, but . . ." She let that trail off, the weight of responsibility hanging on her. "That poor boy. He wouldn't lift a hand to defend himself. I have to find a way to clear him."

"I know." He clasped her hand briefly. "We're doing the best we can."

A spurt of gratitude went through her at Leo

aligning himself with her. Would he still feel that way when she'd told him?

She took a breath, steadying herself. "There's something I have to tell you. I don't know how you'll feel about it, or if it's something we can use, but I've reached the point that my mind is going in circles, and I need your opinion."

"Of course. You know I'm here for you."

Leo had known her a matter of weeks, but he was here for her. The gratitude deepened.

"Bobby managed to trace the pendant. He found that it had been purchased nearly two years ago from a dealer in Pittsburgh. The credit card used to pay for it was a business card belonging to Trey's father." She rubbed her temples, trying to wipe away the pain. "You see how it looks. If Trey's father gave the pendant to Cherry—"

"He wouldn't." Leo sounded sure. "Jessica, I knew the man all my life. I know what he was capable of, and believe me, he couldn't have been involved with that girl."

"That's what Trey said, too. But if he didn't give it to her, then who did?"

Leo frowned. "Wait a minute. Didn't that friend of hers, the McGowan woman, say that she had received it fairly recently, and from a boyfriend she was keeping secret?"

Jessica struggled to recall that conversation. So much had happened since then. "That was certainly the implication she gave," she said slowly. "But if Trey's father bought the thing, how did someone else get it to give to her? It could only . . ." She stopped.

"Be Trey?" Leo finished for her. "That's what you're really worrying about, isn't it? That's what's clouding your judgment."

"I suppose it is." Leo was right. Her mind had been spinning in useless circles because of her fear that Trey had been involved.

Leo gripped her hands firmly. "Stop and think. If the person who gave Cherry that pendant is the same person who left the threatening note for you, the person who ran you off the road, the person who killed her . . . can you seriously tell me you think Trey is capable of that?"

"No." Her heart answered without any doubt at all. "No, he's not. But maybe . . ."

"Maybe what? Someone killed Cherry and left that symbol behind, so subtle that it almost wasn't spotted. I find it hard to believe that it's not the same person who gave her the pendant. The long arm of coincidence just won't reach that far."

"You're right. Of course you're right." She shook her head, shaking off the negative thoughts that had been paralyzing her. "So someone else had to have access to that pendant."

Leo frowned, leaning back in his chair, fingertips drumming on the desk. "You said that Bobby came to you with the evidence. When was that?"

"Yesterday afternoon."

"After the television interview ran."

"Yes. Why? What connection could that have?"

"I'm not sure, but . . . Did you actually see the record of that sale?"

She shook her head. "Bobby just told me about it." What kind of lawyer was she, anyway? Why hadn't she asked to see the material for herself?

Because she was emotionally involved, that was why.

"So it all depends on Bobby's word," Leo said slowly, as if he were turning it over in his mind. "Bobby handled all the financial records for Trey's father, just as he does for Trey."

"You think Bobby . . . ?" Quiet, unassuming Bobby, with his dogged devotion to Trey—how could that be?

"I'm not accusing anyone," Leo said. "But I think we ought to have a second check on this." He picked up the phone. "Let me give Trey a call. See if we can get access to those business-card receipts. Then we can move forward from there."

It was what she should have done, if she hadn't been so tied up in knots over her feelings for Trey. She could hear Leo's voice, talking to Geneva, apparently, but it was Trey's face that filled her mind. Even if nothing could come of the feelings she had for him, she had to admit them to herself.

There was a click as Leo hung up the phone. She looked at him, to find him staring back at her, his face so devoid of any expression that it shocked her. "What is it?"

"Geneva says Trey's not there. He had a call from Bobby. He's gone to the cabin to meet him."

Fear gripped her heart—instinctive, primal fear. She bolted from her chair. "We have to go there. If Bobby—"

She didn't finish the thought. She didn't have to. Leo was close behind her as she rushed to the door.

CHAPTER TWENTY

TREY'S HEAD THROBBED. He sagged forward, something cutting into his wrists. He fought to open his eyes, but his eyelids refused to cooperate. It was a dream, a nightmare . . .

He jerked his head back, earning a fresh stab of pain. A nightmare, maybe, but only too real. He forced his eyes to open, attempted to focus.

The cabin. He was at the cabin. He'd come . . . The darkness threatened to sweep over him again, and he beat it back. He'd come to meet Bobby. When he walked in the door, something hit him.

Not something. His mind worked sluggishly, like the truck's motor on a below-zero morning. Someone.

Bobby. Bobby had been waiting for him.

He struggled against the realization. Bobby couldn't have, wouldn't have—

The door opened, letting in a shaft of light that hurt his eyes. Bobby walked in, carrying a metal gas can in each hand. Trey couldn't argue with himself about it, not when the truth was in front of him.

"Bobby." His voice came out in a harsh croak. No point in asking what he was doing. That was only too obvious. "What—why are you doing this?"

Bobby didn't answer. He busied himself with

the gas cans, setting one on one side of the room, the other opposite it, in the precise, fussy manner that kept everything he touched in perfect order. Then he straightened and looked at Trey.

"Poor Trey. He asked me to meet him at the cabin where his father committed suicide. But when I got there, the place was already on fire. I could see him, slumped over. I tried to reach him. Maybe I even got some burns on my hands." He held his hands up, inspecting them. "But I was too late. He'd killed himself, just like his father."

Bobby looked the same. That was the thing that turned Trey's stomach. He looked like the same Bobby they'd all taken for granted for the past fifteen years. That mild facade—Trey could see now what it hid. Hatred.

"Except that my father didn't commit suicide, did he?" The truth seemed clear now, when it was too late. "That never made sense to me. You killed him. Why? Did he catch you cooking the books?"

It was a shot at random, but he saw the truth flare in Bobby's face. "He made it almost too easy. You and your father were so trusting. 'Bobby will take care of all the dull, boring, financial stuff.' Too bad he got suspicious. It really was the cancer that killed him, you know. Because of that, he suddenly decided he had to get his financial house in order—started looking through the books and stumbled on my little deception."

"So you killed him." Bile came up in Trey's

throat. "He wouldn't have sent you to jail. He wasn't like that."

"Oh, no. He told me that, in such a pitying way. He was being magnanimous, letting me go quietly, promising never to tell anyone." Bobby's mouth twisted. "That was thoughtful of him. Made it easy to arrange his suicide."

"I thought we were friends." Trey twisted his hands, trying to loosen the knots. He couldn't just sit here and let Bobby kill him. He had to fight.

"Friends?" Bobby's eyebrows lifted. "Because the golden boy who had everything condescended to stop his little buddies from bullying me? That made a nice story, didn't it? I could see Jessica just lapping it up."

Jessica. Pain lanced Trey's heart. He was never going to see her again, never have a chance to tell her what he felt for her . . .

"I don't get it. Why did you do all those things to chase her away? You were the one who brought her here."

"Only because your mother insisted. I told Henderson we didn't need his high-powered talent—just some lowly young attorney who could plead the case out quickly. He sent Jessica. Who would have guessed she'd turn out to be such a fighter? I'll be doing something about that, you realize."

Bobby turned away, walked to the closest gas can and unscrewed the top. With a swing of his arm, he began splashing the gas across the floor—over the rag rug, on the wooden planks that would burn so easily . . .

The acrid scent filled Trey's nostrils, choking him. From outside, he could hear Sam start barking. He must smell it, too. Someone might hear him, might come. But the Miller place was the closest house, and it was nearly a mile away.

"You couldn't resist leaving your signature, could you?" The ropes were loosening, Trey could feel it. Say something, anything, to buy a little time. "That raven symbol. What was the idea behind it?"

"Don't talk about that!" Fear flashed in Bobby's eyes, jerked his hand so that the gasoline spilled on his shoe. "Never mention that." He gave a furtive glance over his shoulder at the open door. "I shouldn't have done that. They wouldn't like it."

"They?"

"The brotherhood," Bobby's voice dropped to a whisper. "They mustn't know."

Fear trickled down Trey's spine. The brotherhood, an organization that had been dust for two hundred years? Bobby was crazy. That was the only answer.

"Was that why you killed Cherry? Because she knew about the raven?"

Bobby picked up the second can, splashing the gas on the other side of the room, over the table where Trey's father died. Trey jerked at the ropes, fighting them.

"She was too greedy. She thought she could use the things I told her against me. So she had to go." Bobby looked at him then, dropping the empty gas can on the floor. "Like you." He pulled a gun from his pocket, shifted it to the other hand, fumbled with a box of matches. "Goodbye, Trey."

JESSICA'S CAR BOUNCED OVER the ruts in the lane. Please, please, let us be in time.

They burst into the clearing, and Jessica hit the brakes to keep from running into Trey's truck. Sam was in the front seat, lunging at the window, barking furiously. Beyond the vehicle, the cabin door gaped open.

Bobby stood in the doorway, his back to them. Her heart stopped. He held a gun. He lifted it, aimed, she couldn't be in time, she couldn't—

She shoved the car door open, raced the few steps to the truck and yanked its door wide. Sam exploded from the front seat. As she ran after him she could hear Leo shouting into his cell phone, could see Trey beyond Bobby in the cabin, tied and helpless, the gun—

Sam flew into Bobby, snarling. Bobby fell, the gun going off. A small flame arced through the air. It hit the floor, flames blossoming in its wake.

Trey—she had to get to Trey. She plunged into the cabin, feeling heat already from the flames.

The whole place would go up, Trey with it. She had to get him out. She veered around man and dog, stumbling, nearly falling, surging forward.

The smoke was choking her. Coughing, blinking away tears, groping forward an endless time until her feet hit something that moved. She dropped to her knees, fighting to see.

Trey's chair had tipped over. He squirmed, struggling with the ropes around his wrists, trying to get free, coughing and choking. She grabbed his hands, yanking at the rope, feeling it give. In an instant it fell away.

"Go." Trey gave her a push. "I'm all right."

She didn't argue, just grabbed his arm and pulled with all her might. Trey lurched to his feet. He tried to push her away. She pulled his arm across her shoulder, put her arm around him. Through the flames she could see the oblong of daylight that was the door. She propelled him toward it.

A few more steps, the room on fire behind them . . . and then they were out, stumbling across the porch, and hands reached out, helping her. Leo, Jonas Miller . . . the wail of a siren from the lane.

"Sam!" Trey rasped the dog's name. Sam came bounding out, leaping off the porch as if he were a pup. He barreled into Trey, nearly knocking him over.

"Bobby." Trey tried to push away their hands. "We have to get him out."

Tires shrieked behind them as the township police car skidded to a stop, doors flying open.

"Put the gun down, Stephens." Adam had his own weapon out, pointed at the doorway where Bobby stood against a background of flames. "It's no good. Put the gun down and come out."

For a moment Bobby stood there, gun waving as if he couldn't decide what to do. Then, before anyone could move, he put it to his head and pulled the trigger.

JESSICA SAT ON A BACKLESS bench in the rear of the Miller barn, Geneva next to her, row after row of Amish women and girls in front of them. Across an aisle between the benches, men and boys sat, with Trey and Leo directly across from her and Geneva.

Elizabeth, on her other side, patted her hand. She had been appointed to sit with them during the worship service, explaining in whispers.

It was no easy thing to sit on a backless bench for close to three hours, especially when you didn't understand a word of the language. But they had been honored with an invitation, because Thomas was finally free, completely cleared of all complicity in Cherry's death. By craning her neck just a little she could see him, sitting next to his father and brothers about halfway up the aisle, looking just like every other man here in his plain black suit, except for his battered face. Thomas was restored to the spot where he belonged.

How long would it take him to heal? Not just physically, but emotionally? It was hard to tell. The boy was probably still in a state of shock. Still, the old clichés were probably true. He'd be all right, given time.

They'd been fortunate, and the thought was sobering. If Adam Byler and Jonas Miller hadn't arrived in time to see what had happened at the cabin, would they have been believed? Certainly the process would have been far more complicated. As it was, a conference in the judge's chambers had brought out the truth, as well as a decision as to how much of that truth would be revealed to the public. As long as Thomas was completely cleared, it didn't matter to her how much dirty laundry the D.A. wanted to hide.

So the case was completed, and she was out of a job. The future looked blank, but strangely, that didn't terrify her. She'd come to terms with her lack of a relationship with her father. She might always regret that, but she could move on.

Elizabeth leaned over, compressing them to the squashing point. "Bishop Amos is going to speak to all of us in Englisch." Her awed whisper made it clear that this was unprecedented.

The bishop stood in front of his people. No platform, no pulpit, no stained-glass windows proclaimed this a church. It was simply a barn that would be restored to its normal purposes tomorrow. Today it was a house of worship.

"We cannot conclude our time together without thanking God for the deliverance of our brother Thomas Esch. And we must thank Him, too, for those Englischers He sent to be His servants in this matter."

He raised his hands, looking like an Old Testament prophet with his long white beard.

"Father God, we praise You for your faithfulness to each generation of those who follow You. Thank You for delivering Your child Thomas from the hand of evil, and restoring him to those who love him. Thank You for sending us gut friends from among the Englisch to accomplish this act of your power. We will not forget to praise You."

Jessica discovered that tears were dripping on her clasped hands. She never cried in public. Never. Until now. But now tears of thanksgiving seemed only right.

"I STILL THINK THE FACT that Bobby had me trussed up like a Thanksgiving turkey while he tossed gasoline around would have convinced a judge, even if Adam hadn't been there in minutes when Leo called," Trey said.

Geneva paled. "I called Adam, too, you know. That's why he was so close. I just . . . after I heard Leo's reaction to Bobby's calling you, I just knew."

After the lengthy worship service and still-more-lengthy lunch, they'd finally come back to Geneva's place to relax. Jessica hadn't argued the point. If Trey found it awkward . . .

The truth was that she had no idea how Trey felt at this point. The past twenty-four hours had been busy, but he could have found time for a moment alone with her if he'd wanted that. He hadn't.

"I'll trust your instincts from now on." Trey, sitting next to his mother on the sofa in the family room, gave her a quick hug. "And don't look so worried. I'm fine, thanks to Jessica and Leo."

"And Sam. Don't forget him." The dog came to nose against Jessica's hand, and she stroked him.

"And Sam," Trey added.

Geneva clutched her son's hand as if she'd never let go. "I feel as if we've hardly had a chance to talk since all this happened. I still don't understand what all that business was with the hex sign."

"I doubt anybody ever did, except Bobby." Bleakness shadowed Trey's eyes. He'd be blaming himself for not seeing what was happening with Bobby, probably.

"The Brotherhood of the Raven doesn't exist nowadays except in his imagination," Leo said. "I'm sure of that. A psychiatrist would probably say that it made him feel important, thinking he was part of some powerful secret society."

"It was such a foolish thing to kill that poor girl

over. As for Blake, he'd have forgiven in a minute." Geneva held Trey's hand tighter, and the diamond in her ring winked in the light.

At least Geneva had her faith back in her relationship with her husband. She was hurting, but eventually this nightmare would fade, and she'd be left with the knowledge that her husband hadn't willingly left her.

"He said something about Cherry being greedy." Trey frowned. "I don't suppose we'll ever know exactly why he killed her, but she knew too much about him."

"Or why he decided to frame Thomas. At least he's safe now." Leo glanced at Jessica over the top of his glasses, eyes twinkling. "How does it feel to win a big case in such spectacular fashion?"

"I'd just as soon win them less dramatically," she said. "In fact, I'd settle for some nice, boring land disputes. Or writing wills. That would be safe."

"It's funny you mention that." Leo exchanged looks with Geneva. "You know, I've decided I'm not quite ready for the scrap heap yet. I'd like to go on with the practice, if I could get a bright young partner to work with me. What do you think, Jessica? Would you like that?"

"Please say yes." Geneva reached across the space between them to clasp Jessica's hand. "I can't stand the thought of you going out of our lives. You'd like it here, really."

The longing to say *accept* was so strong it nearly forced the word out of her mouth. But how could she do that? How could she stay here, seeing Trey, knowing how close they'd come to having something real between them?

"I'm honored, Leo. Can I have a little time to think about it?"

"Of course. All the time you want." If Leo was offended that she didn't jump at the offer, he hid it well.

Trey stood suddenly, holding out his hand to Jessica. "You'll excuse us, I know. Jessica and I are going for a walk."

"We are?"

"Yes." He grabbed her hand and pulled her to her feet. Sam, responding to the word *walk,* was already at the door, his tail waving.

Jessica could feel the others watching as they walked out the door, crossed the porch and started across the lawn. Trey held her hand firmly in his, as if he'd forgotten he had taken it.

Sam at their heels, they walked across the lawn and under the shade of a gnarled old apple tree. Trey stopped, turning to face her, still holding her hand. "There's something I have to say."

"I'm listening." Her voice sounded calm, but her heart was thumping so loudly she could hear it.

"You saved my life yesterday. I thought I was protecting you, and you saved my life."

"Turnabout is fair play," she said, managing to

keep her voice light. "You saved my life that night Bobby ran me off the road."

"Yes." His grip tightened painfully. "When I think how close we came to losing each other . . . Jessica, you already know all the bad things about me. I'm bossy, and overprotective, and stubborn." He paused. "Maybe stubborn isn't all bad. It means I'm not willing to give up on what we might have between us. I love you, Jessica. I don't want to lose you. Please stay."

She looked up at him, her heart swelling. It wasn't over. "You really are all those things," she said softly. "But I wouldn't change any of them. Because I love you, too."

A smile trembled on her lips. Trey pulled her toward him, wrapping his arms around her, and then his lips found hers. The kiss was warm and loving and filled with promise, saying all the things that didn't need words.

Trey drew back finally, looking at her with a question in his eyes. "Does this mean the answer to Leo's proposal is yes?"

"It does."

"And mine?"

"Yes to that, too." Happiness bubbled up inside her. "I guess I can't get Geneva for a mother on any easier terms, can I?"

"We're a package deal," he said, pulling her close.

Center Point Publishing
600 Brooks Road ● PO Box 1
Thorndike ME 04986-0001 USA

(207) 568-3717

US & Canada:
1 800 929-9108
www.centerpointlargeprint.com